Dirty Laundry

By
Stephen Murray & Darin Jewell

authorHOUSE

1663 LIBERTY DRIVE, SUITE 200
BLOOMINGTON, INDIANA 47403
(800) 839-8640
WWW.AUTHORHOUSE.COM

This book is a work of fiction. People, places, events, and situations are the product of the author's imagination. Any resemblance to actual persons, living or dead, or historical events, is purely coincidental.

© 2005 Stephen Murray and Darin Jewell. All Rights Reserved.

No part of this book may be reproduced, stored in a retrieval system, or transmitted by any means without the written permission of the author.

First published by AuthorHouse 01/05/06

ISBN: 1-4259-0390-8 (sc)

Printed in the United States of America
Bloomington, Indiana

This book is printed on acid-free paper.

To my good wife Kate for putting up with me and replenishing my glass during the writing process and to my family, Steve, Connor, Michelle and Jade. It's also dedicated to all my loyal customers and to the good people of Strathaven, especially those who frequent the 'Castle Tavern'. Will this unsolicited testimony get me a free drink? Worth a try.

Acknowledgements

Many thanks to my agent, The Inspira Group. I could not have published this without them. A special mention to Michelle and Kris Paterson for their help in the promotional side of the book.

Contents

Chapter 1
Pull The Udder One 1

Chapter 2
Cabin Fever 11

Chapter 3
Ghost 39

Chapter 4
One For The Road 77

Chapter 5
An Expensive Bargain 99

Chapter 6
Champagne And Tears 111

Chapter 7
Going For A Song 125

Chapter 8
Have Yourself A Very Merry Christmas 145

Chapter 9
A Bit Of A Do 173

Chapter 10
The Evaluation 203

Chapter 11
No Smoke Without Fire......................................215

Chapter 12
Up The Creek 237

Chapter 13
R.I.P. 245

Chapter 14
Heads I Win, Tails You Lose 261

Chapter 15
East, West, Home's Best 283

CHAPTER 1

PULL THE UDDER ONE

Here's a recipe for disaster. Take one feckless individual, add a generous measure of strong alcohol, a pinch of bravado and finally, one dumb challenge. A word of caution though, stand well back. Yes, there's a lot of stupidity out there and I'm afraid to say I contributed to it, but I still blame the wife, or to be more exact, the ex-wife for the unfortunate accident I suffered - the Friesian cow in the middle of the field was merely incidental.

I was celebrating the first anniversary of our divorce (acrimonious) with a few close friends at the Auldhouse Arms - a quaint pub that's not changed it's style in years, it remains a bastion for good taste and old fashioned values and puts two fingers up to the generic blandness of most of the other 'watering holes' in East Kilbride with the exception of the Montgomery Arms.

It's the type of pub you can sit and chat in front of an open fire without loud music assaulting your eardrums or some inebriated idiot belting out a karaoke number thinking that he or she is perfectly in tune and the rest of the audience is somehow captivated by the performance - most of them have Van Gogh's ear for music.

A few single malts, a couple of beers, the obligatory pepperami snack and I was relaxed as Perry Como in his rocking chair on a lazy Sunday afternoon. The big mistake I made was to accept a generous piece of cannabis to chew - smoking pollutes the body. Neil seemed to have an inexhaustible supply of the stuff, which was strange considering he was unemployed and allergic to work, I think the word he used was 'ergasiophobia,' which he explained as 'a fear or aversion to work, diffidence about tackling the job.' After a lump of the golden brown substance your mind becomes emancipated from the confines of normal thought and rational, it's the only euphoriant I allow myself because it's not addictive, (I should know, I've been using it for years) although they do say its leads to passivity and apathy.

The conversation seems to be raised to a higher, more intellectual level regardless of what you're discussing - simple things become profound, problems and anxieties melt away like snow gently falling on to a river, and women in general become more attractive somehow - a fat sweaty woman with a distinctly hirsute upper lip begins to resemble a supermodel. I think cannabis was invented so that ugly people could get laid.

I say that with honest conviction because someone once commented that I was the absolute double of 'Shrek,' not the colour obviously, just the looks and physical demeanour - now I'm stuck with the bloody nickname.

The occasional imbibing is a luxury for someone like myself who's fiscally challenged - but what the hell, I needed a night out to take my mind off the divorce and her rapacious lawyers who hung me out to dry. Bastards! I swear to god their type could follow you into a revolving door and still come out ahead of you!

I lost the house (okay it was hers but I still contributed generously) and everything in it with the exception of my own personal belongings, which sadly didn't amount to much. Ten years of marriage gone just like that - thank god we didn't have any children.

The conversation between myself Neil and Stevie went from the profound to the imbecilic, everything from conspiracy theories, illegal substances, cows, the meaning of life and the greatest conundrum of all time, which came first, the chicken or the egg?

Stevie ruined a perfectly good conversation on the origin of life by telling a truly awful joke - he said, and I quote, 'a chicken and an egg were lying in bed, the chicken was smiling, smoking a fag, and looking rather satisfied while the egg looked miserable. The egg muttered, 'well I guess that answers the question!'

The conversation about drugs was insightful and rather animated as usual - Frank Zappa was right when he said, *'a drug is neither moral or immoral, it's a chemical compound. The compound itself is not a menace to society until a human being treats it as if consumption bestowed a temporary license to act like an arsehole.'*

I'm ashamed to say, under the influence, I acted like the proverbial 'arsehole,' when we finally left the Auldhouse Arms and the fresh air hit like a slap in the face. I had convinced Stevie and Neil that if you approached a cow at night (the bovine type, not human) and it was sleeping, you could easily push it over. Cows are like sheep, I reasoned, basically stupid and docile. I had read that somewhere in a book and I was determined to prove my theory to two unbelievers who were openly mocking me. It was Stevie that kept on goading me as we walked down the road towards East Kilbride.

"Come on Jack, prove your theory, there's a field of cows over there, do your thing."

Neil sniggered, "It's not a field of cows, it's a herd - go on big man, you can do it!"

It's one thirty in the morning in the middle of Auldhouse, it's minus five degrees, frosty, biting cold and dark, and I'm under pressure to prove a ridiculous point to two equally drunken idiots who can't even walk in a straight line.

"It's a four foot fence guys," I said nervously, "and it's got barbed wire on the top."

"Chicken," Stevie replied as he made the perfunctory fowl like noises, "you're nothing but a big quakebuttock!" Neil started giggling, he found anything amusing after a few and chipped in with his tuppence worth.

"What's a quakebuttock?"

"It's a coward, a person whose arse quivers because of fear. I think, I read that somewhere, anyway, Jacks bottom is quivering through fear of the cow!"

Neil added to my discomfort, as if it wasn't bad enough to be called a quivering arse.

"You're not scared of a few …cows Jack, are you?" he slurred. The two of them were teaming up against me and I was beginning to feel the pressure. Stevie lit up a cigarette and continued the verbal assault. He lit the filter end of the fag and complained about the poor quality of it

"Look Jack, you're a big bloke, it would be no problem to leap over that fence if you really wanted to - I think you're scared and the theory sucks!"

"I'm not scared," I said indignantly, "I'll do it to prove you guys wrong."

"Before you do it, wait a minute," Stevie replied. His cigarette fell from his lips. He turned his back to us, unzipped his trousers, fumbled for a minute, then proceeded to urinate against a post as we kept watch, not that there was anyone around, apart from a few cows.

"Christ it's cold, better hurry up before it drops off," he moaned, "right, I'm ready for the demonstration of cow pushing." Neil started giggling again, which was beginning to get on my nerves. With great reluctance I took a few tentative steps towards the fence then gripped the top carefully avoiding the barbed wire then leapt over in a single bound - I landed with a squelching sound underfoot. They applauded the effort and I turned and took a bow.

"I wish I could video this, maybe something will go horribly wrong," Neil said.

Stevie shook his head in disbelief at the stupidity of it all, "go on Shrek, go for it!"

"I hope it bites his big hairy arse." Laughter erupted.

"Sshh! You'll frighten them," I complained, " they will stampede!"

"I don't think three cows in a field running constitutes a stampede," Neil reasoned, "anyway, it's only buffalo that stampede you idiot, I've seen that 'Dancing with wolves' film."

"Quiet guys, I mean it - I need to have the element of surprise on my side." I was getting annoyed, they were not on this side of the fence facing danger or uncertainty, and Neil's incessant giggling was beginning to wear a bit thin.

"Jack! Jack!"

"What?" I turned around quickly, I sensed danger (cannabis makes me a bit jumpy, even paranoid)

"I hate to tell you this mate, but there's a big bull moving towards you over there, and he looks angry!"

Dirty Laundry

"Where?" Panic set in and I started to run back the twenty yards or so to the fence - I lost my footing and fell face down in the field. Panic. A sweaty panic that induced genuine fear.

"We're only joking you nutter!"

"You bastards, that's not funny." More giggling, uncontrollable this time.

"Look Jack, get on with it, we're freezing out here, I can't feel my toes."

"And we're getting bored."

I was livid but decided to save face by trying again - with great stealth I nervously approached the cow -I was intimidated by the sheer size of it close up, they are big beasts, and must have weighed at least 35 stones I figured. Animals have always given me the creeps, they're unpredictable - even as a child I was scared of them, stroking a horse made me nervous, even worse was holding your hand out with sugar cubes for the horses - I was convinced they would take my fingers off with one bite. They have very big teeth. Now as an adult, I'm close to a huge cow and I can see the steam coming out of it's nose. What if it bit me? What if it suffers from one of those debilitating cow diseases like spongiform encephalopathy, would I end up with 'scrapie' or even mad cow disease?

I'm suddenly not so brave now, but their constant barracking spurs me on - the fact that I'm pissed also helps, it might even be funny tomorrow.

I held my breath as I neared the great beast then I slowly placed my hands on it. The daft cow jumped involuntary, let out a snorting sound right into my face and decided to attack me. I let out a girlie scream and ran like hell toward the fence, to add insult to injury I could hear them laughing hysterically. In one fear driven leap I mounted the fence, snagged my trousers at the arse, and landed in a heap over the other side. A searing pain coursed through my body - something was broken.

When the merriment and mirth had subsided I managed to convince them I had done some serious damage to my ankle and was in need of a hospital.

Neil phoned for a taxi - the pick up point? somewhere in the middle of the Auldhouse road, next to the big field with the cows in it.

When I arrived at Hairmyers I was in a terrible state for a man of thirty-nine, I was ashamed ,my trousers were ripped and caked with mud and cow shit and I had lost my new mobile phone and a shoe somewhere in the field (even worse there was a large hole in my sock, thank god I had clean underwear on). They had refused to look for it and said they were too scared to go into the field with the fierce cow. Cowards.

The attending nurse was not too pleased, nor did she try to hide the fact - no sympathy, not even for someone with a broken ankle.

So as you can see, all of this was my ex-wife's fault for divorcing me. I'm still right about the 'cow pushing' thing by the way, and one day I'll prove it to them when I work up enough courage.

CHAPTER 2

CABIN FEVER

I think it was T. S. Elliot that said, *'what is hell? hell is oneself, hell is alone, the other figures in it, merely projections. There is nothing to escape from and nothing to escape to. One is always alone.'*

It's bad enough being alone, add incapacitation, then the situation really is hellacious - I feel like I'm imprisoned in my upper bedroom as I stare vacantly out of the grimy window on to the street below. The square is devoid of life apart from a dog crapping on the grass - I imagine a gun with sights trained on it. It has even got to the stage I find cloud formation quite interesting.

How on earth am I going to endure another five weeks of this, there's only so much daytime television you can digest without becoming mentally devitalized, it's chewing gum for the brain.

The problem is compounded because I live in a dingy room approximately 12 feet by 12 feet - it's not been decorated in years, plus it lacks a bit of feng shui. The wallpaper is a delightful combination of brown and yellow flowers that's matched with an orange carpet that comes with it's own cat hair. It's 1980's décor, it's not kitsch or retro, it's just gaudy, completely rank. A pink shade with a 60 watt bulb adorns the ceiling and illuminates my life. I can actually put a date to the carpet and probably the last time it was decorated - 4th of June 1982. How do I know? - I lifted up the carpet to hide a key for my money box and found an edition of the 'Daily Record' from that date. It was quite a fascinating read actually, especially the pope coming to Glasgow which doesn't happen that often. I found myself lifting up other sections of the carpet to see what was underneath, there was a copy of the 'Sun,' which I read, 'The Peoples Friend' which is for old boring people, and an edition of the 'Sunday Post.'

I share the facilities with my charming landlady who chain smokes, drinks gin and tonic for breakfast at the weekends and has the unnerving habit of wandering about in a state of undress. I think she fancies me.

Sandra Potter is about 55 years old, divorced, has dyed red hair, wears too much makeup and has rather large breasts that look like two puppies fighting in a sack when she moves. They're quite hypnotic really.

I've lived in this symbiotic relationship for a fortnight for which she charges the reasonable price of sixty pounds per week, 'with no other bills,' as it was advertised. I would have loved to sub let a small flat in

Dirty Laundry

Strathaven or even East Kilbride but the prices were too exorbitant and I was desperate to get away from my parents who were kind enough to take me in for a while until I found my feet. Anyone who has moved back in with their parents after being independent for a while will know how truly awful it is, it will probably scar me mentally.

It's amazing how quickly your life can turn around, not that long ago I was living in a beautiful old sandstone house in Lethame road, the posh bit of Strathaven and it had just been renovated at considerable cost and we had it looking wonderful. As a couple we went on foreign holidays twice a year, and enjoyed the benefits of a joint income. Money was never an issue -Jill worked as a personal assistant to a lawyer and was climbing the corporate ladder so to speak, she was also, to my utter consternation, involved in some horizontal gymnastics if you know what I mean. Bitch!

When we divorced I found myself on a downward spiral, I was put out of the house, lost access to the car and was left with some crippling credit card bills that were in my name - she even got the two gold fish. I did however leave with my dignity in tact, my clothes, a Yamaha acoustic guitar, a keyboard, and a selection of knickknacks and photos- scant reward I feel for ten loyal years of marriage. It's hard to think about her now without my blood pressure rising or coming out in hives.

Now I'm stuck in a single room in Laurel Place which Stevie said was, and I quote, 'a bit on the rough side.' He said that people there install double glazing by nailing on a second sheet of plywood and that one way of telling you are in Greenhills is that the Somerfield trolleys are usually up on bricks. A slight exaggeration I think, it's one of those places that gets a bad name, yet it's no worse than anywhere else in East Kilbride I can assure you. So there we have it, I'm in sunny Laurel with a broken ankle, up to my eyes in debt, indisposed staring at four sickly walls listening to the Ken Bruce show on radio two - isn't life one big bowl of cherries!

The worrying aspect of this unfortunate downturn is the financial one, being self employed means the government in all its generosity pays me the princely sum of fifty-three pounds per week for my incapacitation. Fifty-three quid. I used to spend that on a night out at the weekend. I have exactly five hundred pounds in the bank so I'm just about reaching the panicking point if I can clear all my bills and keep a roof over my head - sitting on a street corner with a Styrofoam cup in hand asking for money is not an option yet.

I dread to think what Mrs Potter would say if I informed her I had no money to pay her. Would she put me out? Would she make me sleep with her for payment? Would she demand excessive interest if I defaulted?

Things are going to be tight for a while so I decided to be extra vigilant with my resources - no more alcohol or comfort food, curries.

I sat on the bed and my mind began to wander, it's been doing that a lot recently, I think I'm suffering from a mild dose of cabin fever. How can I earn money? Rummaging through the drawer I found a pencil and a piece of paper and started jotting down some suggestions - they came thick and slow.

1.Music lessons

I could get Sandra to put a few adverts in the local shops, maybe in the papers, and charge a reasonable fee for tuition. I'm proficient at guitar and piano, a legacy I owe to my parents. I played in a few bands when I was a bit younger and had more hair so teaching the basics to learners or even advanced theory should not be too difficult. I put a tick against number one.

2.

I pencilled in number two and waited for some inspiration, nothing was forthcoming. I know it sounds pathetic, but after a few minutes racking my brain (I've not used it much recently) I wrote, 'BABYSITTING.' Not the best of ideas, who would want a giant (I'm six-foot six) middle aged bloke who looks like Shrek to watch your precious offspring. People constantly tell me I'm quite intimidating looking, anyway I hate snotty nosed kids, even my sisters weans are still frightened of me and they are both teenagers. A cross went against that suggestion.

I needed a coffee to kick-start the old thinking processes, so I hobbled down the stairs in discomfort, cursing along the way. I kicked the cat up the arse as it sauntered past me - that's another thing I hate, the wee bugger crapped on my carpet the other day and that was a swift reminder to stay out of my room, I don't care if it was hers before. I pay sixty pounds a week for the privilege so no cat's defecating in my space. The cat, by the way, is named 'Fanny,' which is the worse possible name for a feline and it's also hugely embarrassing listening to Mrs Potter shouting it in from the garden or even just listening to her talking about her beloved Fanny. She seems completely unfazed by the name and the obvious 'double entendres' it throws up, I honestly think she named it that for a laugh, although she said it was named 'Fanny' after her auntie, Fanny Furtuck. What a strange family.

I got into the kitchen and opened the cupboard that was allocated to me, it was a depressing sight that greeted me, two tins of beans, not even Heinz, a packet of porridge, (the only oats I get these days) tuna, peas, a pot noodle, and half a tin of cocktail cherries. I bet the master chefs on 'ready steady cook' could not concoct something out of that lot. I had run out of coffee so I borrowed some of Mrs Potters, I knew she

Dirty Laundry

wouldn't mind, she told me to help myself to tea or coffee anytime.

Her spirit of generosity emboldened me to pinch a few of her ginger nuts - anyway I gave her a muffin last week so it's a fair arrangement I think. Armed with caffeine and biscuits I struggled back upstairs to my personal prison to continue the quest for additional income. I looked at my pathetic notes, 'music lessons'- not too bad, then 'babysitting'- who am I kidding. Number three was a bit slow in coming.

3. Sell my body

I wrote that one down half joking then decided otherwise, I had the body but not the looks unfortunately, someone once described me as having a face that could turn milk sour, I personally think that was a bit cruel. Some other so-called friend said that when I was born the nurse slapped my mother! Just as well I'm thick skinned, the caustic remarks are now water off a duck's back.

I sharpened my pencil again and stared out of the window looking for inspiration. I saw the bearded face of Jesus in the clouds which transmogrified into a chicken or was it a turkey? The cloud gazing killed five minutes. Still nothing. Zilch. I then remembered something I read recently that would get me moving. It was an old horse dealers trick to make a tired, broken down animal look lively by inserting a piece of ginger into the horse's anus, hence the phrase, ' to ginger up', which meant to put spirit or mettle into it, I wonder if Sandra has got any ginger downstairs?. If not I could improvise, maybe a piece of red hot chili, I'm sure that would do the trick, it would certainly enliven me. Number four, come on think, another suggestion for number four. Ah!

4. Stuffing envelopes

It's just about all I can manage at the moment physically but it would be better than nothing, without a laptop or computer I'm limited in my options.

After draining the last of the coffee I had what they call 'writers block,' a constipation of the mind, I had exhausted all avenues, which didn't say much for the range of my talents.

So there we have it, I can stuff envelopes all day (monkeys work) or I can teach music. The first suggestion was the best by far and I was determined to make a go of it. The door slammed downstairs, I knew it was Mrs Potter, she could not close a door quietly - I heard her coming up the stairs.

"Jack, are you in?" She pushed the door open. Sandra had the unnerving habit of just waltzing in unannounced, the last time she did that I was in my boxing shorts - "nice shorts," she said, and continued unabated. I know it's her house but I still need a bit of sanctuary.

"Hi Mrs Potter."

"Call me Sandra for goodness sake."

"Sandra, what can I do for you?"

"Nothing really, just checking to see you are alright, if you need anything - I'm off to the shops for a few things." A few things meant gin and fags normally.

"Actually you can do something for me, can you put this advert in the Spar shop, I'm thinking about tutoring, music tuition to make some money since I'm housebound at the moment. I thought of a few other ideas but I couldn't come up with anything else."

"Sounds a fine idea, but it might take a while before any interest is generated. Listen I realize the situation you're in. You're self-employed, money is tight, so if the 'dig money' is a bit late don't worry you can pay me whenever you get back on your feet again. Back on your feet again, get it!"

She let out a loud rasping laugh, it was infectious. Her presence immediately lifted my spirits, it was good to have someone to chat to after being stuck inside all day. I felt like I was suffocating in boredom.

"That's very kind of you Mrs Potter, eh Sandra, I think I should be alright for a while, but yeah, money is tight at the moment. One other thing, could you possibly bring me back two of those microwave dinners, curry or something?"

"Sure darling." I handed her a fiver. She was about to leave the room and turned back and remarked, "You know I had a friend who was once housebound for a while, she was bored and found that time really dragged, do you know what she did to earn a little income?" Being a man I immediately thought of prostitution, selling her body, just like my idea.

"No, tell me, I'm open to suggestion."

"She wrote a book."

"Did she?"

"Yeah, she eventually managed to get it published and made herself about two thousand quid - not bad eh?"

"Excellent, but my long list of talents doesn't stretch that far I'm afraid, I'm not a writer."

"Neither was she, but she did it -why don't you try something like that while your waiting for a few clients, it will keep you busy and your mind off your problems, it will give you something constructive to do in the interim."

"It sounds a good idea but I'm not qualified."

"Who needs qualifications? Have you heard of the author Sue Townsend?"

"Of course, she wrote the diary of Adrian Mole and countless other tomes."

"That's the one, she's a prolific writer, books as well as screen stuff, very talented, very funny, down to earth - in fact I've got one of her books upstairs if you wish to read it - its called 'Public confessions of a middle aged woman aged 55 and three quarters.' The point is Jack, she left school with little in the way of qualifications and went through no formal training in writing, basically she just blagged it, wrote a book, found a publisher and the rest is history as they say."

"I'm sure that happens to few people Sandra."

"It's only a suggestion."

"I suppose I could give it a try, what have I got to lose, and as you said it will keep me busy in the meantime," I said with a bit of enthusiasm, "but I wouldn't really know what to write about."

"Well they say you should write about what you know."

"God, it's going to be a very short story then."

"You're a window cleaner right?"

"Yeah."

"Why don't you write something about that, how long have you been doing that job?"

"About twenty years or so, I dropped out of university, I was studying philosophy at the time and became increasing disillusioned with it all. I realized philosophy was as someone once described, 'like a blind man in a dark room, looking for a black cat that doesn't exist.' After that I bummed about for a while before cleaning windows - it was only supposed to be for a week or so to help out a friend, the week or so turned out to be twenty years, I think I might be stuck in a rut, I'm not particularly the ambitious type, mediocrity has its attractions, it's a lot less demanding than success."

She smiled at my honest comments and then suggested, "look you must have a few stories to tell after cleaning windows for 20 years, you've probably seen a few sights heard a few juicy stories."

"Yes I have Sandra. I've seen and heard a lot over the years, life, death, scandal, some sad events, some inspirational as well, not to mention some of the characters and the situations they have been in."

"Well, there you are then, surely you could fill a few pages with that and the rest you could embellish - you could call it - you could call it 'What the window cleaner saw' - or something as equally brilliant!"

"Sounds good, I'll think about it," I said warming to the idea.

"Right then, advert in shop and two microwave dinners, any brand in particular?"

"Not really, as long as it looks palatable."

"Jack they all look wonderful on the front cover, but they usually taste like shite!" She smiled at me then walked out the room talking to herself. Adding the 'e' to shit somehow made the word more offensive. She had a colourful way of expressing herself, a spade was a spade to Mrs Potter. I was really beginning to warm to her and her certain peculiar idiosyncrasies. Yeah, I definitely think she fancies me. A few drinks and she might even come across as attractive, as they say 'beauty is in the eye of the beer holder.' At my age, and with my looks, I can't be too picky these days. I really must get around to having sex again before I forget what it is and what the limp appendage hanging between my legs is for.

Mrs Potter is in a very good mood today, she mentioned that her friend is coming up tonight for a 'night' as she calls it and she promised to introduce me to Irene Black. I'm very curious what she looks like, what age she is and would she be susceptible to my animal magnetism. I have already formed a plan of action, I'll dig out my best jeans, put on a fresh shirt, shave and splash on the aftershave, this in theory, should make me irresistible, well, that's the theory anyway.

I heard the downstairs door slam and I watched from the window as she headed for the Spar shop in the Whitehills, she had her Fanny on a lead, which I can assure you was a strange sight to behold - the poor cat struggled to keep up with her frenetic pace, Sandra always seemed to be in a hurry, she was a bundle of energy for a middle aged woman.

I thought about her suggestion as she drifted out of sight, I harboured some doubts whether I was actually capable of writing a novel or if I would be wasting my time with this particular flight of fancy. They say everyone has a book in them, maybe mine is a booklet, what the hell did I have to lose? It would give me something to do that's constructive and take my mind of the insufferable tedium I was experiencing, no more cloud gazing or staring out the window waiting for something exciting to happen.

I decided to unplug the television, I felt like I was unplugging my life support system, its been on constantly since the accident, goodbye Trisha, GMTV,

Richard and Judy, and black and white films on channel five, no distractions, time do something positive, be creative.

I organized a pad of A 4 paper, a sharp pencil and a rubber, and was now set to write a literary masterpiece. One thing was missing, something that provided inspiration, afflatus - a small drink, I've read that most creative artists occasionally imbibe, it lubricates thought.

This was the last of my supplies, once the bottle of single malt was finished, that was it, as I said, money is tight and this now represents a luxury. The smooth whiskey burned as it slipped down and I stared at the blank piece of paper waiting for the words to flow - the flow unfortunately didn't even constitute a trickle, the river bed of the mind was dry and dusty. I could now visualize tumbleweed rolling in the distance. I stared at the blank piece of paper and it stared back, it was like it was teasing me, daring me to write something on it. I suppose the first few words are the hardest, I think it was Quentin Crisp that said, *'there are three reasons for becoming a writer, the first is that you need the money, the second, that you have something to say that you think the world should know and the third is that you can't think what to do with the long winter evenings.'*

I embodied all three reasons. Surely something will come, the conditions were perfect, I have five weeks, a good pencil, paper and rubber, no distractions like a phone or television and more importantly, no wife. When I think of Jill my mind turns to murder mystery novels, something that contains heinous crimes, blood and guts for some reason, but I quickly dismiss the thought, that would be too difficult, I'll leave that up to Ian Rankin, I don't want to muscle in on his genre of writing.

I jotted down the title Mrs Potter suggested, 'What the window cleaner saw.' It didn't look too bad, although it sounded like a soft porn movie from the seventies, but it certainly conjures up some interesting images and thoughts - yeah the working title would do for now unless I came up with a better title myself.

A breakthrough at last, I've actually got words down on the paper, even if they were not mine. I was so delighted with the progress I poured myself another small malt whiskey, hard work should always be rewarded my father used to say. Sandra's suggestion was actually quite good, there was a lot of scope for such a book considering the time I've spent in the job, the characters I have met and the situations I have been in, it runs the whole gamut I suppose from life to death, laughter and tears, to hope and despair with a good measure of banality in between.

I've seen a lot in the twenty years or so cleaning windows, and witnessed many changes,for instance, the close community where you were acquainted with everyone in you street is now a distant memory, with the exception of your immediate neighbour - many of us don't know the names of the people across the street from us or what goes on behind the lace curtains, maybe it's just as well. Trust and openness with neighbours has been replaced to a certain degree by suspicion and wariness.

Imagine you lived next door to the quiet, unassuming chap called Denis Nilsson, his neighbours said he was a hard working man that was employed in the job centre in Kentish town. Pleasant, well dressed, quiet spoken - then in February of 1983 a neighbour reports a bit of a smell and a blocked drain in Cranley gardens, Muswell Hill. A 'dyno rod' employee is sent to investigate the blockage and finds to his horror the decomposing remains of a human. When the blockage was traced back to no 23a, Nilsson's flat, the police were called in, broke down the door and discovered human remains everywhere - in the wardrobe, under the bed, even chilling in the fridge. Sixteen people died in his flat and it was later found out he had a penchant for young gay boys.

I suppose it could be worse, you could have lived next door to Fred and Rosemary West. On the upside you could have been fortunate enough to have lived beside someone who was a pillar of society or someone famous like George Orwell, I'm sure neighbours were oblivious of his prodigious talent as he worked in the local store and bookshop to supplement his income.

Dirty Laundry

As I said you just don't really know who's in your neighbourhood ,I personally think that good neighbours are the ones you don't see. Cynical? Probably.

I don't think I can promise something as sensational as the Nilsson story or someone with the talents of Orwell, it's more likely to be 'kitchen sink' material with one or two surprises thrown in.

I scribbled down some of my experiences and some of the people that made a lasting impression on me over the years, and would eventually separate the wheat from the chaff as there was quite a lot to choose from. One of the first to be committed to paper was a woman called Rose from Glen Cannich who read palms and tarot cards and attended the spiritualist church in Glasgow, every time I think about my experience with her I still get goose bumps,that would be a good story to start the book I'm sure.

John, the town drunk from Glen Moriston is another character worthy of mention - the situations he's been in would be difficult to make up, some of them even defy belief. I think you could describe him as 'colourful.' He has now sadly departed from this mortal coil, so I'm sure he won't mind me recounting some of his inebriated exploits, and to be fair to him, some of the positive aspects of his life. John eventually drank himself into an early grave, not a bad way to go I suppose.

I was now beginning to enjoy the experience - words and ideas actually flowed and the general outline of the book was beginning to take some form. I would use Sandra as a sounding board for ideas as well as constructive criticism as she was, in my opinion, very well read - her library was as impressive as it was diverse, it ranged from Franz Kafka to Stephen King, Michael Creighton to Stephen Hawkins - she always had her nose in a book and a glass in her hand, she worked hard and played hard, not a bad philosophy.

Speak of the devil. I heard the door slam and the footsteps approaching. The door was pushed open.

"Here we go darling, sorry I took so long, I forgot to say I had an appointment to get my hair cut." She thrust a Spar bag in my hand.

"Your hair is lovely Sandra, you suit that style."

"Thank you, it makes me look ten years younger doesn't it?" I was obliged to agree although ten years was a bit hopeful.

"That Lisa does a great job," she said running her fingers through it. " Hope you like these Chinese noodles, couldn't find anything curry wise in your price range, there's a bit of change and the receipt in the bottom of the bag."

Not high on my list, noodles, they have the taste and consistency of rubber bands in a sauce, but when you're ravenous you'll eat anything.

"Yeah these will do fine Sandra thanks."

"Your ad is in the Spar shop and I got Lisa to put one in her window, no charge, its cause I always give her a good tip."

"Brilliant." I saw her eyeing my bottle of Glenmorangie. " Would you like a small malt, it is the afternoon?" It didn't take much convincing.

"Oh that would be lovely darling, just a small one though, I'll nick down and get a couple of glasses, drinking whisky out a tumbler is quite socially unacceptable. Do you want me to put that in the microwave for you when I'm down?"

"Please if you don't mind."

I smiled as she left the room, what an eccentric woman. I noticed in the cupboard all types of glasses and she would only serve a drink in the appropriate one, for instance a Guinness would only be served in a genuine Guinness glass, wine in fine crystal glasses and whiskey in the proper chunky glasses. She came back up five minutes later with my noodles which smelled pretty good, and two slices of bread and butter which I thought was very kind and two Jack Daniel glasses. I poured her a generous measure.

"You've been busy I see," she said taking a sip.

"Well I thought I'd make a start on the book, god that sounds a bit pretentious, I've a few ideas already, its just a matter of getting them in some type of order," I said sounding like an experienced author.

"Good for you it will keep your mind occupied until you get a few replies back from your advert, if you write a few more out I could put them on the notice boards in my work if you want, that might help."

"Thanks I'll do that."

"Oh listen, I meant to say to you I've got an electric typewriter in the small bedroom, its only about six months old, its never been touched, you're welcome to use it if you like. I bought one of those computers and I've no need for it now."

Her generous offer was accepted with thanks and I refilled her glass, we chatted for a while before she departed downstairs to prepare dinner for her girl friend Irene. She promised to keep me some chilli con carne, which she modestly described as ' the best in the world.' We will see. It certainly would be better than hot rubber bands in a spicy sauce.

My interest was once again piqued by the mysterious Irene Black. Sandra spoke very highly of her and was obviously fond of her. I've already visualised her as a cross between Helen Mirron and Sharon Stone, someone who's attracted to ugly blokes, has a great sense of humour, big bosoms, and is financially secure. I wonder if that's just too optimistic and hope I'm not too disappointed when I finally get to meet her.

I've not had much luck in the last year or so with women since splitting up with Jill, my confidence took a bit of a beating and it was about ten months until I had my first date, or to be completely honest a blind date through the pages of the local paper. It turned out to be an unmitigated disaster.

I know some people might view it as a little sad, even needy, but I thought I would try my luck through the lonely hearts column in the East Kilbride news, it did say and I quote, ' Finding your ideal partner has never been easier - phone 09069 169 001 to find the perfect match.'

It was exciting trawling through the 'women seeking men' section, for some reason all the women sounded attractive, even exotic, just what I was looking for. Initially I had some bother with the 'dating jargon,' WLTM, I worked out as 'would like to meet'; GSOH, 'good sense of humour, and as far as I could make out, OHAT was 'own hair and teeth' or it could be 'own house and tent'- I'm not too sure to be honest. I'm afraid the jury is out on, DKFF. I asked Stevie what it represented and he said it was, 'drowns kittens for fun.' Surely not!

Anyway to cut a long story short, I arranged to meet, and I quote once again from the paper, ' attractive, cuddly, blonde, forty one years old, five foot three, WLTM honest male, over six foot, between 30-40, NS, who is able to offer friendship, possibly a LTR.

I didn't seek Stevie's help on LTR, I reckoned it meant, 'long term relationship'. We had arranged to meet at eight o'clock in the Bonnie Prince Charlie lounge, (not exactly the most romantic place in the world, it could certainly do with a fresh lick of paint and a few discreet air fresheners) for a few quiet drinks then a romantic, candle lit dinner somewhere, depending on her taste. She gave a brief description of herself which sounded wonderful and said she would be wearing a black dress by 'missoni' and a red jacket and would be carrying a magazine. She sounded really nice on the phone, very well spoken, educated, even a bit flirtatious and I was really looking forward to meeting up with her.

I gave her a quick description of myself which, as you would expect, was on the flattering side, the fact that I was six foot six and had a shoe size 12 seemed to impress her. It all sounded very intriguing and exciting, a chance encounter or amorous liaison with a perfect stranger, it's the stuff of romantic fantasy, Mills and Boon. My imagination was working overtime, double time!

I had spent a lot of time thinking up some smooth lines to impress her as well as some humourous anecdotes and stories so that I would come across as someone windswept and interesting. I ran a few by Neil to test the water so to speak and he just collapsed in a paroxysm of laughter, I genuinely thought they were very romantic, was I really that out of touch? 'Do you believe in love at first sight, or should I walk by again? There must be something wrong with my eyes. I can't take them off you. Is there an airport nearby, or was that just my heart taking off?'

I can't help it, I'm a romantic at heart. Women like to be told these things, fussed over and to be the centre of attention. Neil's suggestions were downright crass, needless to say I rejected them all, even I found them offensive, 'Nice arse doll, can I wear it as a hat?' 'How are you doing babe, the word of the day is 'legs.' Let's go back to your place and spread the word.' 'Would you like a gin and tonic or would you prefer a scotch and sofa?'

Unrefined and discourteous, and from a former figure of authority, no wonder there's concern over our kids future.

I arrived at the Bonnie Prince Charlie at 7.15 a.m. I know it was a bit early but I was keen and I needed a drink to settle the nerves and take in the ambiance. I ordered a lager and sat in the corner so I could see everyone coming in, it was a good vantage point. As eight o'clock neared, and the door opened, my eyes darted in that direction waiting for a glimpse of my blind date. For some reason every woman that walked into the lounge was extremely attractive, and I was beginning to salivate into my Fosters lager.

Excitement was mounting, and I was hoping I would be doing the same later on in the night.

That is until my blind date walked in, or to be strictly accurate, wobbled in, giant thighs chaffing against each other, without being too unkind you could have parked a bus in the shadow of her backside, I think the word I was looking for was 'steatophgous,' a word I learned from Stevie, which meant very simply, 'big bottomed.' I didn't know designer dresses were made that big, I thought they only sold them in size 6-10.

To say I was disappointed was an understatement, I actually felt my jaw drop (and my testicles) when I saw her - cartoon like.

Here's a word of warning for anyone contemplating a blind date and reading the description in the ads - if it says *'cuddly'* it means positively endomorphic; *'emotionally secure'* usually means, well medicated; *' average looking,'* is ugly; *'open minded'* usually translates as desperate and *'tanned'* means wrinkled and leathery looking.

My blind date for the night spent most of the night making excuses for her weight problem as she picked the meat of her chicken chat and shovelled pakora into her mouth. It reminded me of those boiler workers on the steam trains shovelling the coal into the furnace at great pace to keep the engine going. She said she was 'big boned,' then it was a problem with 'water retention,' she wasn't retaining water, it was more like retaining fatty foods.

To be absolutely honest I think she was crestfallen when she first set eyes on me, she was expecting someone a bit better looking, I had probably built myself up as Mel Gibson whereas in reality I was more like Mel Smith - but that's a blind date for you, potluck.

It wasn't by any means a wasted night, we both enjoyed ourselves, had a wonderful meal over some good conversation, had a laugh then exchanged phone numbers and promised to keep in touch. At least I got a kiss at the end of the night and for a big girl she was a fantastic kisser.

When Mrs Potter finally departed from the room after a chat the hot noodles were stone cold and decidedly unpalatable. I couldn't eat them in front of her, it seemed rude, and I don't think they could take another burst in the microwave. I was hungry so I had to do something. Brainwave, epiphany, call it what you like - I poured the last of the Glenmorangie over the lifeless noodles, hoping for some cuisine resurrection. They were now cold and wet but I ate them nevertheless with the bread and butter. Bon appetite. I miss Jill's cooking.

I reviewed the initial notes I had made when I was reasonably sober and they looked quite impressive, the main body of the work was established, I had an idea for an introduction, so overall I was pleased with my endeavours. Sandra's idea looked pretty good, it should be interesting, provocative, possibly polemic if it's written properly.

I could enlist the help of Neil and Stevie for the final proof reading of the work as they are suitably qualified, being teachers. I hasten to add Neil is an ex-teacher still looking for gainful employment. I trust their judgement and value their friendship equally.

I have about 16 short stories to tell, interspersed with some anecdotes and my own personal viewpoints and observations of life all within the small community of East Kilbride and Strathaven - from the rich to the poor, the educated to the great unwashed, the young to the elderly. A genuine slice of life.

Sixteen insights from:

The canteen con lady
Two customers caught in 'flagrante dilecto'
The town drunk
A cannabis factory in a living room
The corporate thief
The senile lady
The teenage suicide
The tarot reader
Jehovah's witnesses
The obsessive compulsive woman who collects strange items.
A pensioner sitting on a fortune
The doctor struck off for wife beating
The drink driver
The drug pusher
The town lush
The toddler that died of cancer.

Yeah, it looks good, all I needed to do was flesh it out, conduct some research, and make it as interesting as possible.

The huge mental strain of thinking, a few malts, a full stomach and I was feeling drowsy. I drifted off to sleep with the aroma of chilli con carne in my nostrils and the sound of Tom Jones reverberating in my ears. Not a bad combination actually.

My last thoughts were that of Irene Black. When I meet the enigmatic lady I might rehash some of the old chat up lines to see if they work with a different person. I just hope she's not a 'big boned' person, or 'retains water.'

CHAPTER 3

GHOST

I woke up to the sight of a huge bosom alarmingly close to my face, it looked like someone had shoved two pink balloons down a jumper. It must have been an epic struggle. Mrs Potter was leaning over me, fag in mouth.

"Jack, Jack, ... it's the phone for you - I shouted up but you must have dozed off." Horrible feeling when you wake up and you don't know what day it is.

"Thanks Sandra, must have nodded off...I'll be down in a minute." Once again she breezes right in, no chap of the door, no warning - I'll get my own back one of these days and see how she likes it. I hobbled down the stairs with the aid of the crutch, walked into the living room and lifted up the receiver.

"Hi, Jack Wilde speaking."

"Good evening Mr Wilde, you have just been selected out of thousands from your post code area to receive a substantial discount on a fitted kitchen from our latest design." I interrupted.

"Actually that sounds good, I'm looking for a new kitchen at the moment, oh could you hold the line for a second, someone has just chapped the door."

"No problem Mr Wilde." I left the phone off the hook and wandered into the kitchen. I usually tell them their call is important to me then play some quiet background music before disappearing -I detest with those bloody nuisance sales calls, especially when it's a real effort just to get down the stairs.

Sandra was in the kitchen perched upon a stool, glass in hand watching the news on the portable television. Her face was flushed, probably a combination of the heat during cooking and the Gordon's gin.

"Smells nice Sandra," I commented.

"Thanks, anyone interesting on the phone?"

"No, not really just a sales call."

"What were they offering this time, a free kitchen, bathroom? They must think we are thick, you get nothing for free in this world Jack, trust me." I nodded in assent. "Here, before you disappear again try this and see what you think." She reached for a wooded spoon and proffered a sample of the dish, it was wonderful, quite hot and spicy.

"Oh yeah, that's good, very good."

"Thanks, see that small pot there, that's yours, you can pinch some of my rice if you don't have any yourself."

"Great, that's very kind. So when is your friend coming up tonight?"

"About eight o'clock ,listen, you must come down and meet her, have a quick blether."

"I don't want to impose."

"It's no imposition at all, as I keep telling you, the living room is for your use as well, you don't have to shut yourself up in your room all day."

"Alright I'll stop in for ten minutes, I won't stay too long if you're having company. Bye the way, the typewriter is excellent, it looks brand new."

"It is new, I just bought myself a computer so I don't really use it - how's the book coming on?"

"I've got it well organized, so I think I'll make a start this evening, it's just getting the first words down, that's the most difficult bit."

"Good, it will keep you busy, keep you out of trouble. Right, better check my pie." She lifted an apple pie out of the oven, the aroma was wonderful, I felt myself salivate then felt short changed with the Chinese noodles.

"Looks good Sandra - you're a bit of a chef alright," I remarked.

"Before I worked at Avex, I was in a restaurant for many years, the Hilton in Glasgow, so you could say I know my way around a kitchen, I'll keep you a bit of pie as well."

"You're a darling, thanks -right I'll get out of your hair and I'll see you later on tonight, I'm away to write a best seller."

Before starting the 'literary masterpiece,' I decided to make myself respectable for Sandra's guest - I showered, washed my hair, brushed and flossed my teeth, in an attempt to impress them , copious amounts of aftershave was splashed over my body. I was feeling great, truly awake now and ready for the first story. I made myself a cup of black coffee, loaded the typewriter with paper and was ready for some serious work. The introduction for the book was already written on a pad of paper and would set the scene, it ran to about eight pages and it would just be a matter of typing it up later.

I wanted to start the book with one of the strongest stories, one that would immediately grip the reader, hold their attention and keep them turning the pages - well, that was the theory anyway. I decided to start with a customer called Rose who stayed in Glen Cannich in St Leonards and entitled the chapter, 'Ghost.'

I know it's a tired, hackneyed phrase, 'never judge a book by it's cover,' but it remains a cautious piece of advice as people are not always what they seem. On first impression Rose was an ordinary unpretentious housewife going about her business. She was polite, soft spoken and always paid on time which I was grateful for. She was also a very good tipper which showed the generous side of her personality.

The neighbours felt the same except that she was maybe just too private, even reclusive. Rose kept to herself and rarely socialised, which in this day and age isn't too unusual. She was widowed and lived by herself for the last three or four years along with her two black cats.

Rose Hume was anything but ordinary. She was extraordinary.

When I think of the things she said and what she performed, my blood still runs cold and for a while after our meeting I suffered nightmares - I thought that nothing could faze me and I treated people with 'supernatural' gifts with casual contempt, sometimes even ridicule, but not now. For a while, I'm ashamed to say, I slept with a lamp on at night much to the annoyance of Jill.

But she wasn't there. She didn't experience what I did.

It was a cold December morning with a wind that could cut right through you, I had only been working for about an hour when it started to rain heavily, I finished Rose's house and decided to call it a day. As I walked down the path, thoroughly depressed and cold, she kindly asked me in for a cup of coffee. I normally declined because I'm usually too busy, but the thought of a hot coffee was very appealing this morning and I gratefully accepted her kind offer.

I don't think I've even had a conversation with Rose before, just the usual pleasantries were exchanged, banal stuff, usually weather related.

She went into the kitchen to make the coffee (real percolated coffee that smelled superb) and I walked over to her impressive bookcase that positively groaned under the weight of the tomes, the bookcase ran the length of one wall and it looked like she had a very interesting collection. You can tell a lot about a person by the books they read, I personally think that a room without books is like a body without a soul. Some of the volumes looked antediluvian but very striking, there was a certain redolence off them, the smell of weathered leather, you felt like you were touching a piece of history when you handled some of her books. Maybe she was a book collector, a bibliophile, some of them appeared to be worth something judging by the date of publication.

I lifted out an old black leather volume entitled *'A system of magick, a history of the black art'*, and was astonished to note that is was published in 1727. It was 278 years old! It pre dated events like William Bligh and his ship ' the bounty' sailing to Tahiti; the invention of the spinning mule by Crompton; the great famine of Bengal that took 10 million lives; the Jacobite victory at the battle of Falkirk; Dick Turpin's execution, and even the appointment of the great composer Handel of the Kings theatre in London!

I carefully flicked through some of its pages - there was disturbing images and illustrations, one page was a document said to have been signed in reverse Latin as a pact between the 17th century priest Urbaun Grandier and the demons, headed by the great demon, Lucifer, the shining one. There was pages of incantations, spells, conjurations, alchemy and other material I was completely unacquainted with.

Fascinating, but slightly disturbing.

I put it back and lifted out a beautiful reddish leather bound book called, *'Hermetic order of the golden dawn,'* 1887, by Dr W Westcott. It was a work on transcendental teaching, whatever that was.

Most of her collection could be classified under 'supernatural' or the 'occult', there was everything from Jung, geomancy, Kali Yuga, astral planes and I Ching. One book caught my attention, written by Aldous Huxley entitled *' The doors of perception.'* I had read that book when I was at university. I remember the book was controversial at the time as it encouraged experimenting with mind-expanding drugs.

Rose came in with the coffee and I complimented her eclectic collection of rare books -many of them were first editions and were worth a considerable amount of money - she had taken out extra insurance for them. She had devoted a lot of her time to 'the quest of the unknown' as she called it ever since her twin boys and her husband died of a rare blood disorder. Rose had even written a book on the subject of the afterlife which she proudly showed to me and I was very impressed with her knowledge and her 'religious' devotion to the subject.

I remained unconvinced however, and was still suspicious of all the 'hocus pocus'and the rituals and symbolisms involved, being a catholic I had seen enough of it to last a lifetime.

During our conversation I learned that she was unemployed at the moment and spent her time studying and researching for another book which her publisher was desperate for, she had created a great deal of interest with her first tome and the second one would be a natural progression, and I would imagine, a good source of income, she had already been given a two and a half thousand advance. She supplemented her income by reading palms and tarot cards, a 45 minute reading of tarot cards cost £30.00 which I thought was a fantastic remuneration.

I made the mistake of gently mocking her. I possibly offended her although she took it in good spirit. My view of life and death was simplistic, when you're dead, you're dead, that's it, nothing more, nothing less, a bit nihilistic. If there was an afterlife, why the hell has no one come back and told us what it's like? Where's the evidence? I was sceptical and I proudly told Rose I was a pragmatist.

Show me, prove it to me.

She smiled and refilled my cup and offered to read my palm or perform a reading of the tarot cards which

I refused because they were too damn creepy for my liking - who wants to be involved with images of a horned goat devil crouching on a pedestal with a naked woman and man in chains, or a hooded monk holding a lantern - even worse the death card that depicts someone hanging upside down on an inverted cross

No thanks.

I decided that an innocuous palm reading would be sufficient. She sat down beside me and I was quite amused by it all but decided to go along with it in case I offended her again.

I reckoned Rose was about 40 to 45 years old, very nice looking, but there was an inherent sadness about her. Her eyes seemed to reflect that, I also thought she was lonely or reflected too much on the past which weighed her down, made her restless. I got the impression she wanted to be somewhere else.

Before she read my hand she explained a bit about it and asked for some silver as it represented good fortune. I handed her a few pounds. She carefully explained that palmistry or chiromancy, is based on lines, texture, colours and the pads of the hand and that it was originally taught in India and China more than 3,000 years ago and was even practiced by the ancient Greeks.

So far I remained unconvinced but appreciated the lesson on palmistry. Rose went on to elucidate about the uniqueness of finger prints, and that palmistry was not so much of a divinatory art but a type of scientific character analysis. Physical characteristics were revealed in the hand, a doctor for example can look at your hand or nails and detect if there is something wrong with you physically - a single crease on the hand at birth could indicate downs syndrome, and a number of skin diseases are directly related to mental stress.

There was a germ of truth in that I concluded. She finally went on to explain that each finger is 'ruled' by a particular planet - the index finger represents Jupiter, the middle one Saturn, the third finger the sun, and the pinkie represents Mercury. The fleshy parts of the hand represent other planets. Even the shape of the hand was significant. She explained about the importance of the elements, the earth fire and water. In all fairness she made a pretty convincing case for the art but I still harboured some doubts. She smiled as she took my hand. It was surprisingly cold to the touch and she was wearing a beautiful diamond ring that belonged to her great grandmother.

I felt like I was involved in a bit of street theatre but went along with it nevertheless.

Five minutes passed before she uttered a single word, the hand was studied meticulously, every papillary ridge, every fold, line, fingertip, nail and pad. I watched with growing interest as Rose jotted down some notes, I thought she was finished when she released my right hand. Wrong.

She proceeded to do the same with the left which puzzled me because I thought that both hands were basically analogous, she later explained although there were many similarities, the other hand contained nuances that were useful for interpretation and prediction,- according to her, the left hand stands for the 'natural' and the 'fated' things, and the right hand for what we do with them.

The results left me disquieted, probably because of the accuracy, I felt as if she had known me intimately for years. I had always got the impression that all palm readers and fortune tellers were like the 'end of the pier' type. You went along for a laugh, and paid your tenner for some old gypsy to stare into a crystal ball and offer you some vague, generalised half-truth that could be interpreted in any way whatsoever.

Her notes revealed some staggering truths.

Large wide hands showed method, detail, kindness and sympathy. My finger of Apollo was well developed (whatever that meant) and this indicated artistic tendencies, Rose correctly stated that I played the piano or guitar. She also pointed out some of the illnesses I had, going back to when I was a young child and some accurate comments about my upbringing and family. I knew she was no charlatan when she mentioned my twin brother Gary. He died shortly after he was born and there was no possible way she could have known that fact. No way on earth.

After dwelling on the past she turned her attention to the future and by now I was feeling more than a little apprehensive, I asked her to be honest and not hold anything back, give her credit, she didn't exactly sugar coat it.

I was to suffer some kind of accident that would incapacitate me for a time. Rose forecast trouble ahead in a close relationship, she mentioned that marriage was indicated by a large cross on the mount of Jupiter. This unfortunately had crossed the heart line in the plain of Mars, which in most cases tells of a separation. (I doubted that one, Jill and I were very close, so I assumed it had to be in another relationship with someone I knew well) On the upside there would be a change of career (as if window cleaning was a career) and that my future would eventually become secure, that comment gave me some comfort.

She also predicted that someone with the initials I.B. would pass away peacefully and I would be the last one to see him or her and offer them words of comfort. I knew immediately whom she was speaking about, her prediction was so precise, it would be my aunt Isobel Barns who was very ill at the moment and bed ridden. We were all concerned about her failing health - the fact that she was 93 maybe had something to do with it. But once again how could she possibly know about her and her fragile state?

She finished by commenting on my 'aura' and said that it was very positive, whatever the hell that meant. She explained a bit about it but I was still too disturbed, dumbfounded to take it all in - too much too soon -it was like being released from a darkened prison into the bright light, I was finding it difficult to adjust and assimilate all the information.

After the twenty minute reading I was astounded and disquieted in equal measure, she was so accurate that there was no logical, rational way to explain her abilities. I was at a complete loss.

If I had just left after the palm reading things might have been different, but I'm afraid I was intrigued, maybe even beguiled by this quiet spoken women and her gift of cognition, I wanted to know more, I was completely drawn in. I made the mistake of asking her about the latest book she was working on and she was delighted that I was taking a genuine interest in her and the book.

I sat on the comfortable leather chair, still in a bit of a daze, as she went upstairs to the upper bedroom. I heard her talk to her mother and she sounded concerned, although I couldn't really hear much of the conversation ,not that I was trying to eavesdrop. She came back down a minute later with the manuscript in her hand and muttered something about her mother. I took it off her and Rose walked back into the kitchen for something.

I eagerly opened it up and turned to the first page.

It didn't make sense, it appeared random and incoherent, it looked like it was written in ancient Egyptian hieroglyphics with complex symbols interspersed with numbers. I turned the page a bit disappointed and even more confused - it was basically the same, nothing made sense. When I reached the fifth page I finally recognised standard English - the first twenty lines or so were made up of the indecipherable symbols then just below it the words, *'I can not understand you, please help me, this is too difficult.'* This was followed by lines of symbols, numbers and shapes then another plea for help written in English - it said, *' no, no slow down, I still don't comprehend, translate, nothing is making sense, nothing.'* More symbols and numbers, then over the page a large black symbol I understood perfectly well, an inverted cross.

I felt a sudden chill as if someone had opened all the windows and a blast of artic air entered and goose bumps appeared on my forearms, I was experiencing genuine horripilation, it was a frightening sensation and a stony coldness permeated my body. I think I was just overreacting to the whole situation, the reading had freaked me out, then perusing this disturbing manuscript with its demonic images just tipped me over the edge. I manfully composed myself, then flicked through the rest of the pages which were basically the same with an increasing sense of frustration on the part of someone who couldn't translate it , the last lines in English read, *'no stop, can't go on, need to rest, this is too much at the moment, I'm in pain, I'll try later, please don't leave, I need to know please don't go.'*

I closed the manuscript and put in on the coffee table, it made me feel uncomfortable, the content was somehow dark, malevolent, that's the only way I could describe it.

Rose came back in with a small sherry and I didn't want to offend her by suddenly departing. I noticed that she also felt the cold. She had a shawl around her shoulders.

I asked her what the manuscript was all about, and what language it was written in, was it Babylonian, possibly some Hittite script? I was at a real loss and didn't see any sense of logic behind it without a constructive exegesis.

Her succinct reply stunned me.

It was a message from a repentant angel, spirit, call it what you like, named Zohar, that has visited the earth before the great flood and was banished by god himself into Tartarus for his iniquitous acts. It wanted redemption. Rose explained that she put herself into a trance like state and the spirit worked through her although she expressed difficulty in understanding the message. It had previously worked through her in English but she was granted some esoteric knowledge that only a few chosen ones could receive and she had to translate it herself to fully understand it.

She was confident that she would decipher it in time and that the ethereal writing would prove to be very significant some day in the near future. The spirit had told her that.

Rose explained that the particular gift (I would call it a poisoned challis) was not uncommon and that psychic or automatic writing had produced many volumes over the years and that it wasn't all connected to the occult or demonic activity. She sighted someone called Johannes Greber who produced a version of the bible that way, or to be more precise, his wife did - she fell into a trance and in that altered state received information from the spirits that Greber wrote down.

She asked me if I wanted to see one by Blavatsky that was in her library , I declined her offer. What had started off as a bit of fun had now, as far as I was concerned, degenerated into something potentially serious, even dangerous, something that was out with my control, and I speak from experience when I say that. Anyone who has ever tried an Ouija board will probably testify to that.

I think Rose could sense my rising unease and apologised for being a bit pushy, she wasn't. It was just that I couldn't handle the situation and was feeling uncomfortable.

I sat and had the good grace to finish off my sherry as we talked about more banal things. In the middle of the conversation I noticed that Rose was rather distracted and her eyes kept glancing to the other side of the room to a single leather chair. She said her mum was cold and I commented on the sudden chill a while ago. Her mum probably needed a shawl, so she excused herself and went upstairs to fetch it for her. She came back down with a tartan shawl and I asked regarding her mother. 'Just cold' she replied, I thought she had seen to her mother and the shawl was for her.

'Here we are mother,' she said sympathetically. Rose walked over to the empty chair and carefully placed the shawl over it.

It took the shape and form of thighs and legs and physically moved when Rose sat down next to me.

The colour drained from my face and for the first time in my life I could feel my scalp tighten. Genuine foreboding. Fear. The temperature in the room dropped again and my hands began to shake.

I didn't remember leaving the house, I must have been in a state of shock.

As I have said previously, never judge a book by it's cover. Rose was a remarkable woman, but I don't know if she was gifted or cursed, only time would tell I suppose. Six months after the incident she moved house to somewhere in the Scottish borders, the name of the place now escapes me. I often wonder how the book was coming on and if she finally deciphered the language it was written in, some might view it as the ramblings of a senile mind, although it might even prove to be significant. Who knows? I just hope she finds the inner peace she's been searching for, she deserves that much.

The predictions she made on my behalf have all come true so far and this still slightly disturbs me, it's as if some greater power or manifestation has control over my life and there's not much I can do to change or alter anything.

I've spent a lot more time with my auntie Isobel as a consequence of Rose's reading and her health is still a matter for concern. I'm just waiting for the rest of her predictions to come to fruition.

Well, that's the first chapter out of the way - it didn't look too bad and I would maybe add some additional material if I remembered anything else of interest. Chapter one, first draft, what a good feeling.

My reverie was rudely interrupted by Mrs Potters stentorian blast from downstairs, it scared the shit out of me, she's more scary than a ghost sometimes.

"Jack phone, it's a boy called Stevie." Are you still a boy at forty-three?

"Coming!" I yelled from the landing - I must get myself a mobile phone when I get some money together.

"Thanks Sandra."

"Hello."

"Jack."

"Stevie, how are you doing?"

"Great, have you not got a mobile yet?"

"No, I think I must have lost it in the field that night, I can't find it anywhere."

"Listen, Neil just phoned, do you want to go for a drink, he's got something to celebrate?"

"What, has his wife left him?"

"No, he's got a job."

"A job?"

"Yeah, you remember what a job is don't you?"

Dirty Laundry

"Sort of."

"He's got the post of maths teacher at Claremont high."

"Good for him, he's been bumming about for too long, lazy sod."

"Well Karen makes a decent wage, so I don't think he was in any great hurry, anyway he wants to celebrate being back in the land of the employed, it's been a few weeks since we were last out."

" I well remember."

"Are you up for it Jack?"

"Well, I don't know, money is tight…"

Stevie interrupted, "Don't worry about money, he's paying, anyway it's only for a few and he's promised not to bring cannabis,promise."

"Sounds alright then, where do you want to go?"

"We thought because of your disability we would make it near to you so you could get a taxi back no problem, how about the Whitehills or the Greenhills lounge?"

"Greenhills lounge sounds fine, I've never been in there before."

"Great, it's sorted then, the Greenhills lounge in an hour, I'll see you up there, it will make a change from the 'Bonnie Prince Charlie' I suppose.

It was a kind invitation and I needed to get out for a while, I've spent the last two weeks or so cooped up in this dingy room, wallowing in self pity, it would me good to get out for a few hours and enjoy a bit of company.

The only down side was that I might miss Sandra's pal and I was looking forward to meeting her and widening my social circle which had shrunk considerably since I had left Jill and Strathaven. I don't want to be viewed as an aging anchorite, well not yet anyway.

Mrs Potter had made a very special effort for tonight, the living room was looking nice, it was immaculate, no cat hairs off her Fanny, cushions plumped up and it was lit up with scented candles, I just hoped she wasn't going to conduct a séance later on - committing the story of Rose to paper made me feel uneasy again and I now avoid anything remotely connected to the supernatural with the exception of the Justin Toper page in the 'Express' - basically because it's bollocks but a bit of fun, all that psycho babble about the ascending moon in your plain and Uranus rising -I personally think half of them talk out their anus, unless someone can disprove that. After the experience with Rose I think it might be the sagacious course to keep my opinions to myself and my mouth shut.

"Thanks Sandra, it was one of my friends on the phone, I'm just so popular," I said sarcastically as I peered in the kitchen. She was still perched on the stool and the gin bottle had taken a merciless beating. "I'll be going out for an hour or two."

"Oh that's good darling, you need to get out - where are you off to?"

"Just the Greenhills for a quick pint and a chat with the boys."

"Christ," she exclaimed, "it's a bit rough up there."

I was deflated by her acerbic comment -"I've never been there before, surely it can't be that bad?"

"Spit and sawdust place Jack, well, the bar is anyway, actually the lounge is alright I suppose, but it's just the area. I parked my car there for a night with the girls, and a few kids came over to me and asked if they could look after my car for a small fee, five quid, the cheeky wee bastards, I said no thanks, I've got my dog in the back, that's when I had Lucky, the Alsatian, lovely dog, one eye, but a nice thing - do you know what they said?" she said releasing a cloud of smoke into my face.

"No."

"I bet your dog can't put out fires hen! Cheeky wee buggers ,cost me a fiver, never been back since!"

"How very enterprising of them," I remarked, "I'm just out for a short while there because it's the nearest, anyway I like to live dangerously. Tell your friend Irene I'm asking for her, will you?"

" Tell her yourself Jack, she's staying the night in the spare bedroom, it saves her travelling back home, not that you could get a bloody bus back after half past eight."

"Where does she stay?"

"Strathaven, Kirk Street."

"Kirk Street?"

"Yeah, you might even know her Jack, she's lived there for two years now - you know the video shop?"

"Of course, the 'Clyde video,' the one with the good looking girl with the gravely voice that's always talking about her 'dugs' and her Brian that smokes the expensive cigars."

"The very one. She lives near there, it's a beautiful flat, very posh, but a bit noisy with all that bloody traffic."

"There's a good chance I will know her, I've probably seen her in the shops or pubs. Strathaven is a small town," I reasoned

"You'll like her Jack, she's a lovely person, a really lovely girl."

The night was just getting better and better , I was escaping the confines of my personal prison, going for a drink and some socialising, then expanding my social base all in one night, now if there was any chance of sex happening, that would have been near perfect. One can dream. I was now intrigued by the mysterious Irene from Kirk Street, near the video shop, and was looking forward to meeting her.

"Right Sandra I'll see you later, enjoy your night ,can I freshen up your drink before I go?"

" Please, Jack, I think I have mislaid the bottle somewhere." It was sitting on the floor beside her Fanny, she must have fed the cat in an act of kindness. I topped up her drink and hobbled back up the stairs to prepare for a night out.

I arrived at the Greenhills lounge about half past eight and spotted Neil and Stevie sitting in the corner looking very animated, as usual they were the loudest in the pub - what is it about school teachers? Away from their work environment they cast off all discipline and social grace like it's a wet coat, must be a form of release I suppose, imagine teaching teenagers day in day out. I remember vividly sitting in a pub with Stevie as we chatted to some women sitting next to us, one of them politely asked him, ' what do you do for a living?' and he said, 'teaching,'- she replied out of interest, 'what do you teach?' his reply? 'wee bastards.'

"Hey Jack, grab a seat." Neil eased me into a chair as Stevie went for a round of drinks.

"This is for you mate," Neil said enthusiastically, " it's a point d'appui."

"A what?"

"A 'point d'appui,' numb nuts, it's French for a 'walking stick,' isn't it?

"It's very nice," I commented, " it looks better than this NHS effort I suppose."

"Yeah, you look like a big spastic with that thing, this will help your image mate."

"Charming," I replied. Neil giggled and drained the last of his lager, I could tell he was in one of his boisterous moods which didn't bode well for me, I needed to keep my wits about me. "So I hear you're back in the land of the employed," I said gleefully.

"Yes, I'm cured of my ergasiophobia, I start next Monday, back to teaching maths again, the only good thing about this post is I can walk to work now."

"Well done, I bet Karen's pleased."

"Delighted, I think she was getting a bit fed up with me in the house all day, three months was a long time off I suppose, she said it was just laziness on my part but I said I just have a love of the physical calm. She hit me on the head after that comment."

"Don't blame her, that's what you need sometimes." Stevie arrived back with a tray of drinks and an assortment of crisps that were as expensive as the alcohol. I eventually worked up the courage to tell them about my latest project, the novel , I hoped they wouldn't be too critical. School teachers have a very high regard of their own scholastic endeavours and can be dismissive of others. Neil as predicted, giggled while Stevie looked rather bemused .I waited for the caustic onslaught, but the sarcastic comments were surprisingly few.

They agreed that it was a constructive thing to do with my time and even offered to help if they could. It gave my confidence a boost and I would certainly accept any criticism if I felt it would help with the book, Stevie's help would really be appreciated as he was an English teacher and used to all aspects of writing and composition to a very high level. He said, '*verba volant scripta – spoken words fly away, written words remain.*' I liked that phrase and would use that somewhere in my book, it would make me sound intelligent. I found a pencil and wrote it down.

They did warn me that the large majority of people writing a novel will never get it published as it's a difficult thing to break into, most of the decent publishers have their own writers and tend to play it safe, I turned a deaf ear to that unsolicited piece of advice, what did I have to lose anyway?

I related the opening incunabula although they had heard the story of Rose before. In fact I probably bored them rigid with it, but they listened with a degree of scepticism and agreed it sounded interesting for an opening chapter. Damned with faint praises.

Neil was more receptive than Stevie when it came to the supernatural, at least he had an open mind. His good wife Karen had dragged him along to a small establishment near the Waterside in Strathaven, a place called 'the blessed bee', an incongruous name that sounded like it was selling jars of honey rather than dispensing the past and the future in generous measure. It was a shop that sold supernatural paraphernalia, cards, images, ornaments and second hand books. The tarot reading was performed in a small dimly lit room, heavy with incense, at the back of the premises by a clairvoyant called Collette who had an excellent reputation of being accurate and reliable. She had appeared on television many times and had written books on the subject, so her sagacious advice was well sought after hence the long waiting list for a private reading.

The actual shop was owned by a 'good looking hippie bloke' (Karen's description not mine I hasten to add) who was an Irish shaman, equally gifted and endowed with the gift of cognition just like Collette.

Interesting little street in Strathaven, two good pubs The Star Inn and the Waterside, the best bakery in Scotland, Taylors - add a funeral directors, a charity shop, a health shop and a pet shop and you've got a good day out.

Neil related that the 45 minute reading that cost £40.00 was the best money they had ever spent. She gave them advice regarding careers, family and so forth and it was interspersed with annotations and reflections on the past and the present. They were told that they would never have children although they had been trying for many months, which must have been fun. Neil later found out that he was 'firing blanks' and was incapable of producing offspring. That was a great source of amusement for Stevie and I. She also correctly augured that their careers would be stable apart from a brief period of time and they would be financially secure. With no children that was easy to predict. They made it a point to go once every year for their 'spiritual service.'"I've been to one of those spiritualist, evangelical meetings," Stevie volunteered. My interest was piqued. He had never mentioned that before, maybe he thought he would be ridiculed by us.

"You never told us that," Neil said, "where was it conducted?"

"It was in Glasgow, about a year ago, I just went for Lynn's sake, keep her company, she likes that type of thing, you know the preacher, healer type that helps people."

I was genuinely interested, "So what happened, did you witness anything extraordinary, did you feel the spirit?"

"Actually, I did."

Neil laughed, "Yeah right man, the holy spirit descended on you like a dove, or did it manifest itself like the tongues of fire?"

"Don't mock, I really felt something, it's difficult to explain rationally."

"Go on," I said "ignore him, I believe you."

"Okay, it was an American preacher…"

I could see Neil rolling his eyes. "Amen brother," he said sarcastically.

"Shut up Neil and let him finish the story for Christ's sake."

"As I was saying before I was rudely interrupted by this non believer, the preacher spoke for about half an hour on the power of the spirit, the 'pneuma,' then he said that through the grace of Christ he would demonstrate the power of the lord, so that you would believe. He was a very puissant, compelling speaker, very charismatic and the audience were completely captivated. You could actually feel the love in the room."

"Oh god, spare us."

"Shut up Neil, let him continue."

"Thanks Jack. He asked for anyone in the hall that had an affliction and was looking for a cure to come forward and experience the power, the 'dunamis,' of Jesus, the son of God."

I was that engrossed in the story I stopped drinking my lager and listened with bated breath. He continued.

"At first it was silent, I think people were just a little apprehensive, they were Glasgow folk, not evangelical by nature, dissimilar to the Americans who can be effusive, exuberant 'happy clappy,' you know the type. So the minister asked again and reassured them that the spirit of Jesus was in the room and it was capable of performing many fine works so that the non-believers would embrace the word. He emphasised the word 'trust' and 'power.' Eventually two people came forward to the platform , there was a woman who looked about forty and she was on crutches, a bit like yourself Jack, obviously in pain, she hobbled along assisted by her friend and she got up on the platform with the minister, I think his name was Buddy Collins. He commended her for her courage. Another younger man approached the platform and was invited to join the woman with the crutches. He looked alright to me and I couldn't see anything wrong with him, it was when he opened his mouth to speak you could identify the problem, he had a terrible stutter, a very bad speech impediment, you kept trying to finish off his sentence for him. Anyway he got them on to the platform and asked them to hold hands, then he placed his on theirs.

'Do you feel the power of the lord?' he asked them. 'Yes' they shouted. He repeated it again even louder, ' do you feel the power of sweet Jesus?' 'Yes,' they shouted again, he was working them into a frenzy and the audience. The atmosphere by now was electric and Lynn and myself could hear people sobbing and praising the lord.

The minister's assistant, his wife, got on the platform and opened up a large screen directly behind them. The minister now boomed ' do you want to see the power of the lord?' the audience shouted a resounding 'yes' in unison and so did we. He repeated it again even louder and once again the audience responded in kind. Many of them were now standing up and holding hands, it was very moving, very emotional.

The minister directed the woman on the crutches to go behind the screen and have faith in the lord. He asked the young bloke with the stammer to do the same. He then bowed his head and said to the audience, ' behold the power of god.' He turned around to face the screen and raised his hands in the air. 'Behold the power of the lord, young woman throw away your right crutch.' She threw it to the side. 'Now do the same with the other one and have faith in the power of sweet Jesus.'

The tension in the hall was almost unbearable now. There was a loud 'thump' and the minister asked, 'What's happened?' A voice behind the screen replied, 'aaahhh ...think. ssh she's fffell... on hhh her aaa arse!'

Neil went into hysterics and it took a few minutes to dawn on me it was a dreadful joke not a real incident. I fell for it hook, line, and sinker. Bastards!

It was one of those nights which always ends up with Neil trying to get one over on Stevie or vice versa, tonight it just happened to be my turn for a ribbing , it's a guys way of cheering you up, making you look like a chump.

Later on in the night I fell for one of Neil's pranks and it cost me a tenner into the bargain. He had bet me that it was possible to teach someone basic Chinese within ten minutes and that they could actually read phrases unaided. Naturally I scoffed at the idea and proffered a ten pound note. Easy money.

Wrong! You would think I had the word 'sucker' tattooed on my forehead or as they do in school, put a sticker on someone's back that reads, ' please kick my arse' or some other puerile phrase.

He got out a piece of paper and started scribbling down some lines. Stevie was equally as baffled as I was and he volunteered to be the arbiter and also had the great responsibility of holding the two tenners. He decided it was easy money as well.

A group of women at the next table overheard the conversation and asked if they could watch, they also said it was practically impossible to teach someone a language that's so complex -the pictography was too difficult to translate. Being very persuasive, Neil asked if one of them would like to take part and a woman called Carol volunteered. Neil took centre stage as usual.

"Right this is how it works Carol, I will show you this piece of paper, it is numbered from one to ten with different Chinese phrases, I guarantee you will be able to read them. On my piece of paper is the corresponding translation in English, do you understand?"

"Yes, but I don't read Chinese, I don't see the point," she said.

"Well by mind control I will make you understand, I will direct my thoughts into your mind and you will be able to translate"

"Are you going to hypnotise me?" she replied, sounding a bit uneasy.

"Something like that, but you'll be fine don't worry."

Stevie was getting impatient, "Get on with it for goodness sake."

"Don't rush me the build up is important, there's money involved as well. Right Carol, can you sit next to me, I want you to look into my eyes." The other girls laughed at his dreadful patter. Carol moved to our table and sat next to Neil, I think she was enjoying the 'street theatre.'

"Right Carol give me your right hand and let me look into your eyes, I'm going to pass information directly into your mind. Do you understand?"

"Yes," she said nervously.

"You have lovely eyes by the way," he said.

"Get on with it," Stevie said, "stop chatting up Carol or I'll tell Karen"

He spent the next minute or so looking into her eyes and rambling on about the power of suggestion and mind control. " Alright Carol, I want you to read number one on the paper."

She took the piece of paper, looked at it and laughed. I had the feeling by now I was being stitched up.

"Right number one, that's easy it says, 'tai ni po ni.'"

"Correct, number one is 'a small horse.'" Neil held up his paper for everyone to see. The place erupted with laughter. "Now the lovely Carol will attempt number two."

"It says, 'sum ting wong.'

"Correct again, number two is, 'that's not right.'"

I fell for it again this time it cost me a ten pound note - he continued the Chinese lesson amidst hoots of laughter, give him credit it was very amusing. The rest were read out:

3. dum gai – stupid man
4. wai yu so tan - did you go to the beach?
5. ai bang mai ni - I bumped into a coffee table
6. chin tu fat - I think you need a face lift
7. wai yu mun ching? - I thought you were on a diet?

8. no pah king - this is a tow away zone
9. yu stin ki pu - your body odour is offensive
10. lei ying lo - staying out of sight.

At the end of the Chinese lesson we were all laughing at his warped sense of humour and the twenty pounds Stevie was holding bought everyone a round of drinks, which I thought was only fair of Neil, he later admitted the Chinese joke came straight out of the internet but thought it was good to share as it made him laugh. 'He sum gi'! 'Me ar so,' stick that in your phrase book.

We had a wonderful night and it was good to have some female company as well, I must admit, I really liked Carols friend Jay, not only was she good looking she was funny, I could sense she liked me. I just hope she didn't spot me drooling over her. At the end of the night I plucked up the courage to ask her out just as they were leaving. 'No thanks,' was all she said, no explanation or anything - I concluded she must be a lesbian.

Undaunted and with my new point d'appui in hand, I ventured out for a taxi with the boys. I was dropped off first at Laurel place then it headed towards Mull then Salisbury in Calderwood for Stevie's place. It was the only free ride I was going to get. Undeterred by the brutal rejection from Jay, I would maybe try my luck with Irene if she was reasonable looking (I decided to aim a little lower now to avoid disappointment). The few drinks had given me Dutch courage, or was it false bravado?

After a few attempts I finally managed to get the key in the lock and was greeted by a wall of silence.

"Hi Sandra, just me," I bellowed.

No response. I could hear soft music coming from the living room, Nora Jones. I pushed the door open and the place was still lit up like a midnight vigil, the smell of sweet cloying perfume filled the air, it was quite alluring. Where was everyone?

I ambled into the hall with my new stick and shouted up the stairs, "Hi Mrs Potter, I'm back."

No response again. With a bit of an effort I half hobbled, half staggered up the stairs for my bedroom to crash, it was like the Mary Celeste in here, music playing, all the lights on, food half eaten and the biggest puzzle of all, wine unfinished. This was serious, very serious indeed. Mrs Potter never wastes alcohol. I've even seen her take half glasses of wine and pour them into ice cube trays for future use.

I knocked Sandra's door, no reply. The door to the spare bedroom was ajar so I ventured in. The room was tidy but unoccupied. It was then I heard the giggling and laughing from outside. I pulled the curtains back and watched in disbelief as two women dressed only in nighties and trainers were racking through a bin. It was one o'clock in the morning and it was drizzling, what the hell were they doing?

"I found it!" Mrs Potter shouted triumphantly.

"Yea hah," the other mysterious women shouted. She held it aloft as the other one then started to applaud her endeavours. They ran back into the house laughing. I had to find out what was happening, curiosity got the better of me. The time I had walked back down the stairs I could hear raised voices in the living room. It sounded like a party was in full swing and Nora Jones was even louder and more mournful. I chapped the door.

"Hi," I shouted over the din.

"Oh Jack, come in, come in," Sandra said smiling.

I was greeted by a strange yet alluring sight, I was always taught that a real lady, someone of class never shows their underwear intentionally, yet sitting on the sofa was two drunken females attired only in their damp nighties making it impossible not to stare. I think I conducted an entire conversation with their breasts.

I was introduced to the illusive Irene Black and immediately fell in love with her at first sight and I had impure thoughts of a vigorous exchange of saliva with her later.

She must have been a bit younger than Sandra, perhaps about fifty, very pretty, slim with auburn hair, and all her own teeth. Irene smiled as we were introduced and we traded the usual pleasantries before I reluctantly departed into the kitchen for something to eat, the thought of chill con carne was scant consolation somehow.

Yes, I was definitely in love this time and it wasn't the alcohol playing it's tricks again. Although she lived in Kirk Street, I had never seen her before, not in any of the pubs or even the shops.

I asked Sandra what they were searching for outside and they burst out laughing again. It transpired that Sandra had inadvertently thrown out a piece of 'space cake' she was saving for the night when she was tidying up the kitchen. After a frantic search of the kitchen she came to the logical conclusion that it was put out with the rest of the rubbish, hence the desperate search for the illegal cake.

The quest for the 'holy grail' was now on which was assisted by her friend Irene and after emptying the contents of a black bag into another, the cake was found, still wrapped in its foil.

Their joy was unbounded.

In all fairness they offered me a piece but I politely declined, the last time I consumed a moist, light piece of euphoriant all logic went out the window and I ended up on crutches. Thanks, but no thanks ladies.

Sandra's chilli was wonderful and so was her pie. I was tempted to wander back down the stairs to join the private party but thought that it might be viewed as too needy - I would remain enigmatic, mysterious and frustrated.

I fell asleep thinking about Irene and her damp nightie. Her nice smile with all her own teeth and hoped this time it wouldn't be unrequited love. It's not the first time I've climbed to the top of the metaphorical ladder and discovered I have placed it against the wrong window.

This ogre has feelings as well.

CHAPTER 4

ONE FOR THE ROAD

The stretch limo drops me off at the front entrance to the 'Drumclog Inn,' an exclusive little 'watering hole' in the affluent part of Strathaven that's frequented by millionaires and genuine 'A' list celebrities. The doorman performs his usual genuflection as I stuff a fifty-pound note into his top pocket - it's loose change.

As I saunter through the hall way I catch a glimpse of myself in the art deco mirror, and without any exaggeration whatsoever, I'm perfectly gorgeous - the hair is slick, the eyes radiate passion and danger, the jaw line is 'chiselled' and I'm dressed to kill in a black Armani suit and handmade Italian shoes, so highly polished I can see my own reflection in them - god, someone handsome is staring back. The aftershave I'm wearing is intoxicating, probably sexually alluring to any female to within a hundred yards - I'm so hot I'm practically smoking. On a personal note, I have butt cheeks of iron and my penis is 12 inches long (flaccid).

I light up a Cuban cigar and breeze in, awaiting the admiring glances from the men and women alike. Elton John beckons me over to his table but I give him the cold shoulder, I can't be seen associating with a podgy little 'queen' who wears a hair weave and looks like a toad , I don't care how many records he has sold. I tell Mr rocket man to f*** off, and he has the decency to apologise.

I sit down at my reserved table, and a waiter, dressed in black, runs over to me and sees to my needs, which are wide and diverse, I stuff a one hundred pound note into his top pocket because I like him and he makes me feel special, not like Elton.

My table soon fills up with an increasing number of female sycophants eager to please and ingratiate themselves, but I only have eyes for one person in this room, the main act, the woman with a angelic-like voice, who has the power to transport me heavenward ,the inimitable Irene Black.

The stage curtains open and the master of ceremonies introduces her to an excited audience, the sexual tension in the Drumclog lounge is almost unbearable - cue the spotlight, the dry ice effect, and the opening beats of the song.

Irene Black (her name is almost too sacred to utter, its ineffable as far as I'm concerned) is dressed to kill, she's wearing a BHS nightie and a white pair of Reebok trainers, as she opens up with the beautiful, romantic number, 'does your chewing gum lose it's flavour on the bedpost overnight?'

Five minutes into the act, disaster! A small fire breaks out at Elton's table. His hair has spontaneously combusted and the sprinkler system comes on and an alarm sounds. Irene is soaked through, but she's still desirable, beautiful, and she needs to get out of those wet clothes immediately and into a dry Martini in my room. The alarm is loud and persistent and it's just then I hear a voice that scares the bejesus out of me.

"Jack, sorry, sorry."

I wake up with a start, Mrs Potter's burnt something and the damn smoke alarm has gone off and interrupted a very enjoyable dream just as it was getting to the interesting part - thanks a lot Sandra! She barges in and apologises for waking me up then walks into the hallway and starts to wave a towel in front of the smoke detector. She looks like she's trying to attack a swarm of angry wasps. It still blares out and she eventually removes the battery from it. She called the smoke alarm, 'a sensitive bastard.' Charming.

"Sorry, Jack, I've cremated my bacon, sorry for waking you!"

I pulled the covers over me in a protective like gesture, yawned and said sleepily, "it's alright Sandra, it was just getting up anyway." I lied.

"The grill went on fire but everything's under control, well, apart from my bacon, it will need to be a boiled egg now."

"It's not a problem, honest." She's quite scary first thing in the morning before the makeup goes on and the hair's brushed, at the moment it looks like a burst fag. A flustered landlady asks.

"Can I make you as cup of tea, I've got the kettle on?"

"That would be great, thanks, did you have a nice night?"

"Christ, I don't really remember, I think I did. I've got the headache to prove it though."

I had to ask about Irene. "How's your friend this morning?"

"No idea, she set the clock for 7.30 and I didn't even hear her going out. She's working this morning and had to catch the number 13 for Strathaven, she works in that new Smiddy place, the one with the new coffee shop."

It was difficult to mask my disappointment.

"Oh that's a shame, never really got a chance to speak with her, but she seems very nice."

"Oh she's a lovely lassie Jack, you'll see her again soon, the three of us must have a wee drink sometime, you should have stayed a little longer last night, you know you're always welcome."

"Well, I didn't want to be a party pooper, as it looked like the two of you were having a bit of fun."

"Oh we had fun alright," she replied with a mischievous look on her face, "anyway what do you take in your tea again?"

"Milk and three sugars please, I've a sweet tooth."

"Christ, you won't have any teeth left with all that sugar," she laughed. I thought her comment was a bit rich considering she had false teeth, at least I'm sure they were, not that I would ask. She wandered back down the stairs singing to herself which gave me the opportunity to get dressed before she stormed into my room again, one of these days she's going to catch me butt naked. Yeah, I definitely think she fancies me.

I had decided to start the second chapter of my ' best seller' after a spot of breakfast which consisted of two aspirins, two sausages, two eggs and two slice of toast (kindly loaned by Mrs Potter). I wondered if there was any cosmic significance of the recurrence of the number two - maybe not.

Sandra departed soon after to start her Christmas shopping which left me feeling depressed as the festival of cheer was rapidly approaching and my finances were rapidly dwindling. If my situation got any worse I would have to resort to 'making things' for presents which I'm sure would not go down too well with my esurient family and friends, I had visions of knitting woolly jumpers or balaclavas for someone, or constructing something from household items that was held together with 'sticky back plastic, as Valerie Singleton used to say - my 'Blue Peter' days would not be wasted.

Being skint is horrible although it certainly brings out the creative side of you. The thought of penury spurred the thinking processes as I remembered my previous notes for the book. I was undecided regarding who should grace the second chapter, there were so many characters to pick from; the old age pensioner who perpetrated a masterful con trick on her workmates and neighbours; the corporate thief that embezzled thousands from her company; the couple with the terminally ill five year old with cancer; the neighbours caught in 'flagrante dilecto' and the pensioner who supplemented his meagre income by growing cannabis, to name but a few.

After due consideration I went for an elderly gentleman called John , I won't mention his second name or the number of his house, suffice to say he stayed in Glen Moriston for many years before he passed away, but anyone in the neighbourhood will recognize him and his exploits immediately, I think I'll entitle it, 'One for the road.'

I think John was a very complex character, he's been described by family and friends as an old curmudgeon, a belesprit, a wino and an enigma , there must have been many facets to his personality and I suppose the best way to describe him would be 'chimeric,' there was a part of everything in his character. John was the town drunk and at the end of his years he spent more time in the 'Bonnie Prince Charlie' than he did in his own house. People said that he just wanted company after his

Dirty Laundry

wife died, he lived alone and the house was filled with too many memories. His routine rarely changed.

He would leave the house about 11 o'clock just in time for the pub to open armed with a good book or newspaper and would spend most of the day there, the food was good, the pub was warm, there was company and a game of pool or dominos.

According to the next door neighbour, John's life went into a tailspin after his wife died of a heart attack, drink was a comfort, it numbed the harsh reality of life. After a while it completely took over his life and people started talking about him - he was lowering the tone of the neighbourhood, he was a danger to himself and to others because of his drunken antics. But I saw a different side to him after speaking with him and getting to know him a little better. I vividly remember the day he invited me in for a cup of tea, it was a grey miserable February afternoon and I accepted his kind offer - I felt sorry for him, he probably just wanted a chat, and it was one of the rare days he was actually in the house in an afternoon.

It turned out he was a fascinating character - he used to be a lecturer at the Caledonian University in Glasgow and his subject was physics. He had a brilliant mind and was held in high esteem within his own academic circles. He contributed many articles to scientific journals and carried out research for a number of books. His specialized field was quantum mechanics. I remember over a cup of tea (in a china cup with a saucer) and a slice of cake, John trying, and failing, to describe in simple terms what he used to teach and write about. I remember him lecturing that quantum mechanics was the theory that energy does not have a continuous range of values, but is, instead, absorbed or radiated discontinuously, in multiples of definite, indivisible units called quanta. Earlier theories showed that light, generally seen as a wave motion, could also in some ways be seen as composed of discrete particles (photons) and how such atomic particles such as electrons may also be seen as having wavelike properties. The quantum theory is the basis of particle physics, modern theoretical chemistry, and the solid state physics that describes the behaviour of the silicon chips used in computers.

I sat there sipping my tea as my mind went into some type of shut down. It was too much information for someone that cleans windows for a living. John went on to enthuse about one of his great heroes, Einstein. The only thing I remember about Einstein was that he worked as an inspector of patents in Berne, took his PhD at Zurich and became a lecturer at the university and went on to receive a Nobel prize for physics. He had by all means one the most gifted minds of modern times. His equation $e = mc2$ still baffles me - energy equals mass times the speed of light squared - the speed of light being 186,325 miles per hour. What? Come again?

John tried to explain the basics behind the equation but lost me very quickly after saying, 'this stated that if one can annihilate a mass, then the energy emitted (c x c) is enormous, thus the birth of the atomic bomb.' Eh? I started to drift off completely when he talked about polynominal equations of the 2nd degree and Einstein's physics posit events as existing in no absolute state but in a referential flux between varied points of definition equally in flux.

John's 'ignotum per ignotius' (An explanation which is even more obscure than the thing it purports to explain) left me baffled and scratching my head. If his neighbours could hear him now they surely would have been impressed with his scientific mind and his specific recall. They only saw the negative side of him. I was initially stunned by the town drunk, I expected a conversation about more banal things like the weather or what's happening with the football.

Yet John could equally be guilty of some of the most asinine acts when inebriated, and these, unfortunately were what his neighbours remembered him for, as they say, when the drink goes in, all logic goes out.

He had brought shame to the rest of his family the day he buried his beloved Mary. John, in a futile attempt to lessen the grief of bereavement, spent the morning drinking heavily with his two brothers and a friend from Glen Moriston, a Robert Walker, who kindly related the story to me and I think, the rest of the street.

By the time it was 3.30 in the afternoon, John was well and truly 'bladdered' as they say, and in this state went to church for the service.

After the dreary 20 minute talk by the minister, the mourners filed out of the church hall and headed towards Philipshill cemetery. It was cold, grey and wet. The minister offered another few insincere words of comfort from the bible over the sound of crying and mourning. Mary's favourite piece of music was played, Barbers adagio for strings as she was gently lowered into the ground. The breeze stirred the wind chimes which gave the funeral an eerie, almost ethereal feeling.

When Mary was finally lowered into the freshly dug grave and came to rest - the family, each one in turn threw the symbolic piece of earth on to the coffin, then they were encouraged to throw a flower next and then reflect on the significance of life and death. John, as expected, was inconsolable in his grief for his wife of fifty-seven years. He was a broken man. He approached the grave with her favourite flower - a red rose, stumbled, tried to regain his balance, failed, then fell right into the grave on top of his wife's coffin with a thud.

The blow rendered him unconscious and it took three burly funeral assistants to unearth him. He came out with mud on his face, a bloody nose and rose petals stuck to his face, he also suffered the indignity of ripping his brand new trousers.

When I heard the story, I didn't know whether to laugh or cry, there was a certain unrestrained sadness about it, but it also had a rich comical content.

I personally witnessed another 'incident,' that highlighted John's penchant for the bizarre act, it was about a month after I was invited in for a chat and was given a lecture on physics and quantum mechanics , it was like something out of a 'Laurel and Hardy' film.

I was cleaning his front windows when I noticed he was indulging in his favourite pastime, imbibing Jack Daniels straight with a cigarette, it was about three o'clock in the afternoon. I watched as he accidentally spilled some of the whiskey on his shirt-sleeve as he was pouring a measure and I heard a few choice expletives as well which I ignored. He refilled the glass and lit up another fag, he was a chain smoker and a chain drinker. The match fell and landed on his sleeve setting it on fire, in a panic he knocked the refilled glass over himself and the flames quickly spread - it wasn't a raging inferno or a situation that was out of control, but it caused him considerable consternation as the flames refused to go out despite some flailing arms and some bad language.

I jumped down from my ladder, grabbed the bucket of water, ran into the house (thankfully the door was open) and threw the contents over his smouldering body. It quickly extinguished the flames. John was very grateful for my quick reactions and presence of mind and no serious harm was done apart from the shock of the cold water assaulting him.

Undaunted by his 'near death' experience he refilled his glass to steady his nerves and causally lit up again, he didn't even change his shirt. I suggested that a change of clothes would be beneficial or he might catch a cold. I sat with him for about ten minutes just to make sure he wouldn't spontaneously combust again. I was rewarded with a large Jack Daniels that made the rest of the afternoon pass quickly.

That incident was closely akin to the 'sofa incident' in terms of stupidity and farcical value, except it involved a lot more people and had the neighbours talking for weeks.

It happened a few months after the 'fire raising' episode although in John's defence he was not drinking that morning in question and it could have happened to anyone.

I think.

I had just cleaned the top bedroom window and made a start on the main living room one, John waved to me and I waved back ,he looked a bit flustered but I never thought any more of it and continued cleaning the window. He was sitting in his boxer shorts which wasn't a pretty sight. After finishing the rest of the house I chapped the door for the money. No response. Normally I would just put a ticket through his door and return on Friday evening for the money, but it was the look on his face that made me chap the door again just to make sure he was alright. Again there was no response, maybe I was being just a little paranoid. It was then I heard him shout, 'Jack come in to the living room the door's open, I'm in here.'

I thought it was rather odd, maybe he had suffered a stroke and was rendered paralysed or he had taken one of his turns as he called it. I opened the door and walked into the living room not knowing what to expect.

He was still sitting on the sofa in his baggy boxers which made me feel just a little uncomfortable, he was a real wrinkly apparition with possibly the thinnest legs I'd ever seen.

When he explained his predicament I just shook my head in disbelief - he had got his hand stuck down the side of the sofa and could not get it out no matter how hard he tried - he had been in that embarrassing predicament for nearly two hours and was in a state of panic and was very glad to see me. I made light of the situation and told him I would extricate him from the stubborn sofa in no time whatsoever. A pound coin had slipped down the side of the chair and he would be damned if the chair was going to get it (his words not mine, in his struggle with the sofa it had practically taken on a life form and was now engaged in a battle with him for the coin)

His arm was that thin I was surprised it could get stuck there in the first place. I pushed my hand down and managed to grab his wrist and gently tried to free it, it would not budge, not one bit . I tried another position and to my utter horror found my own arm stuck, after four attempts and with my blood pressure rising I eventually freed my own hand. Sweat was running off my brow, and John remained unimpressed with my endeavours and suggested using some of his tools to widen the gap. I suggested using copious amounts of 'fairy liquid' as this might help to lubricate the hand and free it.

It didn't work so I went to his shed for some tools and tried his suggestion but the makeshift tools also failed and to make matters worse he needed the toilet, I was a very relieved person when he said it was just a 'pee.' I rummaged through the kitchen to find something suitable and arrived back with a plastic bucket - I departed into the kitchen to let him perform his 'duties', what a bloody situation to find yourself in!

After emptying the bucket I made one more attempt but I only succeeded in hurting his wrist and I could now see he was in considerable distress and profession help was now needed. John reluctantly agreed and I phoned the fire service which came out within ten minutes. I was sure I heard the operator snigger when I described the predicament my customer was in.

The two firemen tried in vain to release him, which I suppose made me feel a little better. They went out to the fire engine and arrived back with cutting gear and literally cut the side off the sofa to free him, to say John was relieved was an understatement although it was marred by the fact his new sofa had a large chunk out the side of it - his quest to retrieve his pound coin cost him dearly, a new settee, and his dignity, not to mention he was the talk of the town once again.

I've saved the best story about John to the last. It's the type of thing you just couldn't make up no matter

Dirty Laundry

how inventive you are, and like all good stories it's short and simple.

John related this account to me shortly before he died and as you can imagine the demon drink was involved once again, it seemed to be the catalyst for most of his misfortunes. He decided to have a night out at the 'Auldhouse Arms' rather than his local 'The Bonnie Prince Charlie.' I think he had fallen out with one of his pals and needed a break for a night or two. Feeling flush, he ordered a taxi to take him there and he would also get one on the way back as it was a good four or five mile walk (more if you're very drunk as you tend to walk in zig zag lines) and there was no buses available.

He arrived at eight o'clock and parked himself in front of the open fire and ordered a half pint and a half . He got into a conversation with another couple and the night flew past and his money soon evaporated and when it came to 'chucking out time' he realized with horror that he only had some 'shrapnel' in his pocket, not enough for a taxi.

He decided to walk back home. Drink sometimes creates the illusion you're capable of doing anything whatsoever. Anyone that's walked down the Auldhouse road at night knows how dark, twisting and winding it is and there's no pavements to safely walk on.

About two miles down the road he decided to light up as he was desperate for a smoke, the wind was blowing in his face as he attempted to strike the match, after two attempts he turned to face away from the wind and managed to light the cigarette and he carried on walking as the rain started to fall and the wind increased. He cursed himself for not having enough money for a taxi.

About forty minutes later he saw the encouraging sign of lights ahead and he knew he would soon be back in East Kilbride. It was when he got closer to the lights he realized what he had done, he had arrived back at the Auldhouse Arms, -disoriented by the alcohol and turning away from the wind to light up, he arrived back where he had started much to his consternation!

When he related the story I laughed until it hurt. What an interesting man he was, John was a contradiction in terms, he could be brilliant but equally stupid, he was a living oxymoron.

Now new people have moved into the house but every time I clean it I can't help thinking of him and his hilarious exploits.

Just before he died he gave me a book to borrow (I still have the book) by Elie Wiesel, the human rights campaigner that was born in Romania. He was held in the infamous Buchenwald concentration camp during WW II in depraved conditions that were designed to destroy the human spirit. But he was a survivor and assiduously documented the atrocities against the Jews in an effort to alert the world to the dangers of racism. John was always quoting him and recommended that I read the book as it would give a glimpse into a great mind and a compassionate human being - its only when you read the book you fully understand the context of the quotes. His words really touch the heart - Johns favourite quote?

> *'the opposite of love is not hate, it's indifference,*
> *the opposite of art is not ugliness, it's indifference,*
> *the opposite of faith is not heresy, it's indifference,*
> *the opposite of life is not death, it's indifference.'*

I was greatly impressed with his words on neutrality and his comments on forgiveness, he wrote, *'Take sides. Neutrality helps the oppressor, never the victim. Silence encourages the tormentor, never the tormented. God of forgiveness, do not forgive those murderers of Jewish children here.'*

I greatly enjoyed our conversations and I always came away with something of real value, something to make you think, especially his stories of the war. I think it saddened him that the memories of the suffering and the sacrifices made by a generation was beginning to fade. He made the salient point that one million people died at Auschwitz, yet according to a survey carried out recently, nearly half of Britons have never heard of the Nazi concentration camp. Among women and the under thirty-fives the ignorance was worse, with 60% unaware of it's history of mass murder. Six million Jews, nearly seven out of every ten living in Europe before the war, were shot, hanged or killed in specially built gas chambers during the holocaust.

I was grateful of the reminders and it made me appreciate the freedom we have today and the sacrifices that were made by his generation.

Anyway here's to you John, the next time I'm in the pub I'll have a large Jack Daniels in honour of you and I'll make a point of keeping back from anything that's lit. Chapter two went quite well as far as I was concerned. Who said writing was difficult? My stomach was tactfully reminding me it was well past lunch time so I struggled back down the stairs in search of some sustenance, hopefully there would be a bit of Sandra's chilli con carne left over, if there wasn't I had the choice between tuna or beans. Maybe I could make a tuna surprise, just add the beans and stick a few cocktail cherries on the top.

Damn, all the chilli was finished, it would have to be tuna. I made a mental note to get some decent shopping in this afternoon or I would become severely emaciated.

The phone rang in the living room and for once it wasn't a nuisance.

"Hello?"

"I'm looking for a Jack Wilde. It's in regard to the advert in the local shop."

"Yes, that's me. How can I help you?"

"Well, Mr Wilde, I've got two teenagers aged 13 and 15 that are very keen to learn the guitar, they have been playing for about 6 months now and they really need proper tuition to bring them on. They know the rudiments but that's about it."

"That's fine, I would be pleased to help."

"So what styles do you teach?"

"Basically whatever they want to learn, jazz, blues, folk, finger picking."

"Sounds good Mr Wilde, another question."

"Yes."

"Do you teach how to read the basics of musical notation?"

"Of course it's a necessary part if they want to be really proficient rather than average, at the end of the session I would give them some homework to take back, but I don't want you to think it's all technical or all theory, the pupils must be able to have a good time, it has to be enjoyable for them so they view it as educational fun rather than a chore" (I hadn't a clue what I was talking about, but I sounded convincing).

"I agree, that sounds reasonable."

"Listen, if you want to sit in on the first session and see what it's all about you're more than welcome and it will give me a chance to meet you personally."

"Okay that sounds great, now what about the cost?" I hadn't even thought about it, thinking quickly on my feet I said.

"I charge ten pounds per hour per pupil."

"That's very reasonable, I phoned one from the yellow pages and she was charging eight pounds for a half hour session, yeah that's fine, when would you be able to fit us in? -the weekend is the best time for the boys obviously."

"Pick a time that suits you. Sorry, I didn't catch your name?"

"Pete Townsend."

"Well that will be easy to remember," I remarked.

"I know Mr Wilde, I've heard all the jokes before believe me. Saturday afternoon would be good, how about two o'clock?"

"Two o'clock today?"

"Is that too short notice?"

"No, not at all." It was, but I was not going to turn down an easy twenty pounds for an hours work in the comfort of the house. I gave Pete Townsend my address and told him it was cash only and looked forward to meeting him and his sons. The money would pay for my shopping. I phoned Sandra on her mobile to inform her that I would be having some clients for tuition and asked her if it was possible to use the living room. As always she was very accommodating and was pleased I was back in the land of the employed. She informed me she would be back home when the shops closed. I didn't know if she was joking or not. Can woman really spend that long wandering around the shops?

The hour session with the boys turned into an hour and a half but I must admit it was very enjoyable and I think Pete was quite impressed by the relaxed set up and my playing. It was made a lot easier for me as the boys, George and Paul, were very keen to learn and had a reasonable grounding in the guitar. At one stage their dad even joined in much to the embarrassment of the sons. You can always rely on your dad to show you up. He promised not to return next week.

I can't wait to tell Stevie and Neil I'm now a teacher earning twenty quid an hour, okay it's only one hour per week but it might pick up, we all have to start somewhere. If I could only get forty hours a week I reckoned that would be £800. I think I could live on that at a push.

CHAPTER 5

AN EXPENSIVE BARGAIN

Someone once wrote that 'only the poor can feel for the poor' - there's an element of truth in those words, although I wouldn't classify myself as 'in forma paupers,' I'm not exactly rolling in it either.

With Christmas looming I decided it was time to sit down and work out the finances to see what I couldn't afford - the credit card is going to take a pounding this festive season as I'm faced with the usual problem of having too much month left at the end of the money ,sound familiar? But I'm trying to remain upbeat, positive, in less than a month or so I hope to get back to work and I've now expanded my client base to four a week which brings in an extra forty pounds on top of the incapacity benefit.

It's just over a week since I started writing the novel and it's going better than anticipated, probably because I'm isolated up here in my room and there are very few distractions, the only distraction I would welcome would be to see Irene Black again. She's becoming more involved in my thoughts every day.

Five chapters are now completed, five stories that will hopefully captivate the reader and I pleased because they are so diverse - there's Rose, then John, the town drunk, then I thought it would be good to change the tempo and mood of the book by introducing the story of Chloe, the teenage loner who committed suicide - I just hoped it was written with compassion and a degree of dignity .I would obviously have to seek the permission from the family if the book was ever considered for publication, but I don't think it would be too much of a problem as they were very open about it and shared their grief publicly to make others aware of their sad loss. It was strange, just after I had finished the story of Chloe, I received a phone call from Grace, her mother, asking when I would be back to clean the windows - I explained my situation to her. Chapter four was devoted to the corporate thief from Calderglen Road, the posh part of East Kilbride where people rarely tipped and always complained about any small rise in the price of their window cleaning. Mrs Bickeet siphoned off £175,000 from her employer's bank account over a three-year period by signing company cheques in her name, she was the personal assistant and had established herself as a trusted employee. The sheriff Dawn Mc Conville sentenced her to nine months. I'm not too worried about this story if it ever gets published as it's already in the

Dirty Laundry

public domain and I've no money if they decide to sue me - you can't get blood from a stone.

Every good novel needs a bit of intrigue and a generous measure of sexual content so chapter five was devoted to the dubious exploits of the street lush, a woman in her sixties who thought she was twenty or thirty years younger and hot, mutton dressed as lamb as the saying goes. She would have been attractive maybe a few decades ago but you can't hold back the ravages of time nor can you disguise it, she was now what you would describe as 'jolie laide' as the French say. Jean had a bit of a reputation in the street, no man was safe from her clutches, not even the window cleaner because she had a habit of wandering about half naked which can be very distracting when you're 25 feet up the ladder and you've got your applicator in your hand. Her language was very coarse and was peppered with 'double entendres', when I met her for the first time she casually asked without blushing, 'how far do you go up love?' Any one in Loch Striven was fair game for old Jean, and a collective sigh of relief went up when she moved house although some of the men folk were sorry to see her go I think.

I decided to write chapter six today once I had a few things sorted and was in the frame of mind for it. I poured myself a cup of strong black coffee and examined the bank statements that came in this morning , it didn't make for pleasant reading and without exaggeration it was the leanest period in my entire life.

Being rendered ' hors de combat' was really frustrating, all that work out there was going to waste and my financial situation was slowly deteriorating, damn that cow in the field and the one living in luxury in Lethame road. I wonder if Jill would be magnanimous enough to give me a small interest free loan? Forget it, bite the bullet and move on.

My spirits were lifted by the thought of seeing Irene again, she was coming up for a night with Sandra and I was invited downstairs for a few drinks which I thought was very sociable of them. Sandra had went to a lot of trouble again, she had bought in some good wine and food. She is definitely on my Christmas list as well as Irene, although the thought of buying something for two older women was quite daunting, I didn't want to be predictable and dull, you know what I mean, the wicker basket full of soaps or the scented candles. I might phone Karen or Lynn for a few suggestions. I had decided to do all my Christmas shopping tomorrow, which was Sunday, in the forlorn hope that it would be quieter than normal, maybe people would be attending church or chapel. The plaza in East Kilbride resembles a Serengeti sometimes with people roaming in packs, looking flustered, stressed and ready to kill. It's actually quite a scary place when its very busy, its easy to get caught in the slipstream of people moving quickly and its very difficult to take a right or left to where your shop is, you can get pulled along for hundreds of yards before you manage to get out, its like a fast flowing river, you can't fight against the flow. People in East Kilbride are always in a hurry and they shop like it's the last opportunity on earth and stock up on items with a siege like mentality, especially at Christmas or New Year. What's happened to the spirit of Christmas? God I miss Strathaven, shopping there is a pleasure, people actually have time for you, they're helpful, the parking is free, and best of all, you can get a really great cup of coffee at the Tudor house or Taylor's café, none of your Starbucks rubbish.

I wrote down a list of the people that would benefit from my Christmas spirit and allocated each of them £20, which I think would be enough, it's at times like these you sometimes wish you were a Jehovah's witness or a Jew then you wouldn't have all the hassle and expense of the celebration of Christmas.

The only problem I faced was where to spend Christmas, it was 'officially' my sisters turn this year and the thought of celebrating it with the most boring couple in the world didn't exactly fill me with joy, all they do the entire day is sit in front of the television, eat drink and vegetate and gossip about everyone in the street - what makes it excruciating is the fact that neither of them drink alcohol, and they frown upon anyone that does, so its like undergoing an operation, fully awake because of a mistake of the anaesthetist. Yes it's really that painful.

I had an offer from Neil and Karen but I suspect it was done out of sympathy but I still appreciated their kindness. I would politely decline and prepare myself for my sisters by drinking copious amounts of alcohol before I arrived and chewing gum to mask the smell of the demon drink.

Fifteen minutes later my finances were sorted and it was time for some serious work. I had just loaded up the typewriter when I heard the ominous footsteps of the landlady approaching , cue the door being pushed open without an invitation to enter.

"Ah Sandra, how are you?"

"Fine darling, just fine. I see your writing, how is it going?"

"Very well so far," I enthused, "I'm just about to write chapter six."

"Good, good ,now what are you doing for Christmas?" she said rather abruptly, no protocol, no time wasting, straight to the point.

I groaned, "probably going to the sisters, it's her turn this year, it was my parents last year."

She picked up on my lack of enthusiasm, "Well, if you were not doing anything special you're welcome to come to my sisters (oh god, there's another Potter?). She always does a great Christmas party and the foods brilliant, but on the down side she's a bit of a snobby bitch sometimes, but she's a lovely person."

"Its very kind Sandra, but I'm not family and I'd feel a bit awkward…."

"Don't be daft," she interrupted, "I'm supposed to bring along a few friends, they are always glad of some new company, you know how boring these things can be sometimes if it's just family all the time." I had visions of sitting in front of the television with a pile of snacks on my knee listening to my sister bellyache while her husband Ian went into a coma because of the amount of food he had just eaten, he was like one of those bloody big anacondas, you could see the bulge in his belly and it would be days before it was completely digested - no wonder he's fifteen stone. Fat bastard.

"Irene's going this year," she said, "so you will know someone at least."

My reverie was interrupted and her comment piqued my interest and I replied a little too quickly, " I would love to come, where does your sister stay?"

"Broadlees, Chapleton, the posh bit."

"I know it well, must have money."

She smiled, "Loads, he's a corporate banker, that sounds like some rude rhyming slang doesn't it?" she let out a hoarse laugh. "Bob will pick us up on Wednesday about five o'clock, is that alright?"

There wasn't a lot going on in my diary. "That's fine Sandra, excellent."

"No problem, listen I'm just nicking out to the Spar shop for a few things, do you need anything?"

"No not really."

"Right then I'm off, hope the writing goes well, remember to stop in when Irene comes in and we'll have a natter."

"Great." Her thirty-second appearance lifted my spirits and it was time to get back to some work again. I decided chapter six would be about the unostentatious pensioner who succeeded in defrauding many of her work colleagues, neighbours, and myself out of a considerable sum of money. I still can't believe I was taken in by the smooth talk, the tempting offer - maybe it was because you intrinsically trust an old age pensioner, especially a woman, or possibly it was just the way she skilfully used those factors in her masterful deception.

It's an embarrassing situation to find yourself in when you've been conned, you don't know whether to complain to the authorities or keep quiet to save your savaged pride especially when the perpetrator is a decrepit old sod. Nancy Burns, in my defence, did not look the criminal type, she had ill fitting false teeth that looked two sizes too big for her, wore a wig that looked like a birds nest, and was slightly bent over when she walked. I suppose the description of her is not relevant but it just builds up a picture of someone that doesn't look like a career criminal or an evil genius, but underneath that clever disguise was a shrewd, calculating old bastard that cost me about £185 and the trusting community of St Leonard's approximately £5,000 give or take a few pounds.

In my defence, I think it's true to say that we have all been victims of a con trick at some time, anyone that's frequented the 'Barras' will vouch for that, the words 'pig in a poke' spring to mind. A confidence trickster, to give them their correct definition, basically plays on a persons edacity, getting something at a really cheap price, a bargain, which is dissimilar to gambling, which is getting nothing for something. So when a tempting purchase is offered by someone plausible you're automatically drawn, it's human nature, it's like those' pyramid schemes,' they look enticing and sound convincing but are ultimately a complete waste of money, again it appeals to greed or the lure of quick gain.

Let me illustrate the point, and this is a true story as well. I fell for this con and even knew the culprit, although in all fairness he refunded my money when I complained to him. Like all good scams, it was simple and had a certain appeal. He had self-published a slim novel entitled '101 cons, the book the police tried to ban' Intriguing title, and you could see the attraction. The book was shrewdly wrapped in cellophane (Like some of the top shelf men's magazines which prevents perusing so I'm told) so if you wanted to know about some of the great cons and how to make a quick killing all you had to do was buy this book which was reasonably priced at £4.99, a small price for potential gain. Sounds good.

Wrong! When the unsuspecting victim (sucker) opened the book there was only one page of print which read,' to con people, play on their greed, it works every time. Thank you for making me rich.' The book was also sold on the internet and made Alex Boyd a few thousand pounds before it was taken out of circulation, but by that time he had already made money out of it.

So back to the original story of Nancy Burns, the master of jiggery pokery and skulduggery. This was a plan that couldn't possibly fail because it had universal appeal, it involved cut price alcohol, reliable brand names like Smirnoff, Glenmorangie, Gordons and so forth, no cheap imitations or homemade moonshine, and large slabs of cigarettes.

Nancy causally mentioned to her workmates that her son, Frank, who worked with her majesty's customs and excise, had access (illegal) to cases of seized contraband and was selling it off. She fabricated the story that much of it was destroyed rather than reselling to customs staff, hence her son was doing the community a service, he made a few quid out of it and his customers received cut price drink and cigarettes. Where was the harm in that?

Initially Nancy had made a loss, she would buy in a few litre bottles of vodka, gin, whiskey and cigarettes and sell them 50% cheaper than the retail price. As you would expect word got around very fast and a great deal of interest was generated. The few that had bought Nancy's bargains attested to the quality of the product, and more importantly, the superb price it was selling for along with the reliability of delivery. Old Nancy had built up trust among her work mates and neighbours.

The timing of 'the sting' was perfect, just two weeks away from Christmas, the time when people generally stock up on the booze and fags and have that bit of extra money in their pocket.

She took orders from many of her work colleagues, neighbours and basically anyone else who was willing to part with their money in advance for the sake of a bargain. Like one of those dreadful pyramid schemes you get sucked into, I got a few of my friends involved who were looking for some half price drink courtesy of Frank Burns from the customs and excise department. It was supposed to be a 'festive steal', unfortunately it did turn out to be just that. Just like before, Nancy asked for the money up front and people were only too pleased to give it to the old age pensioner with the stoop, they even received a receipt which made it look totally legitimate and were told the consignment was due next week, three days before Christmas. After collecting a sizeable amount of cash, the police later revealed it to be about £5,000, Nancy Burns vanished into thin air. She never returned to work and she moved house. No one has seen her since.

There were probably others that were fleeced but were too embarrassed to do anything about it, that included myself, so the figure could have been even higher. The people that contacted the police aggrieved, were simply informed that buying illegal alcohol and cigarettes was a criminal offence, so no charges were ever made. I handed her £185.00, which included money from a number of my friends who were only too keen to buy cheap booze and fags for the festive season. I had to repay all the money back which really hurt. The old bugger also owed me 'two cleans,' which was £5 which only added insult to injury. Every time I see the flat in Glen More it makes my blood boil, just the way the wool was pulled over my eyes - I won't fall for anything like that again I can assure you. I think.

After a few finishing touches to chapter six, and a quick bite to eat, I had to prepare for the students this afternoon which wasn't a chore at all, I found it very relaxing and enjoyable work and more importantly, profitable. The adverts I had put in the papers would hopefully bring in some more people looking for tuition.

My mood was ebullient, the thought of having a few drinks with the girls (I use that term loosely) and getting to know them really lifted my spirits, as they say, 'fortune knocks once at least at every man's gate.'

CHAPTER 6

CHAMPAGNE AND TEARS

It was Shakespeare who wrote, *'give sorrow words, the grief that does not speak whispers the o'er fraught heart and bids it break.'*

A single word can destroy or it can build up, it can alter the past or change the future. It's often difficult to verbalize words, especially the ones that cause pain - its easy to tell someone you love them, it's much more difficult to say that you don't. Its easy to be the bearer of good news while relaying bad news is an onerous task often fraught with complication. The spoken word, like a double-edged sword has to be handled with extreme care.

When the oncologist uttered the words ' it's back,' the pretty brunette's world fell apart and there was no hiding her devastation. Just two words, that's all - words that filled her with dread and with a sense of hopelessness. The fight was finished, it had won.

The personal battle that had been waged for over a year was now over and it was time to face the harsh reality, the cancer had metastasized and invaded the tissues nearby, spreading to the liver and the lungs by means of the lymphatic system. Radiation therapy had failed. Chemotherapy was basically the last hope but this also made little impact on the silent killer.

In her heart of hearts she knew it was back, she was an expert in self-diagnosis, she knew the tell tale signs, the change in the bowel habits, the bleeding, the loss of appetite and the unexplained lethargy. A precursor of cancer.

The doctor had been caring and sympathetic, even tearful as he prepared her for the final eventuality. He offered counselling, practical palliative care and promised to liaise with the local doctor. He was genuine, but they were only words and no matter how well they were articulated or how sincere, they still seemed vacuous.

The pretty brunette wiped away a tear, hugged the oncologist and thanked him for all his endeavours. It could not have been an easy task for him relating the news. He would probably be affected by the emotional fallout as well. Her friend who was sitting in the corridor outside patiently waiting and worrying offered up a silent prayer for some good news, the petition had fallen on deaf ears. When she looked up and saw her coming out of the doctor's room she knew before she had even uttered a word, her body language said it all.

Dirty Laundry

Irene shook her head. Sandra embraced her and they cried together.

"It's back," she wept. The emotion of it all got to Sandra and for once found it difficult to speak, her words came out sounding like a mantra.

"I'm sorry, I'm sorry, sorry," she sobbed as she held her. She knew it would be difficult to offer words of comfort to someone who's dying, anything would seem like an empty platitude, a tired cliché.

"Oh Sandra, what can I say, I knew before I even seen doctor Collins, I told you didn't I?"

"You did, you did."

"What a time to get the news, two days before Christmas, some timing."

"Look Irene, there's no good time." She finally released her from the bear hug and rummaged in her coat pocket for a tissue. "So what exactly did your doctor say?"

Irene let out a resigned sigh and wiped away a tear.

"Just what I expected, the adjuvant chemotherapy failed, all that time on bloody Dexone, then Zofran, what a waste and what I had to put up with."

Sandra interrupted. "Is there anything else they can do? Maybe another treatment, more aggressive therapy?"

"No Sandra, I've tried it all, radiotherapy, chemotherapy, its progressed too far and too fast, even surgery is out of the question, Dr Collins made that abundantly clear."

Sandra started to weep again and it was Irene who comforted her.

"I've put up a damn good fight Sandra, but I've lost and I just have to accept it and so will you, it's not easy but that's the reality of the situation. I've thought about this situation, this scenario, for a long time now."

"It's just so unfair," Sandra wept, "you're so young, it's…" She couldn't finish her sentence, the reality of the situation was beginning to fully register and the tide of emotion overwhelmed her.

"Oh god, what a mess." Irene started to cry again. After she finally composed herself Sandra quietly asked,

"How long?"

"How long do I have?"

"Yes."

"A few months at best, although it's difficult to be certain, but he ran the 'Karnofsky' test to give me a rough idea of the time scale we're looking at."

"I don't understand darling."

"It's based on a scale of 100 to zero, 100 would represent someone with cancer that cares for themselves independently, carries out all normal activities and so forth, then you come down the scale to say, 80, and that means someone's restricted in physically strenuous work, they can only perform light work duties, when the scale indicates 50, then that means the person requires considerable assistance, 40 represents special care, maybe disability, 30 for example would denote that the sufferer would need hospitalization, constant care. Twenty as you can imagine is extremely ill, anything under that is absolutely critical, zero is death. Sorry for being so morbid but you did ask, anyway the doctor reckons I'm between 40 and 50, so I must be doing pretty good eh?"

Sandra didn't laugh, she recognized the seriousness of the situation and her friends attempt to soften the blow for her.

"You should have told me you we so ill," she said.

"I didn't want to worry you, anyway there's absolutely nothing you can do."

"I could have helped more with your housework or just general things."

"Look Sandra," she said quietly as she put a comforting arm around her, "I'm managing, I only do a few hours now in the shop just to keep my mind off things and get out the flat, and my own housework is not that bad, I've only myself to worry about so it's not a problem, anyway Jenny comes up quite often and she's a great help so stop beating yourself up, you do enough for me, honestly ,you're the best friend a person could wish for, I love you."

"You too," she sniffed.

"I've thought about it Sandra."

"What?"

"The worst case scenario, the cancer's back, there's nothing more I can do, so I'm just going to go out with all guns blazing, two fingers up to the world , I' m determined not to wallow in self pity but just enjoy what time I have left while I still have a measure of health. And do you know what else I'm going to do?"

"No."

"I'm going on a spending spree, a shopping day to remember."

A hint of a smile appeared on Sandra's face.

"We should go away for a few weeks Irene, somewhere warm and sunny."

"And where the wine's cheap!"

"Yeah, that's what you need darling, a good break for a few weeks, it will be better than any therapy you'll receive, and you'll get a tan."

"You're right Sandra, that's what we both need, a complete break, a couple of weeks just to indulge ourselves and chill out."

From Hairmyers hospital Sandra organized a taxi to take them back to Strathaven to the Castle tavern for a liquid lunch and a talk, they had so much to discuss now that they knew the seriousness of the situation. The 'Castle' was busy as usual but they were fortunate enough to find a table at the back, it was full of boisterous people in festive mood with money to spend.

The establishment had made a special effort to create a magical Christmas effect, there was two bits of last years tinsel draped over the optics and a cheap plastic Santa that sat in the corner of the pub looking depressed, someone had stubbed out a cigar in his nose and left it there, but what the pub lacked in aesthetic appeal, it more than made up in atmosphere, it was the type of place that was welcoming and friendly and most of the people knew each other, basically it was a home from home - the beer wasn't too bad either. It was, without doubt, the best pub in Strathaven, basically because the regulars knew how to enjoy themselves and were not a shy lot, when they came out for a 'drink' they made the most of it. It was a melting pot of Strathaven society from the affluent to the great unwashed.

"Nice and warm in here Irene, eh?"

"Yes, it's cosy," she replied placing her jacket over the chair.

"I'll get a drink in, what do you want darling?" Sandra enquired.

"Half pint of their best lager please. No, make it a pint, I feel like a drink this afternoon."

"Okay, one pint of Stella coming up, do you want a bite to eat with that, I'm getting a bit hungry?"

"A toastie would be great thanks, that's about all I could manage at the moment."

"I'll have the same, this is like the Castles 'cor don blue' cooking," she said sarcastically. Sandra eased her way to the front of the bar using her ample cleavage to cut a swathe through the men folk, then proffered a twenty pound note after ordering the drinks. Irene sat at the table at the back of the 'bar come lounge' which was difficult to distinguish, enjoying the buzz of normality. People were lively, animated, not a care in the world, sharing a drink, laughing, having a drunken conversation about banal things, and looking forward to Christmas, the most pagan celebration on gods earth, where the god of commercialism is worshipped and many financial sacrifices are offered at a terrible price come January. But this is what Irene desperately needed, a bit of fun, a bit of over drinking, cheap tinsel and cheap perfume assaulting the senses, this is what really made sense in a mad world. For a few brief seconds the thought of cancer and it's devastating effects were actually forgotten.

Sandra arrived back with a pint of lager (quite common in the castle tavern for girls, none of this half pint stuff so you looked lady like and demure) and a large gin and tonic looking very pleased with herself.

"They'll bring the toasties over in a minute, they are being specially cooked in the sandwich maker."

Irene smiled, "Thanks Sandra."

"Cheers darling, here's to you, the nicest person in the whole wide world." Sandra choked back a tear. Their glasses clinked together and Irene took a large swallow of the chilled lager.

"Oh that's good, just what I need."

Sandra grinned and said, "You can thank your friend for the round of drinks, the bloke over the other side of the bar, I think his name was Tiff or was it Biff, something like that anyway, he insisted on buying a drink for us which I thought was very kind of him, he obviously fancies me." She let out a wicked laugh and for the first time today Irene smiled at her friends vanity.

"I'll buy him a drink before we go," Irene said, "that was nice of him." He waved from across the bar.

The flow of conversation was interrupted by Alison the barmaid who brought over their food with a smile, "Enjoy your meal ladies," she said warmly.

"Thanks love." In the Castle tavern a cheese toastie constituted a 'meal.'

"So you plan to see your relatives and your sister tomorrow to let them know the news?" Sandra enquired.

"Yeah I didn't tell anyone I was going to hospital today, well except for you but I thought it would be best to do it face to face, it's going to be hard to break the news and to tell you the truth I'm not looking forward to it, they are very emotional at the best of times especially Jenny, she's very protective of her older sister, always has been."

"It won't be easy pet, but at least you know they will all be there for you," she said reassuringly.

"It's always been like that Sandra." She took a consoling sip of lager and added, "anyway, that's my plan for Tuesday and I'm going to enjoy myself on Wednesday at your sisters, then we are all getting together at Jenny's for boxing day so that will keep me busy, keep my mind off of things."

"Good for you darling, you're sounding very positive and I'm going to make sure that we have a wonderful time together, as you said, all guns blazing!"

"Here, here! Your glass is nearly empty, do you want the same again?"

"Please darling, awful small measures you get in a pub, try and smile at the nice gentlemen and they'll buy you a drink, it worked for me!"

"They are infatuated with your bosoms, that's all, but we know who's the good looking one don't we." Sandra laughed and drained the last of the gin and tonic. She lit up a cigarette and watched as her closest friend approached the bar, she noticed how thin she was getting and was suddenly tearful when she thought about the results from hospital. The thought of losing her was unbearable, a part of her would die as well. She tried not to let dark foreboding thoughts enter her mind but concentrate on positive things, difficult as that would prove. Sandra was determined to make whatever time they had left truly memorable, it would be filled with fun and happiness, together they would battle against it and continue to defy convention. They would not give in to it and the cancer would not completely take over their lives. She had always said to Irene that true friends are made in wine and proved in tears, this was now going to be a testing time of their resolve and their friendship.

Irene arrived back with a bottle of champagne, two decent glasses, crystal ones that made a genuine clinking sound and a bucket of ice. Sandra looked perplexed and exclaimed.

"What's all this about, did someone buy you this?"

"No."

"Thank Christ, you would probably have to sleep with him for that!"

"No one bought me a drink, I told you I have smaller boobs than you, I don't get noticed, no, this is for us, a kind of celebration if you like."

"What are we celebrating?"

"Life, or to be more accurate without sounding morose, what's left of it."

"Well, I'll drink to that."

The champagne was poured with due pomp and ceremony and attracted a bit of attention, Irene watched as Sandra lit up another cigarette.

"Pass me a fag will you?"

"What?"

"A cigarette."

"You stopped smoking two years ago."

"And I'm about to start again, god I miss them, and please don't tell me they are bad for your health." Sandra smiled and passed the packet over to her, she lit up and inhaled deeply.

"I've been thinking darling, what would you like to do before you go? I know we talked briefly in the taxi but I think we should really start planning ahead, sorry if that sounds a bit morbid but I want us to enjoy our time together, its precious."

"I've not really had time to think about it, I'm still in a haze at the moment, I don't think it has really sunk in yet. What would you do Sandra?"

She mused for a moment then replied.

"Things I would like to do before I depart this mortal coil,let me see,- the first thing would be a date with George Clooney then some good sex although I admit, I can't really see that happening could you?"

Irena laughed and shook her head.

"Doubt it, you're too busy at the moment, anyway you could do a lot better I'm sure," she said releasing a cloud of smoke and enjoying the instant gratification of the nicotine.

"I would love to go to Paris for a long weekend, a good five star hotel and have dinner in a fancy restaurant, you know, the candle lit thing with romantic music."

"Sounds great," Irene enthused, "you know what I would love to try Sandra?"

"What?"

"Go on a naturalist holiday, somewhere exotic, not that one in Loch Lomand, somewhere tropical."

"Are you serious?"

"Of course, does that not sound wonderful? Let it all hang out, that would be great, liberating, and you would get an all over tan. We should definitely do that."

It would be a blast."

Dirty Laundry

"Well that's something for my 'to do' list ,depending on the money I suppose."

"Irene darling," Sandra said breezily, "money does not present a problem now, buy everything on credit then you'll never have to repay it , take advantage of those greedy stores and companies that are always asking you if you want credit or a loan, then cheerfully charge you 33% bloody interest, get your own back, that's what I would do, but then again I'm more wicked and devious than you are."

There was a glint in her eye as she replied, " you know Sandra you're absolutely right, it's payback time, the number of times the banks have fleeced us, overcharged us or treated us shoddily, payback! Fill your glass up, let's plan a mega shopping spree for next week, it will be like Christmas all over again except a lot cheaper!"

"That's a brilliant idea, and do you know what else you should do?"

"What?"

"Stick all you bills in the bloody bin, or better still, get them all together and set them on fire, that would be kind of symbolic don't you think."

Irene smiled at her friend's devious nature. "It's true what they say, every cloud has a silver lining -I'm not going to worry or stress ever again about money, bills, tax whatever, absolutely nothing - what a wonderful feeling that is, I'm free, liberated!"

"You're intoxicated darling," Sandra laughed.

"God that champagne really does go straight to your head doesn't it?"

"Brilliant!"

The conversation, like their emotions ebbed and flowed as they discussed their future over the champagne, the time they had left together was precious, every moment would have to count, because life is like a candle in the wind, or hoar frost on the tiles, it's finite, it's unstable, uncertain, and it's a wise person who enjoys it to the full and appreciates what they have. The ominous words, 'it's back' was all it took to galvanize Irene and Sandra into positive action and to carefully plan the rest of their days, however long or short they would prove to be, and with family and friends by her side it was a comfort that would keep her sane and give her the fortitude and inner strength to fight her last battle with quiet dignity.

CHAPTER 7

GOING FOR A SONG

Isn't life grand, it's two days to Christmas and I'm in a rhapsodic mood, I'm in such a good mood I'm whistling to myself, mostly Christmas type songs as I prepare the next chapter of my novel.

The snow is falling gently outside the window, great big flakes that are hypnotic to watch as they descend effortlessly from the sky and carpet the ground in a glorious white blanket. I've a song in my heart and I'm in love (yes, once again, but I'm one of life's optimistic suckers that has a short memory and a forgiving spirit). The self-imposed drinking ban has been temporarily lifted because of the festive season and partly because I write a lot better with a sherry in hand, well if Van Gogh painted better under the influence of absinthe why shouldn't my mediocre writing become elevated with a glass or two of Harvey's Bristol cream? (I've removed any sharp cutting instruments from the room).

It was wonderful to meet with Irene on Saturday and I stayed for nearly two hours before reluctantly departing upstairs. We have a lot in common, she's divorced and stays by herself in Strathaven, loves rock and blues music, good food and wine, black and white movies and has a certain animus towards lawyers and officials in grey suits.

Sandra was a very good host and the night went very well, so well in fact I decided that when we met up again at Christmas at Sandra's sisters I would ask her out on a date, nothing too formal, just a quiet drink in the Waterside and a nice relaxed meal at Mario's in the common green as it serves good food in nice surroundings although it's a bit pricey for me in my current state of affairs. But what the hell, I honestly think it's love this time, what more could a guy ask for? She's very pretty, big brown eyes, brunette hair and very slim with, dare I say, pert bosoms.

I feel I have a real commonality with Irene and I'm more than sure she liked me, her obvious body language gave it away, we even share the same sign of the zodiac, Aquarius. All in all it was a very good weekend, Saturday of course was sublime and Sunday wasn't too bad either considering it involved what most guys normally hate - shopping for presents. Its depressing enough normally, but trying to shop with a broken ankle with my new 'stick,' could have proved to be a nightmare. The problem, however, was solved by Neil's wife Karen who had phoned up the 'Shop Mobility' place in East

Kilbride and ordered a motorised wheelchair for myself. I thought it was a joke and remonstrated until Neil sat in it and drove it about like a big kid, it didn't look too bad and would take the hassle out of the shopping. I didn't know if they were being extremely kind and thoughtful or were taking the piss, however I squeezed my ample backside into the chair. It proved to be brilliant and had a top speed of 10 mph - Neil suggested that it could be improved by putting spikes on the wheels, a bit like the Ben Hur chariot thing to scythe down annoying or tardy shoppers especially the elderly who generally walk at a deaths pace and hold everybody up. He thinks there should be a special time for old people to shop, the blue rinse brigade, preferably after 6 o'clock. There's a man with a mean streak in him, thank god he's got Karen to rein him in and temper his asocial behaviour, but that's a school teacher for you.

Karen was an absolute darling, I had six presents to buy for females and she took all the strain out of it by volunteering to buy for me, that way, she reckoned, each one would get a practical present at a reasonable price. I had always worked on the premise of purchasing the same present for every female, for example 'soap like things,' or fluffy slippers that looked comical, it takes a lot of pressure out of the shopping, eliminates thought. For guys it's a hell of a lot easier and predictable and it's guaranteed not to be returned the following day - alcohol, or anything alcohol related, no one ever returns booze, you can't lose. So Sunday afternoon went like clockwork, Karen bought 6 individual presents to the value of £20 each (extravagant, yes, but that's just me) and I had purchased 6 bottles of Jack Daniels, plus a big load of wrapping paper, pink for the girls and blue for the boys, you need a system. After shopping we went for a pub lunch at Shenanigan's and had just a little too much to drink, afternoon drinking really hits you quick and poor Karen was press ganged into driving us back home.

Driving an electric buggy half cut was quite hysterical especially with Neil sitting on my lap. We returned the electric wheelchair with a bump in it. The shopkeeper thankfully didn't check it over, she obviously trusted Karen who looked a little embarrassed. The only down side was the fact it took us twenty minutes to get out of the bloody car park as it was so busy, no wonder people's blood pressure rises when they come into East Kilbride, they should offer you a free drink or Prozac when you walk through the doors.

So I'm sitting here, in good spirits, it's 6.30 in the evening on the Monday and I have the house to myself, god it's quite without Mrs Potter. She phoned from hospital and said she was visiting a friend and wouldn't be back until Christmas Eve, Tuesday. She was kind enough to tell me to use up the chicken pie in the fridge which had to be eaten and reminded me to feed her Fanny and lock up, she sounds like my mother sometimes!

Dirty Laundry

I was tempted to phone Irene but I didn't want to come across as pushy or needy, so decided just to wait until we met at Christmas day. I could hardly wait, as they say, 'absence makes the heart fonder,' a phrase used by the Roman poet Propertiu way back in the first century, then unashamedly plagiarised by the British poet Thomas Bayly. I'm suddenly moving into writing mode once again!

I shuffled over to the other side of the room, grabbed the bottle of sherry and poured myself a generous measure of 'Jerez's' finest, you cant beat a glass of it served with a slice of orange and ice. Down to the serious business of writing as the next few days would be taken up socialising and ingratiating myself with some of the more affluent ones in Strathaven society.

I looked at my list of stories and decided to write about a dear old soul who lived in Loch Goil. She was about 75-90 years old I reckoned, it's difficult to judge how old people really are, let's just say she was well past the bloom of youth. Mary was a delightful person, which I'm afraid can't be said for a lot of old folk who constantly carp on about their pension, the price of a loaf, poor bus services and the good old days (yeah, two world wars, food shortages, famine, the Spanish flu and powdered eggs, say no more!). She was kind, considerate and always had a good word to say about everyone. Her husband died about two years ago, so being widowed left her like a lot of pensioners, 'financially challenged', money was tight and her house was spartan to say the least, I think she worried about bills, the rent, council tax and anything else. The houses in loch Goil were warmed by gas central heating, yet hers was never switched on, old Mary used a single bar electric fire only when it became cold, false economy I think. It reminded me of that old joke about the poverty stricken family - the old buddy recalled when it was cold the family of eight used to sit around a candle, when it got really cold, they used to light it!

But she was not mean or tight-fisted, every Christmas time she would tip me, the house cost £2.70 to clean and she always insisted that I take £3, thirty pence was by no means a massive amount of money but it was the gesture that was appreciated and the spirit in which it was given. If Mary had problems with any of her bills she would always ask me for help when it came to filling out any forms, council tax rebates, housing benefits and so forth, I was only too glad to help, some of the forms were very complicated and problematic, a Philadelphian lawyer would struggle with some of them.

The window cleaners function is a diverse one, apart from the obvious, I have cut grass (lawns not drugs I hasten to add) cleaned gutters, carried out numerous painting jobs, roof work and even wallpapering for a modest fee, but the most unusual and the most satisfying work I have ever undertaken for a customer has to be an evaluation of old Mary's possessions from her loft, and if I had been unscrupulous or exploitative I could have ripped her off big time. But that's just me, as

Dirty Laundry

honest as the days long, but for one fleeting moment, just a heartbeat, I was tempted to take advantage of her obvious ignorance for monetary gain, and I can tell you this, it was a considerable amount of money I could have appropriated dishonestly.

When her husband died she decided to move from Busby to East Kilbride to be beside her family who rarely visited her or even kept in touch. The onerous task of clearing the loft was dutifully performed and a lot of the stuff was either discarded or given to some of the local charity shops, there was the usual assortment of miscellaneous items that were transferred to the loft in Loch Goil when she moved in, items that would never be used again, along with some precious family heirlooms in the form of pictures, pottery, old toys, various tack and a violin in its original case.

Her local church was about to organize a 'bric-a-brac' sale for the benefit of its shrinking funds, the roof was in a state of disrepair and the cost was quite considerable. The call went out to its parishioners to provide items that could be sold as well as the usual home baking and sale of plants, hence the loft clearing for Mary who thought she would be able to contribute something for the church.

Here is where I came in, old Mary didn't possess step ladders to gain access to the loft, she would have found it very difficult even if she had ladders, she was very old, and like most pensioners, she did not like heights. I would perform the task of opening the loft lid and pulling myself up, which I thought would be a bit of a struggle. She offered to pay me a few pounds for my services and I gratefully accepted, a cup of tea and a scone as hard as a brick was thrown in to sweeten the deal (to get enough moisture in the fruit scone I actually had to dip it into the tea).

Mary had decided to clear the loft as a lot of the stuff was ancient, some of it was sellable she reckoned and some of it was of sentimental value only, a good clear out would benefit herself and the local church. After three attempts of trying to enter the loft by jumping and pulling myself up I eventually succeeded, sweat was running off my brow before I had even started the task of loft clearing. I didn't even think about taking in a set of my own ladders at the time. She passed me a large lamp which illuminated the damp smelling, intimidating loft - I hate bugs of any description, Jill was always the one who had to beat the spider with a shoe, or chase away 'daddy long legs,' their actual entomological name escapes me, even worse than bugs, are the four legged things that scurry and like cheese, so it was with considerable trepidation I entered the dark, dank hole. She asked me if I was alright and I replied in a butch voice, 'no problem, no problem at all', it was a blatant lie. Once my eyes had adjusted to the light I started the task of removing objects that I thought would be of saleable value, I appreciated her trust in my judgement.

Dirty Laundry

It's amazing how other people's 'loft trash' is far more interesting than your own collection of 'valuable junk' There was without a doubt many items that would be snapped up her church group, an old fashioned cutlery set still in the original box with the pound shilling and pence price still attached; a rocking horse, probably one of her own childhood toys, the value of which I was uncertain; a queens own Cameron highlanders helmet, an officers leather bonnet by W Cater - I suggested that she should hold on to that item as it was quite collectable and in was in pristine condition. There was a box full of 'Just William' books in good condition which I guessed would be worth something to a collector. There was boxes of old clothes, glasses, an assortment of gramophone records, probably valuable, and sitting in the corner of the loft, a brass slide trumpet and a violin box which I presumed contained a violin.

All of the items were carefully handed down to her and after 40 minutes or so we had finished the task of loft clearance. She put the kettle on and I brought all of the loft goods down stairs for her to evaluate and sort out,there was quite a collection. Mary came back into the living room carrying a pot of tea with the with the 'cosy thing' on top of the pot, something you don't often see these days and looks rather quaint, then to my gastronomic horror, another round of scones, why did I say they were delicious, they could be used as a weapon if propelled with force. Over tea and a 'current brick,' we discussed how evocative old possessions really are, how they can instantly take you back to a place or time and trigger many memories. I got a few stories as I politely sipped my tea and wondered how much she was going to pay me, the rocking horse was hers as a child, it was the first Christmas present she remembered and one that was shared by her younger sister. As she was telling me this sweet story I just couldn't, for the life of me, get that bloody Rolf Harris song out of my head - 'Two little boys,'great! now its 'Jake the peg.'

I had casually mentioned in the conversation not to give it to the church until it could be evaluated, I guessed the horse would have been worth some money, so it would benefit her and the church if she was sensible. I told Mary my wife Jill was a bit of an expert in antiques and collectables and she would be able to offer her a rough idea of its actual value if she popped around for an hour or so. She agreed it made sense and thanked me for the sapient advice.

Jill was very good at evaluation, she had an encyclopaedic knowledge of the field, everything from chiparus figures, hat pins, inros, scrimshaw to patch boxes,she actually made banal things sound interesting and had a keen eye for a bargain, for example when we were rummaging through some of the stalls at the 'Barras' she got very excited when she found amongst a lot of junk, one of those 'patch boxes.' She never let on to the stallholder how valuable it was and casually asked what he would want for the four items she had in her hand, three of them were obviously valueless and this clever ploy was designed to 'blind side' the seller. It worked ,still chewing on a bacon sandwich he asked for, 'two quid love,' which was duly handed over. She kept her excitement reined in until she left the stall, it turned out to be a late 18th century oval Staffordshire 'patch box' with an illustration of Buckingham palace on the lid ,she later resold it for £325, not a bad return for £2 I think.

As I said, she made dull sounding things intriguing, for instance the 'patch boxes' were very common up until the 19th century when smallpox was still a terrible scourge that attacked all classes of society. Smallpox was a highly contagious viral disease and was endemic in Europe until the development of a vaccine in 1800, if someone was fortunate enough to survive an attack (the mortality rate was about 45%) they were often left scarred, with a pock marked face. To conceal the scars, fashionable women in the 18th century began wearing tiny patches, usually shaped like hearts and stars on their faces, the fashion proved to be so decorous, so 'comme il faut,' that even women who were not victims of smallpox took to wearing the decorative patches, hence the need for the small boxes to keep them in. The small boxes, usually circular or oval in shape were about an inch and a half wide and were made of silver or enamel and beautifully decorated.

After I had finished my tea, Mary asked if I could take some of the smaller boxes into the living room to clear a space from the hallway. I noticed amongst a box full of thimbles, needles and threads, a patch box which looked very similar to the one Jill bought, this was an early 19th century Staffordshire example in an oval form with a lid mirror and in pristine condition. It would have been the easiest thing in the world to pocket it, she would have been none the wiser, especially when she paid me £3.00 for nearly an hours work, and, I may add, had to endure two cups of tea and two scones. But she was such a delightful old soul and it would have been impossible to defraud her.

When I told her what it was and what it was possibly worth she nearly had an apoplexy and informed me there was another one up in the loft somewhere that was similar, she definitely remembered there was a pair of them as she used to play with them when was a child. Her meeting with me proved to be not only fortuitous but profitable and I promised to come back tonight with Jill to sort a few things out and to give a more accurate evaluation.

I arrived back home at 6 o'clock and I told Jill about my day and she was only too pleased to help out and after a quick bite to eat we headed out from Lethame road to Loch Goil for an evaluation of her 'loft junk' The old girl had made a bit of an effort to do herself up, her hair was neatly tied back and she had her makeup on with the obligatory red lipstick on her teeth which made her look like she had just consumed some raw meat. Mary was the most convivial host, as soon as we had arrived there was a pot of tea and tray of assorted cakes, with not a scone in sight, (I had previously warned Jill about the rock like things with currents that were hard as lead pellet's) and this was accompanied with some small talk before we got down to the serious business of evaluating her goods.

My estimation of the patch boxes was reasonably accurate. It wasn't as valuable as the one Jill had purchased, nevertheless she reckoned it was worth about £250.00 or thereabouts. Jill was now Mary's best friend.

My good wife's face dropped when she saw the rocking horse I had previously described. I've seen that face before when she's about to procure a bargain or rip someone off. The rocking horse, which was made in the 1920's, was basically a donkey, it wasn't worth much because of the poor condition it was in, she would be lucky to get £90 for it, although Jill suggested it might be worthwhile to pay someone to get it restored to its former glory and this would greatly increase its value. Mary didn't let the disappointment show too much and she encouraged Jill to have a quick perusal at the rest of the items 'rescued' from the loft before they ended up in the church fete. The hat, or to be more precise, the highlanders bonnet was worth, in the region of £300.00 if she could find a buyer - I was quite proud of my valuation, Jill's obvious love of the collectables was obviously rubbing off on me. Mary looked absolutely delighted and I think Jill was having a wonderful time rummaging about and looking for items of value, she was really in her element.

We stayed for about an hour examining the rest of the loft stuff and chatting to Mary who was filling us in with some nostalgic stories of the past and memories of her family. It was a very heart-warming experience and she had so many interesting tales to recount. As we were about to leave she suddenly remembered the old violin case which she had put upstairs in her bedroom because it looked 'fragile', I had completely forgotten about it. She insisted that we stay for another minute or so to have a look at it, the violin was inside the case and it had been in the family for many years, and she thought unlike the slide trumpet, it might be worth something as it was in reasonable condition. Intriguing.

She came back down the stairs and handed the case to Jill who looked like an excited child that had just been given a Christmas present, this was Jill's specialist field, musical instruments, she had a wide and varied knowledge of antique violins, cellos, violas and so forth. The case itself was in very good condition and so was the violin, Jill didn't need to say word, her expressive face said it all. It was simple enough to determine the original maker, the name was inscribed on the case, it was Vincezo Sannino, whoever that was, I was hoping it was going to be a rare Stradivarius or at least a Cuarneri, one of the great violin making families from Cremona in Italy. (I learned that from Jill) Stradivarius produced more than a thousand instruments from his family workshops, over 600 or so of them still survive, mostly in America, so the chances of one of them turning up in a loft in East Kilbride would be a bit much to ask for I suppose.

Nevertheless, Jill was excited and that was all that mattered because it meant it was worth a lot of money, she reckoned it was made between 1899 and 1910, and because it was still in very good condition with its own original case it could be possibly worth in the region of £5,000. Mary went a very strange colour when she heard the value of the violin and I thought she was going to pass out. Jill stressed to her that this was only a rough guide and she would have to reference one of her volumes or go on the internet for an accurate valuation. The news of the sudden windfall brought out the generous side of Mary and she arrived back with a decanter of sherry and three good glasses - I watched with mild amusement as Jill checked out the decanter, she just couldn't switch off, finding a Vincenzo Sannino had been the biggest thrill of her life apart from marrying me.

She promised to phone first thing tomorrow with a more accurate appraisal, but unfortunately the meeting with her didn't transpire as Jill was called out on some type of work emergency which took her away for a few days to London. I got a phone call from Mary who had some good news for me, she had read in the paper that the 'Antiques road show' was going to do a programme in Scotland at the Kelvin Hall which was an ideal venue as it sat across from one of the best museums in Britain and was adjacent to the transport museum as well, it was an area rich in culture, and I may add, it was free to the public.

On a whim Mary had decided to visit the Kelvin hall and hopefully receive an evaluation for the violin and if she was lucky enough, to appear on television with the boyish Michael Aspel (that's how she described him).

She arrived on the Saturday morning after getting a bus to George Square then a taxi to the Kelvin hall - as expected the place was heaving with excited people with their family heirlooms and collectables along with a huge compliment of camera crews, floor assistants, directors and producers and the antique experts carrying out the task of separating the wheat from the chaff. Many hours of footage was shot just to produce a half hour programme. Many people went away disappointed that their particular item wasn't as valuable as they had hoped for, it would be back to the grind again come Monday morning, others left with a rictus grin attached to their face, the family heirloom was about to subsidise a good holiday or a new car, so much for family sentiment.

After waiting patiently for nearly four hours, (and five cups of tea) Mary was escorted to a small oak table with four chairs, and introduced to a tired looking presenter, his name, I now forget. She was very disappointed it wasn't Michael Aspel. After a few brief instructions from the production staff they started the shoot, and Mary, in her best pink dress and hat, excitedly proffered the musical instrument to the expert valuator who had looked at the violin prior to going on camera.

The grey-haired expert with leathery hands and a whimsical smile looked genuinely impressed and sounded very knowledgeable - a brief two minute history of violins followed; the cradle of the modern violin was in Cremona, Italy, where Amati developed the design which became the standard for all violins; the founders of other great violin families were the Guarneris and the master of them all, Stradivari who produced the best quality ones, the secret being in the varnish and a combination of fine proportioning and aging. He then spoke about Mary's violin, and its history - the maker, the design, the quality and it's excellent condition. At the end of the appraisal he asked her what she had it insured for (cue dramatic effect). Mary replied that it wasn't insured at all and that it graced a space in the loft for decades.

He politely suggested that it should be insured to the value of at least £7,500, maybe even more, as it was an excellent example of a Vincenzo Sannino which was dated circa, 1900.

The old soul just about fell off the chair and an assistant grabbed her arm to steady her, it made for good television when it was shown about two months later. Mary was a TV celebrity in the St Leonard's community and even made it into the East Kilbride news which gave her instant kudos and celebrity status.

There was however, just one drawback, a down side to the afternoon. It had been a long day for Mary, but a profitable one as she headed back to George Square in a taxi clutching the violin as if it meant her life. The sudden acquisition of wealth emboldened Mary to head for the nearest lounge for a sherry, something she hadn't done for many years, but this was an exceptional day, one to be celebrated, so she ordered a large one and sat in the corner of 'The counting house' enjoying her drink and thinking of ways to spend her money. She left in an ebullient mood.Rather than splash out on a taxi all the way back to East Kilbride, she decided to take the number 20 bus back and save herself £25 in the process. To cut a long story short, the effect of the sherry, the long day and the general excitement made her fall asleep on the bus and when she woke up in Whitehills (she had went past her stop for about two miles), the antique violin had been stolen.

Some punk kid or smack head was wandering about Glasgow with a £7,500 violin, which he would probably sell for £20 or £30 for his next drink or fix, to say she was devastated was an understatement. Rotten things always seem to happen to the nicest people, either that or god possesses a devilish sense of humour , I personally think it's the latter. On the plus side she found the other patch box in the box that contained the needles and threads. You win some you lose some!

Dirty Laundry

Old Mary still lives in Loch Goil and often recounts her one day of being a television star, we all deserve our 15 minutes of fame, but especially her.

I finished chapter eight within an hour and decided to call it a day, too much sherry on an empty stomach, or should I say head? Mrs Potter's chicken pie beckoned me, and I also had the responsibility to feed her Fanny, personally I would like to feed it to the Rottweiler next door. The great escape was on the television yet again and I decided to watch it once again to see if Steve McQueen would make the fence this time. Doubt it.

CHAPTER 8

HAVE YOURSELF A VERY MERRY CHRISTMAS

It's not very often I've seen or heard Sandra flustered, but today she seems a little distracted, unfocused. From up the stairs I could hear pots rattling, doors banging and the occasional curse word which was rather colourful for a lady. I'm in two minds whether to go down stairs to ask if she needs any help or just mind my own business and play it safe. I chose the former and bravely wandered down the stairs. I opened the kitchen door.

"Hi Sandra," I said cheerfully.

"Good morning to you, I hope I didn't waken you up."

"No, not at all, it's 10 o'clock, I've just been doing some reading, bit of research and I'm going to make myself some breakfast, do you want a coffee, I've got Nescafe?"

"God, yeah," she replied sounding exasperated, "Christ, merry Christmas by the way!" She leaned over and kissed me full on the mouth, it was not too unpleasant.

"And to you Sandra, hope it's a good one for you."

The kitchen resembled a war zone, she had been up early organizing some food to take to her sisters for the Christmas party tonight and I suspected she was feeling the pressure as she was a perfectionist when it came to cooking or baking , I noticed two beautiful fruit cakes she had baked a few days ago were sitting on the worktop awaiting the final touches and they were carefully marked 'the girls' and 'the family' which I thought was a bit strange. She pulled a stool over, sat down and lit up a cigarette. Through a cloud of smoke she said.

"I think I'll have a quick break before I get back to it again."

"Are the cakes for your sister?" I enquired.

"Yes darling, they are, it's a bit of a tradition in the family I suppose, without being too modest I'm the best baker, especially Christmas cakes so I always bring one, the secret is to inject plenty of brandy, rum and sherry into it to keep it moist and succulent and not to have too much icing on it or it becomes quite sickening , I've just a few decorations to put on it and it should be ready."

I glanced at her endeavours.

"They look lovely Sandra, and smell very rich."

"Thanks. I used to put money in them…"

"Yeah, I remember that as a boy, it was a sixpence or a shilling and it was a thrill to find it." Sandra continued.

"That stopped unfortunately when an old uncle got one stuck in his throat and just about passed out, we thumped his back until he coughed it up, the poor bugger's false teeth fell out which amused the kids, you can laugh now, but it was touch and go for a time."

I smiled at her wonderful story, she was certainly a colourful character.

"What do you take in your coffee Sandra?"

"Milk and two sugars please."

"Coming up." I poured the steaming water into the two cups and handed one to her.

"So how did your visit go yesterday? you said you were seeing someone in hospital."

"Not well, not well at all, it was bad news I'm afraid…." Her words trailed off and I had the sense not to pursue the conversation any further, if she wanted to talk about it she would in her own time.

"I'm sorry to hear that Sandra," I said sympathetically, " did you have a nice time at Irene's?"

A smile returned to her face. "It was great, we had a few drinks in the castle tavern."

"Are they still as lavish with their decorations?"

Sandra laughed and replied, "Yeah, over the top, we ordered two cheese toasties and they came with a plastic piece of decoration on the plate."

"Maybe you were meant to eat it, it would probably taste better than the toastie."

"Actually they were very nice, we left there a bit tipsy, Irene had bought a bottle of champagne, so it was good fun."

"Champagne?"

"Well, we were celebrating Jack, and I can tell you this, it was a really good bottle, the others in the pub looked jealous as it was poured."

"Sounds good, what were you celebrating?"

"Just friendship, that's all, she's a really good friend and we occasionally do things that are out of the ordinary."

I smiled when I remembered both of them standing out in the rain, dressed in nighties and trainers frantically searching for a piece of cake, they were certainly an odd couple.

"Are we still meeting up with Irene tonight?" I enquired trying not to sound too keen.

"Of course, I've changed the arrangements a bit, we are not getting picked up by Mary's husband Bob, we'll make our own way there, it's no too far, I thought we could go for a quick drink if the pubs are still open, or if not, we could go back to Irene's for a glass or two."

"That sounds great to me. I think that they will close a bit earlier because it's Christmas Day, they usually do."

"Yeah, I would imagine, anyway, you'll need a few drinks before you go to my sisters." The thought of dinner, Christmas dinner at that, with strangers was not sounding so appealing now especially after that last caustic remark.

I asked, "Why do you say that?"

She took a long drag from her cigarette and replied matter of factly, "Don't get me wrong Jack, they are the nicest people you could meet, very generous, kind, but they are just a bit snobby, ostentatious for my liking." I suddenly felt under pressure. I didn't even possess a pair of dress trousers or a decent tie.

"What do you mean?"

"Well, they've got money, serious money. Mary as I have said to you lives in Broadlees, Chapelton in a £900,000 house, drives a BMW and Bob drives a silver Porsche, a big shiny thing."

I laughed at her inept description of German technology and workmanship. She continued.

"My other sister Ann and her husband Patrick, don't call him Pat by the way, it has to be Patrick, they live in Strathaven - you might even have met them before, it's a small town, anyway they live in Newton road, do you know it?"

"Of course, it's not that far from where I used to stay."

"That's right, you were in Lethame road, the nice bungalows. Patrick is a solicitor and my younger sister Ann works for the council, quite high up."

"What do you mean, in a skyscraper?"

She laughed at my pathetic attempt at humour.

"She makes good money and they both move in the upper circles of Strathaven society if you know what I mean."

I knew exactly what she meant. I stayed there for many years and still felt like an outsider. It's the type of small town where everybody knows your business and you have to respect certain protocols and conventions. In other words, they look after their own which is not a bad thing - if you're in the 'circle of trust' you've made it in Strathaven.

"Well don't worry Sandra, I'll be on my best behaviour tonight and I won't embarrass you or make any social 'faux pas.'

"Look, just be you normal self Jack, I'm sure they will all like you."

"Thanks for the vote of confidence." I popped two slices of bread into the toaster. "Do you want a bit of toast Sandra?"

"No thanks darling, just you help yourself."

"So what time do you want to leave for Strathaven?"

"I was thinking about 4 o'clock, which would give us a couple of hours before we go for our dinner, does that sound alright?"

"Fine, what can I take to your sisters?"

"A bottle of wine would be great although don't expect them to serve it with the dinner, they consider that inappropriate, they select their own wine for the meal which is supposed to compliment it perfectly. To be quite honest I couldn't tell a £30 bottle of wine from a cheap one sometimes, as I said to you before, they are a bit snobby, but they mean well."

"Its very nice of them to invite me, I appreciate it."

"My sister is a wonderful cook, even better than myself so you should be in for a treat tonight."

I wasn't complaining, I had intended spending Christmas by myself, the thought of celebrating it with my sister was just too much to bear and although I had received an invitation from others, I just wanted a quiet night in to get on with some writing, I know it smacks of self pity and isolationism but that's just how I felt, anyone that's been through a divorce will know what I'm experiencing, especially at this time of the year, it's just not the same without your partner. I had bought a small turkey breast (reduced to £1.99 at the local Spar shop) for myself and was going to stuff it with some whiskey flavoured haggis, and serve it with mashed potatoes and veg, which I thought would be very 'haute cuisine,' so I was looking forward to being spoiled at her sisters. The day was looking very promising indeed, a few drinks with Sandra and Irene then on to Mary and Bobs for some Christmas nosh and a bit of socialising with the upper classes. I buttered my toast and left Sandra to get on with her preparation and swearing, I intended to do another chapter or so, then luxuriate in a bath and make myself as handsome as possible for Irene, the only thing that spoiled my appearance was the damn ankle in a cast but maybe that would solicit some sympathy from others.

After breakfast I read through the last few chapters of the novel to bring me up to speed and looked at some of the options that were left. I was undecided who should grace the next chapter, the two neighbours having an affair that were caught in 'flagrante delicto' in the middle of the afternoon, they didn't even have the sense to draw the curtains. The customer who had an elaborate cannabis manufacturing process going on in his living room; the Jehovah's witness family that irritated everyone in the street with their constant, over zealous proselytising that gave the impression of being clean cut and wholesome while behind closed doors the wife had taken to drink because of the husbands affairs, or the middle aged woman that suffered from obsessive compulsive disorder. It's amazing the lives some people actually lead and it's sometimes difficult to define with any clarity what's really 'normal,' or socially acceptable. I've learned not to prejudge people, or stigmatise them, as we don't know all the circumstances or issues people have to deal with and because we all react differently under stress or pressure. For example, Bryan the cannabis grower, who was unfortunate enough to be prosecuted by the courts and had his ' cannabis factory' confiscated, suffered greatly from a very virulent form of multiple sclerosis and despite trying every legal 'drug' to alleviate the constant pain and suffering nothing gave him the relief he desperately needed until someone suggested using cannabis. It was the only thing that worked and also had the wonderful side effect of making life extremely jolly into the bargain. Bryan, being a frugal type of bloke, decided to grow it himself to cut the cost of paying a neighbour who used it recreationally and charged him over the odds. When I cleaned his windows I just thought he was a plant lover (the living room resembled a tropical forest) who liked to keep his house very warm, it wasn't until I read in the local paper he was prosecuted for growing the weed that it finally dawned on me. Despite being prosecuted (a slap on the wrist - don't you just love British justice), he's continued to grow it again.

I loaded the typewriter, got comfortable and stared at the blank piece of paper in front of me. Nothing was forthcoming so I hobbled to the window and gazed out of it looking for some inspiration. That didn't help either so I decided to give it a miss for today, I was too excited about the prospect of seeing Irene Black and trying to win her over with my considerable charm and jeu d'esprit. I opted for a bit of piano practice to keep myself sharp. One of my students was scheduled for a two-hour lesson on the 28th of December and he was already extremely proficient and I didn't want to be shown up. He had music exams coming up soon and wanted some extra tuition, Peter was a very polite, likable young man and it was a pleasure to teach someone who had a real thirst for learning. The tuition was going better than expected, after I placed an advert in the East Kilbride news, business increased considerably and it was proving a reasonable income along with the pittance the government provided. I honestly thought that being incapacitated for 6 weeks was going to be a living hell, but my time was taken up and there was no boredom factor at all, if anything I didn't have enough time for all my recent undertakings especially the writing which I'm finding cathartic as well as therapeutic. I'm grateful to Sandra for that one. I might even give her a mention in the credits if it gets published.

I treated myself to some classical sheet music which was a departure from the normal rock and blues stuff and started playing a beautiful composition from the wonderful modern Italian composer Ludiovico Einaudi entitled, 'Le Onde' (The waves) it was a simple, yet haunting piece of music that lifted the spirit. Mrs Potter walked in during my masterful performance.

"Sorry for interrupting Jack…." I stopped playing.

"No problem Sandra, what can I do for you?"

"I like that, no, I love it, what is it?" I was tempted to say it was a little number I had thrown together, extemporaneously. I explained what it was called and who wrote the piece, she genuinely seemed impressed.

"I really like that, it's lovely, can I run something by you?"

"Sure."

She walked out the room and headed back down the stairs without any explanation, I was non-plussed, but was getting used to her strange behaviour and her odd idiosyncrasies. Some would call it eccentric, others, mad. She came back in with a piece of paper in her hand and I patiently waited for an explanation. Waving the piece of paper in front of me she announced.

"I've just had a brain wave!" I bit my tongue and didn't say anything sarcastic. "Every year on Christmas day one of us says a few words or recites a poem in memory of our sister Catherine who passed away ten years ago this very day. It could be anything at all, even something we have made up ourselves, Mary did just that last year, although the poem was naff it was still touching, it's our way of remembering Catherine. It's become a family tradition if you like and it's the most important part of the evening."

"It sounds very touching Sandra, it's a nice way to remember someone, commemorate their passing." I was quite touched by her sentiment. She comes across as brash or even indiscreet at times but the genuine warmth was beginning to shine through and I was seeing the softer side of Sandra Potter even though she spoke with a fag hanging out her mouth that seemed to defy gravity. "What age was Catherine when she died, she must have been young?"

"Forty-six years old, it's so young, so bloody young and she was such a beautiful person, full of life, full of fun until the cancer took hold, she died within six weeks of being diagnosed, it's so unfair….". Her words began to trail off and I could see her eyes welling up at the memory, the emotion still looked very raw and I guessed she must have been very close to her. She still had the paper in her hand.

"So is that a poem you have there?"

"Yes it is Jack," she said wiping a tear away.

"Do you want me to read it?"

"God no, it's only the girls that do that on the night."

"No you misunderstand Sandra, I meant do you want me to read it just now and let you know what I think of it."

"No." It sounded like a sharp rebuke and she continued unabated. "What I want you to do Jack is play that lovely piece of music just like you were doing and I will recite the poem over it, I think that would add something to the moment." She let out a cloud of smoke as she awaited my reply, but she was right, words accompanied with background music can elevate the moment, intensify emotion and make a lasting impression. I harboured doubts over her piece of poetry, if it was composed by herself it could be, as the Americans say, 'god damn awful' or even trite no matter how good the musical accompaniment was.

"That sounds a very good idea Sandra, so how long is the poem?"

"About a minute or thereabouts, so you could do your introduction. I'll recite the poem then when it's finished I'll say a few words at the end and that will be it."

"Great," I enthused, "the piece of music is about four minutes or so, that will give you a rough idea of the timing because you don't want the music to run out while you're still speaking."

"Hadn't thought about that Jack, that's a good point. Would it be too much of an imposition to rehearse it later, it wouldn't take too long?"

"Of course not, I'd be honoured to do it, honestly."

"Right, what I'll do is this," she said emphatically, " I'll write out what I have to say at the end of the poem so we'll know exactly how long everything should take, because as I have said to you, this is the most important moment for all of us. We fill up the glasses, stand up and pay our tributes. Christ, I'm nervous as a plump turkey just before Christmas…"

"You'll be fine Sandra," I said smiling at her considerable unease, "I can improvise on the keyboard and gently wind it down, so don't worry about timing or anything."

She interrupted, "Christ it's not a bloody keyboard you'll be playing, no offence to that thing in the corner, it's the genuine article you'll be tinkering with."

"What do you mean?"

"A Steinway"

"What, a genuine Steinway piano?"

" Of course, Mary plays the piano, she went to lessons when she was younger, she was daddy's favourite, I told you there are a bit snobby, none of your Yamaha keyboard type of thing, no offence."

"None taken." I detected a hint of sarcasm and a soupcon of resentment in her voice. "Well that's fantastic, it's a beautiful instrument and it will sound even better."

"Excellent Jack, and I'll be beside you at the piano and do my thing!"

I had visions of Sandra like Michelle Pfeiffer in the film 'The fabulous Baker boys', spread out, resplendent on top of the piano, all smouldering and whipping up the sexual tension, if Mrs Potter wore a low cut dress she might even pull it off .(not the dress, the theatrical effect)

I was curious (nervous) about her choice of poem she had selected, or even worse, if she had written it herself, homemade stuff is usually excruciating and you don't want to offend them by saying what you really think, it's a bit like song writing, you compose something, play it to a friend and they tell you its good, what they really mean, it's appalling or utterly vacuous and it was a real effort not to snigger. I hope to god Sandra's attempt wasn't like that. For some reason I wanted her to excel tonight, I had the feeling that she viewed her sisters as having 'succeeded in life,' whereas Sandra was struggling to find her own identity, the monetary, financial gap was obvious but it would be rather empty to judge a person solely on 'pounds shillings and pence.' Unfortunately, that's how people view success or achievement. I think Sandra was way better than that. She had a true evaluation of what was worthy or what was important in her life and I remember her quoting Robert Burns on the vanity of pursuing material things and worldly possessions, this was when I was moaning about my situation and my losses - she simply said,

'but pleasures are like the poppy spread,
You seize the flower, it's bloom is shed;
Or like the snow falls in the river,
A moment white- then melts forever.'

Sandra was sometimes capable of rendering me speechless with her sagacious words, but she was equally capable of leaving me stunned with her quixotic behaviour. Her personal library contained every work of Burns and she was constantly quoting him which made me feel inadequate as I knew very little of his works which I suppose was my loss.

I was compelled to ask her, "So what do you intend reciting tonight?"

"Well Jack, I got a poetry book out of my collection and poured over it looking for something personal and realistic, a lot of it was very pretentious, specious, but one really stood out a mile and it really touched me."

"What was it called?"

"It was a poem by a bloke called Paul Meadows."

"I have never heard of him."

"Neither have I, but what he wrote really struck a chord, do you want to hear it?" She held the piece of paper up. "I copied it, I think it's brilliant."

"Yes, go ahead I would love to hear it."
"Okay here it goes, this is for you Catherine,

Go to that place we loved, our secret place
close your eyes and you'll see my face.

Play that tune, the tune we loved to hear
Close your eyes and you'll see me clear

Walk on a beach or climb to the top of the hill
Close your eyes and you'll see me still

Take a sip of wine, of dark red wine
Close your eyes and you'll see me fine

At night go out and look at the brightest star
Close your eyes and you'll see me far

On a day when the sky is blue and cold and clear
Close your eyes and you'll see me near

Take down a book that would have been my choice
Open the book, close your eyes, you'll hear my voice.

When she had finished the recital, come eulogy, I was really touched, she read it with warmth and passion that only a person who had experienced great loss could. I had to compose myself before speaking.

"Sandra," I gulped, "that was really beautiful."

"You're not bull shittin' me?"

The acerbic riposte brought me back down to earth very quickly. "No really, it was very profound, very personal, I liked it."

"Good, I'm glad you like it, cause if you think it's alright, that's good enough for me." With that last comment she walked out of the room, making me feel rather fragile - what a strange woman. After a couple of hours practice I fixed some lunch, Sandra had popped out with her Fanny for a walk and to pick up a few things at the local store. I had a bath, shaved, then ironed my best shirt in preparation for the big night as it was just about time to head out to Strathaven. Sandra had organized all her bags in the hallway so she wouldn't forget anything and she had even written a checklist as a backup, it looked like she was going on a two week holiday. I had one plastic bag that contained a very fine (£4.99) bottle of wine and a few presents for Irene and Sandra that I would give to them before we went to the party. Karen had made sure they were gift wrapped properly, and to be absolutely honest I could not remember what was in each one, it would be a surprise for me as well.

"Right I've phoned for a taxi Jack, it should be here shortly, fill up my glass will you darling and help yourself. I'm just going to double-check everything," she said anxiously. I heard her talk to herself in the hallway, ticking everything off. I tried not to laugh.

"Bag with toiletries, night gown and change of clothes, makeup, spare tights, presents, check presents." I heard more rummaging. "All accounted for, now bottle of gin, bottle of wine, brandy and cigars, that seems to be everything, Oh Christ, I need money, where's my purse?" She came back into the living room looking slightly flustered and I handed her a glass of gin and tonic which she took off me and gulped down quickly. Her purse was sitting on the stereo and she let out an audible sigh of relief. I offered her some friendly advice.

"I think you need to chill Sandra."

"God I know, I'm getting myself all worked up. I do this every year. It's just bloody nerves that's all. I'll calm down when I get to Irene's, honest!"

The taxi sounded its horn and Sandra jumped about three feet into the air and restarted the 'panic thing' all over again, it was amusing to watch. I helped her with some of her bags as best as I could. As I was about to get into the taxi she asked me to double check everything was switched off and locked up which I did reluctantly, I think she was suffering from a mild dose of obsessive compulsive disorder. It was just as well I did recheck, the two splendid Christmas cakes were still sitting in their respective boxes with their labels on them, I lifted them up and smiled the way they were marked, ' the girls' and 'the family.' The kitchen door opened and

Fanny walked in, I think she was looking for food, in her haste Sandra had forgotten the feed the thing, I grudgingly opened a tin and fed her then hurried out of the house with the Christmas cake. I put the label in the box although to be absolutely honest I wasn't certain if it was the right one, they got mixed up when I was feeding the cat and checking up. Sandra was delighted when she seen me coming toward the taxi with the boxed cake she had forgotten, so delighted she gave me a kiss for saving the day. She opened up the box, examined it and said.

"Perfect, thanks Jack!"

It was great leaving East Kilbride and entering Strathaven, I immediately began to relax and enjoy the beautiful countryside and the wide-open spaces. When I get back on my feet (financially as well as physically) I was determined to move back, I miss the place so much and the people, I feel sometimes I'm suffocating in suburban boredom and striving always to come up for air in East Kilbride. Just as those contemplative thoughts entered my mind I was assaulted by the odiferous smell of the farmers silage in the fields, it made me smile.

Strathaven was looking very 'picture postcard' with the Christmas trees lit up and the colourful decorations festooning the shops and buildings, the atmosphere was quite magical, like travelling back in time to when you were young when everything seemed entrancing, beguiling, and it always snowed on Christmas day, I can practically hear Bing Crosby singing 'White Christmas.'

The taxi snaked its way through the common green and turned left at Mario's the Italian restaurant and entered Kirk Street. Sandra insisted on paying and I said I would get the taxi back, it would save any arguing. She was looking a lot calmer now, thank God. I think she needs to be introduced to the wonder of Prozac.

The door to the common hall entrance was left open and we walked in laden with bags and festive cheer. Irene looked delighted to see us and we were warmly welcomed in. Her apartment was absolutely beautiful, it was decorated in light pastel colours with pine panelling on the ceiling and doors that were inlaid with Rene Macintosh glass with expensive looking furniture, the whole ensemble worked very well indeed.

Irene was wearing a black dress (no idea what make) with matching leather shoes, and I just thought to myself, 'wow'. I tried not to stare or dribble. The perfunctory Christmas pleasantries were exchanged and she brought through a bottle of champagne, minus any mistletoe. I had to make do with a peck on the cheek.

"I could get quite used to this," Sandra said breezily.

"It's a bit extravagant, but what the hell, it's Christmas. God, I can't get the damn cork out," Irene complained. Cue muscle bound man with freshly ironed shirt smelling of cheap aftershave.

"Let me try Irene," I said smoothly, "I'm pretty good with a cork in my hand." I heard them sniggering but could not understand why, with a couple of manly twists I popped the cork and it was met with a loud cheer. I poured the champagne into the glasses and watched as it over poured onto the wooden flooring. Irene volunteered a toast just as I was about to drink from the glass. Damn, my first faux pas and I wasn't even at Sandra's sisters. I pretended I was gently inhaling the effervescent bouquet.

"Here's to love and friendship," she announced, short but sweet I thought.

"Cheers!"

"Cheers, all the best!"

"Can I just add," I said feeling bold, "that it's a pleasure just being in the company of two beautiful women, you both look stunning!"

"God, he's a real charmer Sandra isn't he!"

"I think he's infatuated with both of us, and you know I can't blame him."

"Now, now, it's very gentlemanly to pay someone a compliment when it's deserving isn't it? I think it was Mark Twain that said, 'I could live for two months on a compliment,' so please accept my comment without analysing it," I added sounding like it was well rehearsed.

"Thank you Jack," Sandra replied, "it's not very often I get a compliment, well, apart from, 'hey nice knockers.'"

Irene laughed and I just shook my head, Sandra was not one to accept a kind word with a bit of grace, although she certainly did have a big pair of......

I mentally chastised myself, I had to remember my manners, etiquette, politeness, call it what you like. I didn't want to disappoint anyone tonight, especially myself, because the more I see of Irene the more I'm falling in love with her and I want to make a good impression.

"How are you feeling darling?" Sandra enquired.

Irene smiled, shrugged her shoulders and replied softly, "I'm fine honest, a bit tired today but fine, and I'm really looking forward to the night. Jack, her sister is one hell of a chef, Sandra's brilliant, but I have to say your big sister just has the edge and no more, so you're in for a great Christmas dinner."

"So I've heard Irene, it should be fun although I must admit I'm just a bit nervous about meeting other people for the first time, especially the 'haute bourgeoisie' of Strathaven."

"Forget it Jack," Irene laughed, "you'll have a blast tonight, honest. Here let me freshen up your glass, a little alcohol helps." She grabbed the bottle from the table, held my hand with the glass and refilled my drink - I felt a frisson of electricity pass through me when her hand touched mine.

"Thanks," was the only weak response I could muster.

"So what's the plan for tonight darling?" Both Irene and myself turned to Sandra. Thankfully she spoke first, saving my embarrassment.

"Well all the pubs close at 6 o'clock tonight so if you want to go for a quick drink we'll need to go soon, I reckon we'll have over an hour or so - but if you want to stay here and have a small aperitif before we visit your sisters that's fine by me as well."

"Jack?"

"What?"

"Do you want to go for a drink or do you want to stay here?" As far as I was concerned, I couldn't lose.

"I'm easy, please suit yourself, it's your night." Negate all responsibility, it comes across as cool sometimes.

"Sandra?" Irene asked.

"Well we should go for a quick drink, there's always a good atmosphere in the pubs at this time of the year."

"Right then," Irene said with a voice of authority, "it's settled, we'll visit the fleshpots of Strathaven, are you up for it Jack?"

"You bet."

The Castle tavern was very busy, people were packed in like sardines in a can, clutching their drinks to their chests, so we decided to visit the Drumclog Inn (known colloquially as 'the hairy bum,' it rhymes with drum.) which was a leisurely 20 yard walk from the castle just up the hill. It was equally as busy so we opted for the Waterside, it was definitely feeling like Christmas time, there was no room at any of the inns. Thankfully a small group of people were just coming out through the front door and we were fortunate enough to secure a few seats beside a roaring fire. I politely asked a well-dressed woman in her forties if anyone was sitting there.

"My friend's sitting there, she's just gone to buy a drink, but these seats are free," she smiled. I directed the girls to the seats and asked them what they would like to drink. Sandra suddenly took charge.

"Listen Jack, I'll go up for you, you had better watch your ankle, it's busy tonight." I handed her a £10 note and she headed for the bar. Perfect, it afforded me the opportunity to talk to Irene by herself, the two of them seemed joined at the hip sometimes. I was just about to compliment her, when I heard a distinct laugh, one that I recognised immediately - the colour drained from my face although I was sitting in front of a roaring fire and I prayed she would not walk over in this direction. I held my breath and tried to make myself invisible. Too late, she walked right up to our table and stopped dead when she recognised me. Her friend noticed her strange demeanour.

"What's with you, have you seen a ghost?" she said. We just looked at each other as she reluctantly sat down in the very next seat to mine. One of us had to say something.

"Hi Jill, how are you?" I said through gritted teeth. She didn't look too pleased to see me, maybe because the last thing I said to her was ' you're a cheating, lying conniving little bitch in heat, rot in hell!' That might have had something to do with the icy reception and the obvious awkwardness. To give her credit she was polite and complaisant, but that might have been the shock of seeing my face again.

"I'm fine Jack, and yourself?""Yeah, great, couldn't be better, well, apart from the broken ankle." She forced a smile out, or was it wind?

"You always were a clumsy oaf."

"Skiing accident in Switzerland," I lied.

Awkward situation, I was feeling the strain and I thought I better introduce her to Irene who was sitting patiently in silence.

"Er, Irene, this is Jill, my ex wife."

Another uncomfortable silence followed, which was broken by Sandra returning with the drinks, I was going to consume my pint of Stella in one go.

"Ah isn't this lovely, it's Christmas, there's a big fire, I've got good company a large gin and tonic, and a new packet of fags," Sandra said happily. No one said anything. She sat down between Irene and myself. "There's your change darling, not much I'm afraid." It was a handful of silver, no notes. I took the money and introduced her to Jill.

"This is another friend of mine Sandra, Sandra Potter, this is Jill, my ex wife, isn't this a coincidence?"

"Delighted to meet you Sandra, this is my friend and colleague Janis."

"Hi darling, well you're better looking than Jack said and a hell of a lot thinner," Sandra said in her usual loud voice. I just wanted the ground to open up a swallow me, I drew Sandra a dirty look. Thankfully Jill politely dismissed herself, turned her back to us and engaged her friend in conversation. In all the gin joints in town she ends up in here, she usually frequents the Strathaven hotel where the posh people drink. Irene and Sandra had a great laugh at my expense and discomfort but I took it in good spirit basically because there was nothing else I could do. At least we were civil to each other. It's been over a year since I had last seen her and I have to say she's looking very good indeed, there's a new hair thing going on and Jill's lost a bit of weight, probably because she's been pining for me or her latest flame makes her stressed and miserable (I hope).

It's an odd, ambivalent feeling meeting someone you were really close to, someone you have loved and cared for, the person you were intimate with, the one that you shared your innermost thoughts with. Now, in an act of self-preservation, or self-defence, her backs turned to me as if she's trying to shut me out. Suddenly all the anger and hatred for her has dissipated, replaced with a kind of detachment, a numbness.

But I must admit, after meeting with her for only a few minutes I still find her attractive, interesting. I loved my life with her in my old house in Strathaven, I loved her company, she was smart and intelligent and I thought that our relationship would endure, 'in saecula saeculorum' - so much for male intuition, some of the other females I've chatted to since my break up have been mere ' lava lamps'- nice to look at but a bit dim.

Unsurprisingly Jill and her friend Janis left after their drink and there was a collective sigh of relief from all of us, this was followed by some uncomfortable, intrusive questioning from my two so called friends sitting with me, I quickly steered the conversation away from my failed marriage into other less controversial matters, woman can be so personal, it was unfair, it was two against one.

Last orders were called at ten to six and there was the usual stampede for the bar for the last drink that no one really wanted, Sandra ordered doubles again with my dwindling resources, but what the hell, it was Christmas, a time of cheer, splendid inebriation and a free hangover the following morning. We left the Waterside in high spirits and headed for Broadlees, the apprehension and the nerves were now a distant memory, as my mother used to say, *' a cask of wine works more wonders than a church full of saints.'*

I was actually looking forward to meeting her family and more importantly enjoying a Christmas dinner, alcohol certainly gives you an appetite, I just hoped they served big portions, there's nothing worse than being invited for a meal and being presented with portions that would hardly fill a toddler.

Yeah, I had a good feeling about tonight, everything was going splendidly and my intuition (yes there is such a thing as male intuition) was indicating that this was going to be the night for Irene and myself. What a lucky girl!

CHAPTER 9

A BIT OF A DO

Someone once defined human nature as, 'when three astronauts go up in a spaceship and there is an argument about who sits by the window.' Human nature is shallow, base, so when I first set eyes on their house, no, wait a moment, 'house' is too constricting in it's definition, ' mansion' would be more appropriate, there was a just a bit of resentment.

First impressions of the house? Wow, amazing! Second thoughts? I would not like to pay their mortgage. Two cars sat in the driveway, a Porsche and a silver BMW that proclaimed, 'look at me, I've lots of money.'

The house looked on to acres of green fields and trees which gave the place a certain tranquillity and solitude, not bad I suppose for a corporate banker. I was pricked by a small stab of jealousy. The only way I could ever afford something as grandiose as this was to carry out a 'bank job,' with the cosh in hand and the perfunctory pair of tights over the head.

As was customary with Sandra Potter she didn't even chap the door, she breezed right on in, bags in hand and shouted from the top of her voice, "Hi it's me, the good looking sister." Irene looked at me and raised her eyes heavenward. We were greeted in the hallway by her sister Mary who looked very much like Sandra only she had an air of sophistication about her - two steps behind her was Bob, who looked like he was no stranger to the odd glass of sherry. He had a very red nose which made it difficult not to stare, it looked like it had been buffed faithfully every night with a chamois leather. We were warmly greeted and ushered into one of the main living rooms which was positively cavernous and had just about the largest window I had ever seen which offered views on the patio and garden which was roughly the same size as Calderglen park (slight exaggeration). It was really stunning, there was even a stream running through the garden.

Sandra had told me of her sister's opulence and the room reflected that. It boasted a beautiful Italian leather settee and chairs, hand-crafted furniture, object d'art, marble flooring and walls that were adorned with French impressionist paintings. I'm suddenly attracted to her older sister now and think of planning a way to bump off old Bob. My reverie was interrupted.

"So let me take your coats, have a seat and I'll fetch you a drink," Mary said politely. "Patrick and Ann are running a bit late but they will be here soon and Dale and Dotty are just freshening up in their room, I'll introduce you to them." Sandra escorted her sister into the kitchen still clutching the plastic bags that were filled with bottles of spirits and the prized Christmas cake she made such a fuss over. I smiled nervously a Irene.

"Who's Dale and Dotty?"

"A vaudeville double act?"

"I thought you might have known them?"

"I've no idea who they are Jack, but you'll like Patrick and Ann, they are very down to earth and very nice." Bob walked into the room and said with an air of sarcasm.

"I've been instructed to show you to your room by her majesty in case you need to freshen up and leave your overnight stuff." I had no idea we were invited to stay for the night, Sandra didn't even mention it, I was wondering why she had brought so much. All I had was a plastic Morison's bag with a bottle of wine in it and nothing else, not even a spare pair of boxers or even a toothbrush.

All the bedrooms were en-suite and tastefully decorated, my room was directly across the hall from Irene's which I thought was quite fortuitous. The house was that bloody large they should have provided us with a map to find your way about. I had visions of taking a wrong turn and getting lost. I eventually found my way back into the living room after some imaginary unpacking and joined Irene on the settee. Mary and Sandra entered with a hostess trolley full of bottles and mixers looking and sounding very animated.

A pre-dinner aperitif was accompanied with some polite, but strained conversation which skirted anything controversial or in depth. I eventually got to meet the rest of her guests, her other sister Ann, who was very affable and possessed the same throaty laugh as Sandra and her husband Patrick, who resembled the wonderful Shakespearean and Star Trek actor Patrick Stewart, even down to the bald head. It could have been him, the likeness was quite striking. Normally solicitors leave me cold. The conversation usually centres around corporate business and oligopolistic market forces but he managed to steer clear of it and was certainly up for some good natured badinage, which was more than I could say for Bob who came across as a bore with a sherry glass permanently welded to his hand. I got the impression that he desperately wanted to be somewhere else and he contributed next to nothing in the conversation apart from a few sardonic remarks. As for Dale and Dotty? The words that could describe them - outlandish, outer and very eccentric, but nevertheless very personable. They were Americans, say no more. Dotty was in her early fifties, very overweight, very loud with big hair, I mean 'big' hair like Marge Simpson's that seemed to defy gravity, it was a bees hive type of thing, something you would see in a 1960's movie. She was also draped in jewellery, big jewellery, 'bling' I think the term is, she had a diamond ring that made the famous 'Kohinoor' look like a cheap imitation, and earrings so big and circular, a thin person could use them as a hula-hoop.

Her husband Dale was so off the wall. He was difficult to describe. His contribution to the conversation consisted mostly of irrelevant, meaningless facts and figures. Within a short period of time I learned that -

'A sneeze can travel at more than 100 MPH.'

'On average a person had about 2 million sweat glands.'

'When a human reaches 30 they begin to shrink.'

'The male penis extends far into the body, almost to the rectum, you can feel a portion of your penis if, when you have an erection you press a finger up into the area behind your scrotum.'

(I took a few steps back after that last, interesting fact and had visions of him trying it out)

'A polypectomy is the removal of nasal polyps.'

'It's possible to lead a cow upstairs but not downstairs.'

The man was a living, breathing non sequitur and I cowardly retreated from his presence by excusing myself and informing him I needed to use the bathroom. Out of the corner of my eye I could see Ann smiling at me. She obviously knew what he was like and was enjoying my obvious discomfort. His interesting fact about the penis made me smile as I urinated and I hoped that he wouldn't be sitting next to me at the dinner table. I wanted to enjoy my meal without enduring his banal stream of consciousness. What a bohemian group of people!

Dinner was served at precisely 8 o'clock and it was well worth the wait. Sandra did not exaggerate when she said her sister was a master chef. It wasn't the usual Christmas fare I had experienced. There was a choice of food available that I reckoned was very impressive - on display was:

Starter

1.Escalope of hot smoked salmon on a warm new potato, olive and herb salad with crème fraiche and caviar 2. Lightly curried leek and potato soup with a smoke haddock spring roll.

Main Course

1. Fillet of Angus beef with spinach fondant potatoes, roasted cherry tomatoes and deep fried shallots . 2. Turkey breast on puy lentils, with a port and cranberry sauce, celeriac tartlet and kale'n'pine nuts.

Sweet

1. Vanilla soufflé with summer berry sorbets. 2. Bitter chocolate mousse with red capsicum ice cream, sweet sherry and grenadine jus.

This was to be followed with fine Brandy and a cigar. I felt like a 'bon vivant' as I looked around at the wonderful way the table was set, the surroundings, and the wonderful sound of Christmas songs from the likes of Nat King Cole, Bing Crosby, the Platters and others.

I opted for starter number two and when it was served I eagerly lifted the correct spoon and was just about start when Mary suggested that it would be fitting to ask for a blessing on the food - I put my spoon down and looked guilty, Sandra looked across at me and grinned. "Jack, would like to do the honours?" Mary asked politely.

I felt slightly intimidated at the thought of representing this group of people in prayer especially as I was very merry by now, and I was a fully paid up agnostic, or was it atheist? - I was probably a combination of both of them. It went very quiet and everyone looked in my direction, not one to shirk a challenge I answered confidently.

"Sure it would be my pleasure." I stood up and my linen napkin fell to the floor. I lifted up a fish knife and my wine glass and rattled the side of it. Nerves got the better of me and I suddenly remembered that's what you do for a toast - my first faux pas, my savoir faire was shot to pieces. 'Control yourself, say something positive, uplifting spiritually,' I thought to myself. My mind went blank and thirty seconds passed, nothing was forthcoming, I had never done this before in front of people at such a special occasion, I had only seen it done in films, so much for my Catholic upbringing. I cleared my throat and said with an air of assuredness.

"Heavenly Father, bless us and keep us alive, there's ten of us for dinner and only enough for five - Amen."

My attempt of humour was met with a deafening silence and a few icy stares. The only ones smiling were Sandra and Patrick. I regained my composure and spoke again.

"I'm sorry, I'm just a bit nervous, I'm okay now, may we start again with the 'blessing thing.' They bowed their heads and I rambled on incoherently about a 'bounteous table,' 'the grace of god,' 'the holy spirit' and even gave the apostle John a mention, then quickly finished with a resounding 'amen.' I hoped to Christ I would never have to do that again. Once I had got over the initial embarrassment I started the meal over a crisp glass of Chablis- Ann thanked me for the piece of light entertainment.

The food was exquisite and I complimented Mary, I was desperately trying to ingratiate myself after the blessing of the food fiasco but I think it came across as obsequious. As usual I was first finished with the starter, in fact whenever I eat in company I'm always finished way before everyone else, it really used to

Dirty Laundry

annoy Jill -she was always telling me to 'slow down' and 'remember your manners.' I had also drained the last of my wine and was unsure whether to help myself or politely wait -I chose the latter as I watched everyone eat in slow motion - I think it was just nerves.

"You're smoked salmon is perfect," Irene said.

"I got it fresh from the small fishmongers in the common green, it's always very good quality," Mary replied.

"You should try this Jack." Irene cut a small portion of it and gently placed it on my plate. I smiled at her, at least she was still talking to me. It was fabulous and I now wish I had went for that instead of the soup. Mary looked in my direction and smiled.

"There's plenty more in the kitchen, would like some, it won't spoil your appetite?"

"That would be great thanks."

"So Jack what do you do for a living," Bob enquired. Before I had a chance to reply, Sandra got up and stated with a casual air.

"He's a session musician - even played with Clapton, the Stones and Stevie Ray Vaughan (Sandra obviously didn't know he died in 1989), isn't that right Jack? bye the way I'm just going into the kitchen, I'll get you the smoked salmon darling."

"Bring another bottle of Chablis will you?" Mary asked.

The assembled guests were waiting for a reply, what the hell was I meant to say? Yes, then become a grand fabulist, or no, then make Sandra out to be stupid - I did decide however, that when I got her in private I would give her a verbal reprimand. Stevie Ray Vaughan indeed. She would be telling then I jammed with Jimi Hendrix next. Irene looked at me, raised her eyebrows and grinned broadly. She was enjoying every moment of my inquietude.

"Eh, yeah, that's my line of work... line of business, that is. It's not as glamorous as it sounds." A dozen questions followed in rapid succession as I sunk into a pool of mythomania, although I must say, people found me more interesting, if I had said I was a window cleaner it would have been a truncated conversation I think. Lie after lie, untruth upon untruth, the records I had played on, the concerts, the show biz stuff, and the 'joie de vivre' life style it offered. By now, I was actually enjoying it and so was Sandra and Irene who I knew was winding everyone up. It was going well until Bob spoke up.

"So how come then, you're staying with my sister in law in Greenhills?" he said drunkenly, with a sneering tone.

"Don't be rude darling," Mary replied.

"I'm just asking that's all, no harm in that eh?" I was taken aback with his scabrous comment, I put it down to the amount of drink he had consumed. He hadn't even touched the food in front of him. I politely replied.

"Annus horribilis, year of horrors, I'm afraid Bob, divorce, lost the house, lawyers, solicitors say no more, eh, no offence Patrick."

"None taken."

"It's just you don't look like a musician, more like a farmer or a boxer, the size of you and those big hands," Bob slurred. I had the feeling he had taken a particular dislike to me and if continued in his criticisms and sarcastic comments his nose was about to become a lot redder. Mary was looking embarrassed with her husband.

"Well, Bob," I calmly stated, "you can probably tell with the nose I used to do amateur boxing when I was a lot younger, if you don't believe me I'll show you a couple of moves if you like?" The old bugger didn't even smile, he returned to his wine and I watched as his wife gave him a withering look.

"Were you any good?" Patrick asked.

"Not really, when I was looking for sponsorship my coach suggested that I could get advertising space on the soles of my boots." Dale laughed and started a monologue about a recent television programme he had seen on the discovery channel, something about experimental psychology, for once it was reasonably interesting. Dotty smiled and filled in parts of the story he missed. They were beginning to sound like a double act.

The main course was to die for. The fillet of Angus beef just melted in your mouth, everything was perfect except for the size of the portions, and the conversation, like the wine, flowed and was very tasteful. I learned that Dale and Dotty came from a small South-western Virginia town called Richlands, were married for 30 years, had no children and worked together in the same business and that they were related to Bob's side of the family. We had quite a lot in common which I thought was unusual considering the Atlantic divide; they were both very passionate about their music particularly Bruce Hornsby and Bruce Springsteen and still played in a blues band called the Richmond rockers that toured all the small bars and clubs in the area. We decided that we would perform a song or two if our gracious host would let us use the Steinway. Maybe then old red nose would stop his constant carping. They both played guitar and piano.

The dinner was rounded off with a lovely Napoleon brandy and a cigar and we were invited to depart from the dining room area to relax in the other main living room. The most important part of the night, the remembrance ceremony for their sister Catherine was about to take place and I was now feeling nervous about the whole thing being an outsider. I thought it was a very touching thing to do every year, to never let the memory of a loved one pass or even fade but to offer them a place in your heart by means of a few unaffected words.

Sandra was gracious enough to carry my large glass of brandy and the 'Cuban cigar (which I would give to Neil as he was the only one who smoked the things) through to the next room, which was equally as tasteful as the other main room. What caught my eye was the piano beside the large bay window. It was a magnificent example of craftsmanship and looked very old although it was in pristine condition. I actually felt my heart beat a little faster,all that time practicing on a Yamaha keyboard and I now have the chance to perform (I use the word cautiously) on a Steinway, not just any Steinway but a parlour concert grand with open lid with it's original duet stool. I actually wished Jill was here to see this.

At the top of the room a massive antique table was laid out with decanters, glasses and a large crystal punchbowl, which I assumed contained home made punch. As the guests chatted I watched in disbelief as Sandra took a bottle of gin from her bag and poured the whole contents of gin into it when no one was looking. She just smiled at me and raised her eyebrows and whispered in my ear.

"She always makes it too weak, very mean with the spirits is our Mary!"

Everything was done with a generous measure of style and grace. They really put a lot of thought into the meal and the proceedings as well. I sat beside Patrick and Ann and chatted to them for ten minutes or so before Mary took centre stage and announced it was time to think of 'Katie' as she called her. The glasses were then filled for a toast to their loved one. She introduced Sandra to the middle of the floor.

She gave a very touching opening speech about her younger sister, the good times, the bad, and the last days that they spent together as a family, although I had never met her, I actually felt myself welling up (I cry at soppy movies if there is no one in the room). I noticed, and I hoped that it was not an oversight, that Sandra did not have any notes, she must have committed the poem to memory which was no mean feat considering she only had a few hours to do so and she had quite a few gins during the process.

She continued, "I would now like to dedicate this poem in memory of Katie. Ann did such a great reading last year and I thought I would try to do the same. I had selected a poem by Paul Meadows who expresses the sentiments that I feel, and no doubt you will as well. I would now like to ask our new friend Jack to assist me at the piano."

I heard Bob moan but ignored him. I got up from the comfortable leather seat with a bit of difficulty, (ankle and alcohol) found my 'point d'appui' (theatrical effect) and walked slowly to the piano. I hoped it was in tune, there's nothing more excruciating than playing a piano when its even slightly out of tune unless you're Les Dawson - thankfully it was perfectly pitched as I played a few warm up notes. I then started the introduction to 'La aunde' and Sandra came in after a minute or so and started the reading - she spoke with warmth and tenderness which made the piece of poetry come alive, and with the evocative flowing music gently hanging in the air it was truly a wonderful moment.

Go to that place we loved, our secret place
Close your eyes and you'll see my face.
Play that tune, the tune we loved to hear
Close your eyes and you'll see me clear.
Walk on a beach or climb to the top of the hill
Close your eyes and you'll see me still.
Take a sip of wine, of dark red wine
Close your eyes and you'll see me fine.
At night go out and look at the brightest star
Close your eyes and you'll see me far.
On a day when the sky is blue and cold and clear,
Close your eyes and you'll see me near.
Take down a book that would have been my choice
Open the book. Close your eyes. You'll hear my voice.

When she stopped speaking and the last notes faded into the ether, there was a silence that befitted her recital, it was almost spiritual. Her sisters cried and so did Irene, it was a really emotional moment and I was so proud to be a small part of it, no one said anything for at least a minute. Bob broke the silence.

"Well done Sandra, well done indeed, it was moving."

The others soon joined in their praise of her efforts and Patrick walked over to me and shook my hand without saying anything , we drank a toast to Katie who died of cancer at the age of forty-six. I was informed by Ann that it was now part of the tradition to enjoy a piece of Christmas cake which was followed by some music. Sandra cut a generous slice and handed everyone a plate. It was beautiful, rich and moist, a lovely way to end a great dinner. The conversation once again picked up and the mood changed from being sombre and reflective to one that was very festive. I think the copious amount of alcohol played a part in that. Ann interlocked arms with me on the settee and said very quietly in my ear.

"Bet this is a bit different from your normal X-mas party."

"Actually I'm really enjoying myself now, you have a really nice family, Sandra's a darling, she's a very good friend."

"She speaks highly of you as well, is this a self admiration society you two have got going?" I smiled at her comment. "Your playing was beautiful tonight. I've never heard that piece before, what did Sandra say it was?"

"Actually she never said, but it's by the Italian composer Ludivico Einaudi, a good modern day composer. I explained to her what the music represented, the power of the sea, the waves crashing onto the jagged shoreline, the simplicity and beauty of creation and ultimately, the fragility of life. (I was slipping into writers mode again). She was sitting so near and talking so close to me I could smell her perfume, she was a very charming woman indeed, and I may add, very attractive. We were joined by Mary who sat down on the settee beside us, her eyes were still moist and she wiped a tear from her eye.

"Thank you Jack, that was wonderful, very moving, your playing was very good, you must do a few more for us tonight, will you?" she said grasping my arm. Now I'm surrounded by two lovely women, I could get used to this.

"I would love to, it's such a superb instrument and in great condition, my ex-wife would have loved to have seen something like this, she's a bit of an expert in antiques and collectables," I enthused.

She went on to give me the piano's history - it's age (made in 1903) even what they had bought it for in 1992 at Christies auction - the colossal sum of £38,950. She must have seen my jaw drop. That was about the same as my first mortgage for a house! It was bought because she loved the piano and the fact that it would be a sound investment that would never lose its value, she now has it insured for £50,000. I wonder what my Yamaha is now worth?

Out of the corner of my eye I noticed Irene walking up to the table just as Sandra was cutting a few extra slices of her delicious cake, it seems to have gone down well.

Their conversation looked very animated and I could hear laughing. It's hard to eavesdrop from the other end of the room while you're engaged in conversation with another couple. If I was female, I bet it wouldn't be too difficult. I was wondering what the topic of conversation was.

"Sandra," Irene said, "have you tried a piece of Christmas cake yet?"

"No darling I've been a bit busy at the moment. Why do you ask?"

"I think this is ours."

"What? say that again."

"It's ours, our special cake!" she emphasised.

"God no."

"God yes, and by the way Sandra darling, it's delicious as usual, maybe just a little too much cannabis in it."

Sandra put her hand over her mouth when she realized what the guests were consuming. They were even coming back for seconds.

"What should we do?" Sandra asked nervously.

"Nothing"

"Nothing, are you sure?"

"There's no point in panicking them, anyway it's not such a big deal is it? I tell you what you could do."

"What?"

"Find a video camera, the night might prove to be very interesting."

"You're enjoying this, aren't you?"

"Just a bit, anyway they need to loosen up a bit especially that old curmudgeon that's married to your poor sister, sitting by himself, drinking himself into a stupor and insulting everyone, go on take him another large bit over and wait till he eats it all, he's afraid of you Sandra."

"God you're a cruel bitch sometimes Irene." Irene lifted a plate with a generous portion of Christmas cake and walked in the direction of Bob.

"Sandra says your plate is empty, here's another piece, you better eat it or you will offend your sister in law."

"Now, we would…. not want to do that," he slurred. He took the plate, smiled at Sandra from across the room and proceeded to eat the super strength cake. He was already three sheets to the wind at the moment, the cake would send him over the edge and at his age, it was a hell of a drop.

Sandra beckoned me over to the table and I politely excused myself. She looked at me and said.

"Well done darling." She then planted a kiss right on my lips - I actually enjoyed it. I returned the compliment. Her recital was exceptionally moving, and word perfect.

"You did really well yourself, your family will be proud of you," I commented.

"Well I did practice for a solid hour, here, you've got lipstick on the top of you mouth, bet you enjoyed that eh?" She took a linen hanky and wiped my mouth.

Was Sandra Potter flirting with me,?- I definitely think so, and I don't really blame her.

"Hey people will be talking about us," I joked, " the intimate kiss then the sensual cleaning." She let out one of her trademark laughs that could easily light up a room. It was infectious. She then replied very calmly, "Oh they'll be talking all right, dancing and singing and whatever else thanks to your endeavours, you big lump!" I looked non-plussed at her strange comment but put it down to the drink." Jack, can I ask you a question?"

"Of course."

"Now be absolutely certain when you answer."

"I'll try."

"When you lifted the Christmas cake was it the one beside the kettle or the one next to the toaster?" I mentally retraced my steps then said confidently.

"The kettle, yes the kettle definitely."

"Are you sure?"

"Positive. I remember lifting the two labels and put them on the floor to feed Fanny." She interrupted.

"Christ thanks, imagine forgetting about my Fanny."

I continued, "When I fed her I lifted up the labels and I'm afraid I got them mixed up, so I just stuck one in each box, although as I said I lifted the cake that was beside the kettle. Anyway, why the twenty questions Sandra, have I done something wrong?"

"No Jack, but one of them had an added ingredient."

"Oh god, does someone have a nut allergy or something?" I began to panic and had visions of someone having a convulsive fit and collapsing on the floor.

"No, no nothing like that."

"Then what?" Her prevarication was beginning to irritate me. The ridiculous dialogue we were engaging in reminded me of that Danny Kaye film, I think it was called 'The court jester,' and the famous line that was constantly repeated, *'the pellet with the poison's in the vessel with the pestle, the chalice from the palace has the brew that is true.'*

"The cake they are eating is packed with cannabis you numbskull!" She gave me a wicked grin, raised her eyebrows and said, "It's going to be a rather jolly night, my piano playing friend." She then proceeded to slap my bottom as I walked back to my seat. I actually felt myself blush. I didn't know whether to laugh or cry, everyone had cleaned their plate and some had seconds. I watched as Dale approached the table.

"You're still the best darling. This is beautiful, you must give me the recipe Sandra," Dale gushed. I suppose his frame was big enough to absorb a second helping. Sandra shouted over to me as I was talking to Ann.

"Do you want another bit Jack?" She was teasing me. I declined. "I'll keep another slice for Irene, she's fond of my pudding, especially my dumplings," she said just a little too loudly. It was followed by another hearty laugh.

I decided to mingle and share my delightful conversation and I noticed Irene was now sitting by herself.

"Hi," I said cheerfully.

"Have a seat, I think Dale might be a while, he has a thing for Sandra. I really enjoyed your playing."

"Thanks I'm very talented." She smiled.

"Are you going to play a few songs later for us?"

"If anyone asks, I think Dale is quite keen to get up there and give us a song, maybe a duet with his good wife."

"Mary's very accomplished on the piano," Irene added, "she plays every year. Listen Jack, don't worry about old Bob he's an arse hole, oops sorry about the language, Sandra and Ann have been saying to her to leave the old sod, he's not good to her and treats her like a member of his staff rather than his wife."

"Oh, I see. I thought he had taken a sudden aversion to me for some unknown reason."

"Well, that's just Bob, he has no social graces whatsoever and doesn't even pretend to make an effort, and, I may add he's still having his flings - at his age. God what a thought! Did you notice that he never speaks to me Jack, not a single word, unless I speak to him?"

"Can't say I have noticed, but now that you've mentioned it."

Dirty Laundry

"He doesn't like it because I'm close to Sandra and I speak my mind, he hates women that are independent, free spirits, he's an old fashioned, dyed in the wool chauvinistic bugger."

"I get the picture Irene."

I looked over at Bob who was chatting away to Dale, and I thought to myself, go on get more of that cake down you, wash it down with some of Sandra special 'punch,' then we'll have a bit of fun. I know it was wrong to think like that, especially when you're a guest in someone's house and they have been very generous, very unstinting, but he had offended and belittled me, and more importantly, Irene didn't like him, that was good enough for me. I sat and engaged Irene in some lively conversation and I was determined this would be the night I would ask her out on a date, she was lovely company and I think the feelings were being reciprocated.

After some gentle badgering from Dale and Dotty, Mary was encouraged to get the night going by playing a few songs on the piano, and by god, the woman could play, she made me sound like an amateur. She played two classical pieces, one from Beethoven and another from the great Russian composer Shostakovich. Utterly captivating and a hard act to follow. Dale was brave enough to step up next, ably assisted by his good wife and performed a great piano version of 'Born in the USA,' then a Bruce Hornsby number entitled 'The road not taken, and a few other great rock numbers, it went down a storm, they were a real class act.

The night was really beginning to liven up, even to the point of being boisterous as the effect of the over eating, over drinking, and the consumption of Sandra's special cake kicked in. At the end of the night chaos held court - Bob had collapsed in a chair with his glass still in hand when Mary announced with authority in front of all her stunned guests.

"Tonight I want to announce something special. I'm divorcing that old sod asleep in the chair, this is our last Christmas together, good riddance!" She had great difficulty in stringing coherent words together. She then proceeded to walk over to his chair and pour a large glass of punch over his head in full view of her stunned guests. Spontaneous applause burst out. Dale and Dotty were oblivious to the drama that was unfolding before us, they were too busy dancing and looking into each others eyes ,I could hardly believe what was going on, it was like the theatre of the absurd. Bob was too intoxicated to notice anything and didn't even wake up, he will be in for one shock tomorrow when the effects of over indulgence wears off, it's no more that he deserves. Sandra looked very pleased with herself and stated matter of factly.

"I should have brought my special cake years ago, come here Mary give me a hug, we've got a lot to celebrate darling!"

Dirty Laundry

It was an extraordinary night, in fact an extraordinary day. I've attended some weird and wonderful parties but nothing like this, it was a bizarre mixture of 'haut monde' decadence mixed with unrestrained, boisterous merrymaking. I have a sneaking suspicion the cannabis played some factor in the equation, there is going to be quite a few 'fragile' people come morning time.

At twenty past four I decided to call it a day as I could hardly keep my eyes open. Sandra and Irene followed suit while the remaining couples danced away. I was waiting for a window of opportunity to open up so I could talk to Irene for a few minutes in privacy, I had decided this would be the moment as I was, by now, quite infatuated with her and I got the feeling it was mutual. I know I have been wrong in the past, maybe got the lines of communication mixed up, but it was different this time and I was quietly confident. I had thought of this moment for a considerable while now, in fact I had rehearsed it many times, mentally polished my presentation and even thought of some romantic lines that would impress her, nothing too sickly, or trite, but something genuine, something from the heart. Sandra wandered off first and I grabbed Irene's wrist just as she was about to follow.

"Can I talk to you privately just for a minute?"

"This sound very intriguing, you're not going to take advantage of me because I'm a bit tipsy?"

Some iniquitous thoughts entered my mind, a quote from Ogden Nash *'candy is dandy, but liquor is quicker'* but they were quickly dismissed as I looked into her beautiful big brown eyes.

"No, not at all. Look, sit down for a moment will you." She held my hand and said teasingly.

"Yes darling?" I smiled at her inoffensive humour.

"Look, this is quite hard for me to say, so please bear with me, Irene I really like you, you're kind, warm and have such a good nature….I was just thinking… that we, eh, us, you know, us two." Damn, this is not what I carefully rehearsed, it sounded like I was suffering from some type of speech impediment. "I would like to. I want to ask you out to get to know you more intimately, no, no that doesn't sound right, I just mean - god you know what I mean Irene."

There I have said it, not exactly romantic or the type of 'cri de coeur' that would sweep someone off their feet , I came across as a bumbling buffoon. She looked up at me and smiled and I could immediately sense a certain sadness behind the smile, it was just that look I had experienced before. Pity. Sympathy.

"Jack, eh…" It was her turn now to struggle for words. "I'm really sorry, but I'm seeing someone and have been for quite a while now." She shrugged her shoulders and I could sense her discomfort. An arrow penetrated my beating heart, just like the Strongbow advert. Whoomph! I tried to remain calm and unperturbed, but I don't think I pulled it off, she must have seen the abject disappointment in my face and felt the rejection.

"God I'm sorry," I said, "I didn't know, it's just that I've not seen you with someone, and you've not even mentioned him before."

"Her," she replied correcting me.

"Her?" Was the combination of cake and alcohol impairing my auditory senses? "Sorry?"

"I said 'her.'"

"Oh. Right I see, how come you've never introduced her to me?"

"Because you know her."

"I don't."

"It's Sandra."

"Oh, I see, right." Disbelief. Bewilderment.

"AC/DC Jack?"

"Can't stand them, especially the singer." What a strange non-sequitur to thrown into the conversation at this time. It must be a diversionary tactic.

"No, you big lump heap, it's a euphemism for 'bi.'"

"Bi, sorry. Now I understand, bi-sexual." Could she have not just come out and said that in the first place. Why bi sexual, I don't understand, the only advantage it has is that it doubles your chances for a date on a Saturday night. Well, I could actually think of more but that would be too graphic to mention.

My little world had just collapsed, imploded. Unrequited love is difficult to handle and painful to cope with. It's like a question without an answer. You never get used to rejection, I suppose that's the minds defence mechanism kicking in that keeps you trying regardless, or is that just me.

"Listen Jack, you could still take me out for dinner or whatever, it doesn't mean that we can't be good friends, close friends even, I would love that."

"Are you sure?"

"Of course."

"Would Sandra be alright about this, you know, if I took you to a restaurant for a night?"

"Totally, she's not the jealous type. She's the 'live and let live sort,' if you know what I mean." I understood perfectly.

"Well, it's nice of you to say Irene, thanks for letting me down gently."

"I'm not letting you down gently, I really would love to be wined and dined for a night, get a chance to know you better, in fact how does next Saturday sound?"

"I'll need to check my busy desk diary first to see if there's a space."

"Yeah right!"

"That would be great Irene. I'd love that. How about Mario's? Do you like Italian food?"

"Perfect, because Sandra has said to Mary that we'll visit her next week. I think they have a lot to discuss now."

"Was that announcement genuine?"

"What?"

"What Mary said about divorcing Bob?"

"Yes, but I think she's been planning it for some time now but lacked the courage to go through with it. He's quite intimidating sometimes. It must be difficult to break free when you've been married for so many years, your whole life will change drastically."

"Good for her, she deserves better," I concurred. Irene took my hand and said quietly.

"So it's a date then?"

"You bet." She leaned over and kissed me, a genuine warm embrace. I melted.

"I'll see you in the morning Jack."

"Good night."

I watched as she walked away, to say I was jealous was an understatement, what's Sandra got that I don't have, apart from breasts and a vagina? I said my goodnights to the rest of the group and headed for my room ,I would sleep tonight. I later found out that Ann and Dotty performed a complete striptease in front of two excited men before departing upstairs, god knows what happened after that, just my luck to miss that as well, all that female flesh and I get nothing. Lucky white heather? Bob remained in a coma like state in his chair with a blanket thrown over his head like a budgie in it's cage at night.

I lay on my luxurious bed thinking about the recent events. It was a great day, but ultimately disheartening. I just could not get her out of my head. Was I really that blind? Could I not put two and two together without coming up with five? As they say, 'loves the noblest frailty of the mind.'

For the first time in my life I actually thought I wouldn't find someone to share my life with, its been over a year since I've had a relationship, I've asked a few people out, but only received a polite rebuttal or a sympathetic, 'thanks, but no thanks.' Where have I gone wrong? I felt myself slipping into pity mode as I reviewed the last twelve months mentally - rejected by Jill after ten years of marriage, no house, same old dead end job, no financial progress and I'm living in a room with a lesbian, AC/DC, bi-curious, invert, call it what you like landlady that has stolen the potential love of my life. Isn't life one big bowl of f---ing cherries!

I feel like my life is once again put on hold, or stuck in limbo for an interminable period until the gods once again show me divine favour. I eventually drifted off to sleep with my mind in turmoil and my future lost in a mist. Something had to change - and change radically.

CHAPTER 10

THE EVALUATION

Rejection sucks. It's hard to take, especially the older you get and you're nearing the end of your sell by date. Not that I'm over the hill but I reckon in a few years I'll be approaching the brow. It's a long way down so I'm told.

I concluded that the best way to deal with the situation was to keep busy, immerse myself in my writing and try to entertain some positive thoughts, difficult as that would prove to be. I felt like a love sick teenager, but without the acne. Focus on the novel, my music and shut out any lingering thoughts of Irene. Lovely Irene. Lovely, unattainable Irene. Lovely unattainable AC/DC Irene.

Sandra's booming voice (foghorn) shattered the quietude I was enjoying.

"Jack, are you sleeping? if not it's the phone for you, a lad called Stevie!" I hobbled to the door and shouted in response.

"Fine Sandra, I'll be down in a minute." I lifted the receiver. "Hi Stevie, how are you? Merry Christmas, by the way."

"Same to you, did you have a good one?"

"Excellent, very good night indeed, I'll tell you all about it later."

"Well?" he said dryly.

"Well what?"

"Did your considerable charm and average looks win over Irene?"

"It's a bit of a long story actually..." He interrupted me mid-sentence.

"She blew you off!"

"I wish."

"I thought you said you had so much in common?"

"We have a lot in common, too much!"

"What do you mean?"

"We both like female bits if you know what I mean." The laughter over the phone wasn't really helping the situation nor doing my self-esteem any good.

"You're joking!" was all he could say. Disbelief.

"Does it sound like it?"

"Well, not really. Sorry mate, you've been a bit unlucky recently. Oh well, there's plenty other fish in the sea." What an empty platitude.

"Yes, but they are not biting," I remarked.

"You'll need to try a different tact, another subtle approach, maybe a trawl net rather than a rod with a worm on it - think bigger."

"Or just toss explosives into the water and see what comes up," I moaned.

"So what are you doing this morning Jack, are you going to be in?"

"Yes, nothing much planned, maybe some writing."

"Great, I'll pop in soon, I've reviewed you're first 100 pages or so."

"Thanks, that was good of you."

"No problem, I'll be up in half an hour or so. Is there anything you need?"

"A girlfriend."

"I could get you an inflatable one."

"Shut up. Actually, can you bring up a pint of milk, I'm a bit short."

"Sure, anything else?"

"Do you want a biscuit with your coffee?"

"Of course."

"Well could you bring a packet of biscuits, Kit Kats will do."

"Fine, right I'll see you in a bit."

"Oh wait a minute, I don't have any coffee either, I've been pilfering Sandra's, I've not done the shopping yet."

"Christ," he moaned, "what are you like, yeah I'll bring it up don't worry. You have got heating?"

"Very funny."

I put the phone down and walked into the kitchen. Sandra was perched on a stool petting her Fanny.

"Hi Sandra, how are you this fine morning?"

"Very well darling, very well indeed, kettle's just boiled do you want a coffee?"

"I'd love one. Stevie's coming up, my friend, have you met him before?"

"No I don't think so, I've met Neil before, the sarcastic one, the one that fancied me - couldn't take his eyes off me."

"If I recall correctly, you were wearing a nightie which didn't leave very much to the imagination, and Neil, as you know, has a rather vivid imagination," I said sardonically. She just shook her shoulders and smiled.

"Is this the other school teacher you were talking about?" Sandra asked.

"Yes, he's bringing my manuscript up, well, part of it for an evaluation, I'm quite nervous actually."

"Big mistake," she said.

"What's a big mistake?"

She lit up a cigarette and replied,

"It's a big mistake to let someone you know review your work, it's no good."

"Why?"

"Because they're a friend, they are not going to tell you it's naff, they can't be completely honest in case they offend you."

Her reasoning was sound but she didn't know my friends or how brutally candid they could be. "Not in this case, Sandra. Stevie's very quick to point out anything that's sub-standard or exiguous, trust me, he'll offer a frank appraisal, that's why I'm a bit nervous. I'm the same with them."

"Well that's good, honesty is very important." Sandra took another drag from the cigarette and said, "So what do you think of my new hairstyle you haven't commented," she said running her fingers through it.

"It's really nice Sandra, I was just about to say."

"It's not been cut, do you get my point?" Point taken. She stubbed the cigarette out and immediately lit up another one then said.

"I would love to read it when it's finished, I love a good story especially a decent bonk buster if you know what I mean."

"You will be the first to have a copy, I promise, and I would like your opinion when you have read it, I value your judgement."

"Good, because people say I'm very opinionated." I smiled at her humour. I took a sip of the free coffee and was about to depart from the kitchen when she said apologetically.

"Listen Jack, sorry about the confusion, I've not had a chance to speak to you."

"What confusion?"

"About Irene."

"Right," I said.

"I thought you knew."

"I had no idea."

"What?" she said incredulously.

"No, I honestly had no inkling, anyway it was my mistake."

"There's no need to apologise Jack, I just assumed you knew. I thought we were very obvious."

"No, not to me Sandra, I'm a bit slow sometimes." The conversation was becoming just a little bit strained.

"She really likes you."

"That's nice, I still….well, I'm fond of her, I'm sorry, I can't help it."

There was a sad look on her face. I didn't know if it was one of pity or genuine concern with my inability to find a companion of the opposite sex, maybe it was a combination of both.

"You will find someone Jack, of that I'm absolutely sure, you're a lovely bloke and you've got a good heart."

"Thanks for the vote of confidence."

"Introduce me to your friend when he comes in, I'd like to meet him if he's anything as interesting as Neil."

"I'll introduce you as long as you put on some more appropriate clothing, he'll just stare, he has a penchant for the heaving cleavage." She laughed out loud.

"Well, I can't blame him, don't worry Jack I'll behave myself, I'll be the epitome of decorum."

Dirty Laundry

"I'm sure you will Sandra." With that last comment, I departed from the kitchen to tidy my room for my guest and to open a window. Stevie arrived 30 minutes later with a pint of milk, a packet of Kit Kats and my manuscript under his arm. He had forgotten the coffee. Thankfully, Sandra was suitably attired in a pair of jeans and a blue t-shirt that was emblazoned with a picture of Status Quo on it from one of their latest tours, she's a big fan, she first seen them during the second world war she said. According to her, they still 'rock' and Francis Rossi still has incredibly tight 'buns,'-a strange comment coming from her I think. Thankfully she didn't embarrass me or herself and left for Irene's half an hour later after chatting to Stevie and making us coffee. She's not a bad soul really. They were meeting up in the Tudor house coffee place then going on to her sisters at Broadlees for a chat, they had a lot to discuss and I hope it goes well for them. Sandra is staying at Irene's tonight so I have a free house for a wild party or an orgy later if I like. Stevie smiled at me when she departed.

"Not bad looking at all, that's one big pair all right, like two honey dew melons in a sling, I'm surprised she doesn't fall over." I ignored his rabid 'breasts' comment. How uncouth. He sat in the corner chair and reached for my manuscript, I could tell he was switching on to 'teachers' mode so I sat up straight and clasped my hands in front of me. With an authoritative tone he stated.

"Right, let's get down to the brass tacks shall we?"

"Fine."

He looked at me and shook his head. " Jack, you've asked me to review your book and to do it without any personal bias and to be completely forthright."

"Of course," I said nervously.

"Well here's my professional opinion and evaluation."

"Get on with it," I was thinking.

"It's dreadful Jack, I'm sorry, it's vacuous and to be absolutely honest, pretentious." My jaw physically dropped from the vicious onslaught of his appraisal. I wanted the truth but not in such a soul destroying manner.

"Oh, I see," I quietly said.

A grin appeared on his face, "I'm winding you up man. I liked it. In fact, I loved it. It's so original and for a moron it's pretty well written."

"That's good to hear." Relief washed over me.

"I really think you've got something here, it just needs a bit of polishing and some of the rough edges knocked off it and it should be a good first draft to send to any publisher. A few words of constructive criticism."

"Of course."

"Apart from a few grammatical slips and the occasional spelling errors, which I have underlined in red as you can see."

"Great, thanks," I said.

"The introduction isn't 'punchy' enough, a good writer knows that the first few lines of a novel have to grab you're attention, they should be memorable, for instance, my favourite opening for a book is, 'my very first act upon coming into this world was to kill my mother.' You see what I mean? it's compelling, you just have to read on. On the other hand it can be weird or obtuse - another example, eh, I think it was Iain Banks that wrote as an introduction, 'It was the day my grandmother exploded.' Do you follow?"

"Yes I get the point."

"Rework the first few paragraphs and that should give it a bit of an edge. The rest is consistent, it's interesting, it's funny and at times the writing is even poignant, for example, when you recount the story of the teenager who committed suicide. It's good Jack and it will be interesting to see what Neil makes of it -he wants to read it when it's completed and he'll offer another opinion which should be helpful."

I was relieved by his comments. If he had said that it wasn't interesting enough, or the actual writing was sub standard, I would have seriously thought about abandoning the project, but the few words of encouragement was enough to make me redouble my efforts.

"I'll let him have the completed manuscript when it's finished."

"Get me a copy when you're finished, I can't wait to read the rest. I'll leave this one here for you to peruse and you can see what you have to work on. One other thing about the novel...."

"What?"

"The title is truly awful."

"You think?"

"I know - it sucks! 'What the Window Cleaner Saw,' is trite and sounds like a soft porn flick from the 1970's, it has to go"

"It was just a working title that's all, but I suppose you're right. I had a few others in mind. How about, ' Behind Closed Doors.'"

"That's a title of a book already."

"It is?"

"Diana Dors' autobiography. You'll need to think of something else mate, there's a huge scope considering how diverse the content is."

"Okay," I said, "I'll think about it and run them by you later. Thanks for taking the time to evaluate it."

"No problem, it's the school holidays and I'm bored with the television, I needed something constructive to do."

"So how is the lovely Lynn?" I enquired.

"Great, she's keeping well, we spent Boxing Day at her sisters which was excellent and she starts back work on Tuesday. We've got some good news to relate."

"Oh yeah?"

"Listen, don't say to anyone just now, but after many long discussions and soul searching, we've decided we're going to adopt a baby."

"Wow," was all I could muster.

"So what do you think?" he said nervously.

"I'm delighted for you both, it's a major thing, life-altering I suppose, but Lynn has always wanted children."

"We're not getting any younger, she'll be 39 soon and she feels something is lacking in our life, we have both got good jobs, settled in our house, have good friends, but this is the one thing that's missing and I agree with her. It's what I want as well."

I smiled at him and said, "I think it's wonderful although I have certain reservations about your ability to be a father."

"I'll work on it, might even get a book out of the library."

"I think it's a little more involved than that."

"I know it's a challenge, but I'm up for it and so is Lynn."

"Go for it then!" I've never seen him look so excited before, he was like the proverbial cat that got the cream. Ignorance is bliss ,I don't share his sentiments when it comes to children and he knows that, although I did try to be kind and supportive of his decision. I agree with W. C. Fields, I think we have a kindred spirit, he said, 'anyone who hates children and dogs can't be all that bad.'

Stevie's 50-minute appearance fairly lifted my spirits and it gave me the confidence to continue with the novel and with Sandra away until tomorrow it's going to be very quiet. The only company I've got is her Fanny. I wonder what W. C. Fields thought about cats?

CHAPTER 11

NO SMOKE WITHOUT FIRE

If you're a writer, it's the greatest two words in the English vocabulary, 'The end.' After a painful outpouring, which is generally accompanied with blood sweat and tears, it's a wonderful feeling of accomplishment to complete a novel. When it's done and dusted you excitedly flick through the pages and hope that it's all been worthwhile and will be received favourably,

But writers are fickle, prone to moods and sometimes full of doubt and self loathing - an inspired piece of writing reviewed the following day sometimes looses its shine and you wonder how much drink you had consumed the night before when writing it, with a shake of the head and a sigh, the rejected pages are crumpled into a ball, consigned to the bin, and you have to find the drive to start again.

I think it was Juvenal that said, *'many suffer from the incurable disease of writing and it becomes chronic in their sick minds.'* I can relate to that. Five weeks, two days and 255 pages later, the draft manuscript is finished and another chapter of my life closes and I'm optimistic another will open up, hopefully with a happy ending. I hope that the content of the book is strong enough and the individual stories are sufficiently diverse and the actual writing is up to scratch. Thankfully, Stevie and Neil have promised to proof read the finalised work, and give me an honest appraisal before it's submitted to a publisher, I just hope its not the dreaded 'pollice versa' verdict. The final chapter was completed late last night and was devoted to an individual I had a lot of respect for. By all definitions he was a very complex character and someone who was completely immersed in his profession and cared passionately for his patients despite working in a hostile environment. The hostile environment wasn't a war zone or even front line policing but I suppose it came pretty damn close to that level. Colin Evans was the head doctor in charge of the A and E unit in Victoria hospital in Glasgow. He stayed in Calderglen road in one of the imposing houses that looked on to the glen, which he shared this with his wife and two daughters.

I cleaned his house for about a year or so before having the dubious distinction of being the person who discovered his body hanging from a light fitment from an upper bedroom. The moment will haunt me forever.

What possesses a person to commit the 'ultimate self-inflicted blow'?

What inner demons are there that can't be exorcised?

What problems exist that can't be resolved?

What loss is there that cannot be reconciled?

To a certain degree I can understand if the individual has lost everything in life - family, money, self respect, and I can appreciate that a terminal illness must have a devastating effect, but it's beyond comprehension how a person who's highly regarded by his peers, loved by his wife and family and who has a secure future ahead of him, commits suicide.

I remember him describing what it's like to be a doctor and working under those trying circumstances. He said the emergency room is a caldron of raw human emotion, there's relief, comfort, distress and uncontrollable grief. Then there's the disorder of arrivals that flood in creating tension as the staff are buffeted by sudden changing needs. Add to this the constant need to maintain a high level of readiness and you can understand how it must be emotionally draining. The long hours, the stress, the constant levels of awareness and the ability to deal with all sorts of people surely must take its toll mentally and emotionally.

I saved his story to the last as I think it's a great way to end the book, some of his experiences will make you laugh, cry and cringe in equal measure, I just hope I wasn't too graphic in describing the man, high on LSD, who thought his penis was a snake and cut it off with a bread knife; or the tramp brought in to the A and E in the middle of winter, wrapped up in layers of clothing, almost like a 'mummy' that complained his leg was sore and that he kept falling down. When the staff eventually removed the layers of clothing they discovered his leg was infested with maggots. I know for a fact that the humorous stories would be of interest as well, and it would add a different dimension to his account of life in the A and E. For instance, the morbidly obese man that weighed 36 stones brought in by six firemen - a nurse and a technician attempted to place a Foley catheter in his bladder, and after spreading his legs they found a TV remote and a bar of Cadbury's chocolate in the folds of his flesh. Many other of his stories seemed to involve people with the unnatural fixation of inserting things into cavities that were not designed to accommodate foreign objects, I learned an awful lot about the anal sphincter and how quickly it can shut, as well as some stories that seemed to defy belief.

Colin Evans had so many fascinating tales to tell, that I suggested that he should write a book about it. It would definitely be a best seller. Two hundred and fifty five pages, five weeks and two days, blood sweat and tears, and putting up with Mrs Sandra Potter. I just hope the end result is good enough.

It's now the end of January and for the past few weeks I've felt like I've been in a state of hibernation, thankfully the weather's getting a bit milder and the daylight hours are beginning to lengthen. The cast is off and I'm back to work on Monday, two days time, although the prospect of cleaning windows again doesn't exactly fill me with joy. For the first time in many long, cold dark weeks I feel there is light at the end of the tunnel. I think what's lifted my spirits is the prospect of dinner with Irene tonight, third time lucky. She had to cancel our arrangement the last few Saturdays because of ill health, I was hoping that it wasn't a pretext to put me off.

After voicing complaint to Sandra I was told the full extent of her 'illness' as she called it, and was left numb with shock. I was aggrieved that she never confided in me and told she was suffering from cancer or even that it was terminal and only had a few months at best. I took it really bad, but Sandra reasoned that everyone deals with it in their own way and not to take it so 'bloody personally.' She was right, she had more to lose. This was her partner, the one she loved, the one she cared for, and she faced the harrowing prospect of seeing her endure a painful and undignified death. How do you come to terms with that?

We decided to do everything we could for her and to make her last few months fulfilling and happy. I should have known something was wrong, very wrong, in the couple of weeks that had passed I noticed she was looking a lot thinner, her face was gaunt and that she looked tired, lethargic. I put it down to a 'woman's thing,' that's the way Jill used to describe it when she was ill or had the dreaded period. I cursed my own asininity.

I still have feelings for her and if she ever changed her mind about our relationship I would grasp the opportunity in a heartbeat. I must admit that I still find it difficult to accept their relationship, maybe I'm too old fashioned, old school, but as long as it makes them happy, gives them fulfilment, then what the hell, life's too short and you're a long time dead.

"Jack!" A loud voice bellowed from downstairs. Talk of the devil, or should it be the 'she devil'?

"Coming."

"It's for you, I think it's one of you're students, sounds young," she said.

"Thanks Sandra - hello?"

"Hi Mr Wilde, it's Graham, look I'm just phoning to say I can't make it today, my uncle died and we have to travel to Fife today. I'm really sorry it's such short notice."

"It's no problem Graham, I understand, sorry to hear of your loss, phone me when you want another lesson."

"I will, and thanks again."

"Right bye."

Damn I was counting on that money, how inconsiderate of his uncle to die -Graham always booked two hours at a time which was a handy £20 for me, cash in hand. I hoped Irene wasn't a big eater or had expensive taste, there's nothing worse sitting in a good restaurant, worrying about money, trying to enjoy your meal. I think I'll work up the courage to ask Sandra for a small loan just in case. I put the phone down.

"Thanks Sandra, just one of my students cancelling."

"Oh right."

"Listen, are you still alright about me taking Irene out for dinner?.I know we've had this conversation before"

She shrugged her shoulders and replied, "Of course, darling, why shouldn't I be, it will do her good to talk to someone else, she must be bored with me by now."

"I somehow doubt that," I replied sardonically.

"Kettle's just boiled, do you want a coffee?"

"I think I will, thanks. Well, that's me got a free afternoon. I don't know what to do with myself now."

"Do your writing," she suggested.

"I've finished it, just this morning!"

"Great, am I in it?

"Afraid not Sandra, but I promise to give you a mention in the credits if it ever gets published." I should have put Sandra in it somewhere, in fact I could have written a whole book, a weighty tome, about her antics and her outlandish way of life. It would have been very colourful if not a bit adult. In fact it would probably offend the public decency act. I'll say no more, but it's certainly given me an idea for a follow up novel.

"Oh well, a short mention will have to do I suppose."

"Actually I think I'll go for a walk after my coffee since it's quite nice, the ankle's still a little stiff but I think it will do me good to exercise it," I said almost cheerfully.

"You could take my pussy out if you want, she's not been out for a while." I declined her offer. It's embarrassing enough watching her in high heels and the cat on a lead. After a friendly chat and a Nescafe with my delightful landlady, I got myself ready and went out for a walk in the bracing East Kilbride air, by god, it soon puts the colour back into your cheeks and ruffles your hair. A walk is good for blowing off the cobwebs and losing yourself in thought, -quality time to yourself with no distractions.

I decided to walk to Auldhouse which was a couple of miles. The exercise would do me good and I was badly needing it, being off work for nearly six weeks and confined to a single room meant an extended period of inactivity which resulted in considerable weight gain. I must have put on over a stone easily and my trousers testified to that. No exercise, copious amounts of food and drink at Christmas and New Year meant that a vigorous workout was essential or face radical surgery, maybe a bit of liposuction?

Dirty Laundry

I smiled to myself when I thought of Dale's musings. He had an anecdote for everything. I remember him saying with real conviction, 'Did you know Jack there are, on average, 178 sesame seeds on a MacDonald's bun?' How do you respond to that? What a strange person indeed, but funny I suppose. He confided in me that he tried sniffing coke, but the ice cubes just got stuck up his nose! I miss him and his lovely wife Dotty, typical Americans, big and bombastic but a heart of gold and the type that can't do enough for you. They were over here for a month before flying back to Richlands and they were kind enough to give me their phone number and address and insisted that I come over to America for a few weeks to stay with them and meet their family and hit some of the bars and clubs. I genuinely believed they meant it and if I had the resources I would certainly take them up in their generous offer.

As I walked, I reflected on Mary's new found situation which must have been daunting for her, especially after being married for 32 years, but she did it, she separated from the old whinge and managed to keep hold of the house, and more importantly, keep her dignity. Sandra said Bob basically caved in to her demands, which I think meant there was a lot more going on than anyone else realized. She knew of his various tawdry liaisons and his less that circumspect business dealings, so it sounded like some forceful persuasion worked, sounds better than blackmailing I suppose. A bitter divorce is, in effect, a war zone. According to Sandra she's never been happier and has found a new lease in life. I wish her well and I hope that old irascible bugger eventually gets his comeuppance, it's no more than he deserves.

As an incentive when I reached the lofty goal of the Auldhouse arms I would treat myself to one pint of lager and a packet of crisps, just enough sustenance to give me strength for the walk back. My resources were strictly limited for the night, I had just paid Sandra her 'dig money' and was left with about £40 to wine and dine Irene. I didn't work up the courage to ask my landlady for a loan.

I passed the field where I broke my ankle and smiled to myself. I wonder if my phone is still in the field? The things you do while under the influence. I think of what Frank Zappa said, *'it's not getting any smarter out there. You have to come to terms with stupidity and make it work for you.'*

Five hundred yards from my goal the rain started to thunder down like stair rods and when I reached the sanctity of the pub I was drenched and miserable and the ankle hurt. I took off my coat, hung it over a chair, found a seat beside the fire and then went to the bar for my reward. I drank my lager in solitude and munched on the salt and vinegar crisps and thought about the night with Irene. I hoped it would not be too awkward, someone professing their undying love for another could make things very strained especially when the sentiment is not reciprocated. I just decided to go with the flow and to be my natural exuberant self.

When I finally arrived back in East Kilbride, I was utterly drenched and looked like a frightened cat in a bath. I got out of the wet clothes and into a dry martini, filled the bath with steaming hot water and pinched some of Sandra's balls (the ones that foamed in the water and smelled of lavender). I was out to impress tonight. After a luxurious bath I changed into my new blue shirt and tie (a Christmas present from Steve and Lynn which unfortunately was two sizes too small. I hoped I wouldn't pass out with it being so tight, but it did show off my pecks) and went downstairs to make myself a small salami sandwich. I worked on the premise that if I had a small bite to eat just now, I could save myself money by not having a starter, the lack of money is degrading sometimes.

Sandra was sitting in the living room, gin in hand, watching a 'chick flick.' I think it was some banal pap like 'Bridget Jones' or some other equally bland offering with Hugh Grant who had the uncanny ability of playing the same character for every bloody film he appeared in. The range of his acting abilities runs the whole gamut from A to B.

After dinner the plan was to get a taxi back to East Kilbride where Irene could meet up with Sandra and stay over, it made sense, it would have been very awkward to stay over in her flat, not that I would have minded.

Armed with Sandra's Pink umbrella (thank god it was dark outside) I ventured out for the number 13 bus to Strathaven that ran once an hour (a crap service I may add). I got out at the common green and headed for 'Avondale flowers' for a small, hopefully inexpensive bouquet of flowers for my date - flowers make a good impression I'm told, although I always feel a right pansy browsing through a florists. I walked through the narrow lane on to Kirk Street and rang the bell. She looked pleased to see me as I handed the mixed bouquet over - I even got a kiss on the cheek.

After a glass of Chablis and some polite small talk we made the short walk to Mario's. To my horror it was fully booked and we were told that there were no tables available for the night so we left for the 'Bucks Heads,' which was second choice. It had recently been refurbished and it had the reputation of serving very good food, thankfully we were fortunate enough to secure a table, the restaurant was simple, rustic and possessed a certain charm. It was small which added to the intimacy and was beautifully lit up with flickering candles and lamps, tasteful music blended into the background as we discussed the merits of the menu and which wine to order.

She looked very beautiful and was wearing a green coloured, low cut blouse and black trousers which made her look very elegant, I complimented her style and élan. Irene never mentioned my new shirt. She opted for a prawn cocktail for starters followed by the chef's recommendation, which was a baked breast of farmhouse chicken accompanied with a polenta pancake and crispy spinach. I had the traditional steak pie in ale served with new potatoes and a medley of vegetables.

The food, like the conversation, was excellent until I raised the subject of her health, it was something she was reluctant to discuss and I respected her wishes, I think I hit a raw nerve. Changing tact I asked.

"So do you still enjoy working in the gift shop?"

"Actually I had to give it up."

"Oh, I didn't know. So how do you manage?" I hoped the question wasn't too intrusive.

"Well the mortgage is already paid off, it was originally my parents flat before they died, I got the flat, and Jenny, my sister I told you about, received a sum of money. She has a house in Hamilton. She comes up quite a lot to keep an eye on me and does some odd jobs about the house, she's great you will have to meet her and her husband Scott as well. So as you can see money is not a problem, never has been"

"Well that's good to hear," I said sympathetically.

"In fact, you've just reminded me of something."

"What?"

She went on to relate in great detail what Sandra and herself had planed that would strike a powerful blow for consumerism , a frenzied shopping spree using store credit or other form of 'plastic' that would never be repaid - it sounded audacious but ultimately a lot of fun. I liked her attitude, they were beginning to sound like a modern day version of 'Bonnie and Clyde,' without the gratuitous violence or bloodshed, I was just beginning to see the other side of her personality. It was dark with a mischievous undertone.

I often wondered how people reacted to the terrible news that you've only a few months left to live. I suppose some would be so devastated, coherent thought would be difficult and they would be consumed with self pity and despair, yet Irene seemed to have accepted the inevitable with stoic calm and wanted to go out in a blazing act of self defiance having a lot of fun along the way, basically two fingers up to the grim reaper.

Irene also mentioned they were going to book a foreign holiday for a few weeks or so, somewhere exotic (I suggested Butlins) that would be extortionately priced, maybe some type of five star cruise. I casually mentioned to her that I needed to work on my tan and had a fondness for boats.

She was wonderful company and I had a truly memorable night and she even insisted in paying for half, which I thought was very considerate. It was met with the minimum of resistance as I remembered my financial standing.

At the end of the night I did notice she was looking very tired and I tactfully suggested to call it a day, she also needed to get back to take some of her medication. I felt a bit guilty when I remembered on insisting that her glass was always topped up, morphine tablets and alcohol is a potent mixture for someone in such a fragile state physically and I should have known better. Thankfully, it was a short walk back to the flat from the Bucks Head.

We had arranged to get a taxi back to East Kilbride, but when we got in I noticed that she was looking quite ill and she couldn't hide the fact. I made sure she took her meds, poured her a glass of iced water and helped her into bed. I was shocked how quickly her condition deteriorated, it struck without any warning and left her debilitated ,she needed to sleep.

I noticed a bucket beside her bed and presumed she was suffering from bouts of nausea, probably brought on by the combination of pills and the residual after effects of the chemotherapy. I asked her if she wanted me to stay but she insisted that she would cope. I would explain to Sandra that she was too ill to travel ,she would understand.

I locked up the flat, put the keys through the letterbox and waited for the taxi to appear, thankfully it came within a few minutes and I was soon on my way back to Laurel Place. It was an abrupt end to a wonderful night and I couldn't help think about her, I cried on the way back home, to be more accurate it was a bit of a sniffle, I didn't want the taxi driver to think I was an emotional weakling or I had just been dumped. I loved her, it's as basic as that, and I didn't know how many other opportunities I would have to see her again and enjoy her company. I eventually nodded off, probably the combination of the large meal and the wine.

"That's us mate."

I woke up with a start. I must have dozed off for a few minutes.

"Thanks, driver."

"Can't go right into Laurel Place mate, I'll need to drop you here. There's a fire engine in your street."

"That's not a problem, I'll just walk through, -how much?"

"Seventeen-fifty." I handed over the money begrudgingly and walked towards the house, anxious about the arrival of the emergency services. When I got closer to our street I was filled with a sickening sense of foreboding. It was ours that was on fire.

I started running toward it.

The firemen were already tackling the upper bedroom, thick acrid smoke was billowing out of the window and I watched in horror as Sandra was brought out of the house and placed on a stretcher. She was attended to by a paramedic who quickly carried out a health assessment on her, then covered her with a blanket, checked her breathing, put a neck brace on, then put her on oxygen before quickly placing her in the ambulance.

It all happened so fast.

"Sandra, Sandra," I shouted.

She pulled the oxygen mask off a few inches and coughed.

Dirty Laundry

"Jack, I'm alright…. I'm fine. I fell down the stairs to get away from the fire. It must have been a fag end in bed, oh god, I'm so sorry."

The paramedic put the mask back over her face, closed the doors and headed for the A and E at Hairmyers, she would be there in five minutes or so. The next door neighbour Simon and his wife Angela were in discussion with one of the fire crew, they must have alerted the emergency services. I joined them to find out what had happened.

The crew had quickly assessed the situation - where the fire was, who was in the house at the time, where the gas and electricity cut off switches were located and so forth. I couldn't really give them any other information, everything was under control and within ten minutes the powerful jets of high compressed water had extinguished the flames leaving only a cloud of black smoke which was slowly dissipating in the wind.

It was a damn lucky escape for her.

After the fire crew deemed it safe to enter I nervously walked into the house, escorted by a fireman, they had already started removing the blackened objects out of the window onto the grass. There was going to be some clean up job to perform later. The smell was overpowering as I ventured upstairs, all the walls were blackened, there was pools of dirty water, and it was freezing cold. The windows were all shattered and there was glass everywhere.

The officer gave me a list of things to do as it was a bought house not a rented one, so the responsibility lay with Sandra to make it wind and watertight again, she would also need to contact the insurance company and arrange for the upper windows to be boarded up. He also stressed that the gas, electricity and even the water supplies may have been disrupted in some way by the fire, or fire fighting operations, and that under no circumstances should I attempt to reconnect or turn them on myself.

I was advised to contact the gas and electricity companies to ensure that damage to any of the systems was rectified before the power was safely restored, similarly all repairs to water fitting pipes and tanks should be undertaken only by a qualified plumber. If I turned on the water unadvised, he said matter of factly, 'I'll be inviting a flood.' Good advice, but there was just so much to remember, so much to do, and I felt sorry for Sandra coming back to this disaster. She would have her work cut out phoning tradesmen, insurance people, gas, electric companies and various departments if important documents were lost in the fire.

It was a nightmare. The aftermath of a fire is equally devastating.

I informed the officer of what Sandra had said, but I think he already had a good idea how the fire started. As I surveyed the damage he casually informed me that smoking causes more than 5,500 house fires every year in the UK and is responsible for the deaths of 1,500 with more than 20,000 seriously injured in the last ten years. I felt like I was being lectured or suitably chastised for Sandra's mistake.

Sandra had become yet another person for his statistics. Thankfully she was alive and the house could always be repaired. I'll kill her when I see her though, I've told her on countless occasions about her fags smouldering away in the ash tray, or even worse, removing the battery out of the smoke alarm for something else or because she's burnt the toast.

The main bedroom, Sandra's, was completely gutted and I doubt if there was anything that could be salvaged. With a sense of dread I walked through puddles of blackened water and debris into my room, pushing past a fireman.

I just closed my eyes in an attempt to lessen the blow. The fire had spread quickly into my bedroom, the thin plaster board walls put up no resistance, but what was worse than the flames was the water damage. All my earthly possessions were completely ruined, including the guitar and the keyboard which had melted in the intense heat. It now resembled something that could be a contender for an art award at the Tate gallery, it's better looking than sheep preserved in formaldehyde.

Papers were scattered everywhere, or should I say small bits of blackened paper, my manuscript. Six weeks of toil, hard work, personal outpouring, literally gone up in smoke. I was devastated, I had put so much into it, I was hoping the book would open up an opportunity for me to do something else if it was successful. It was totally ruined and there was no copy made, no disc, nothing stored on a computer.

My clothes were smoke damaged and drenched in water, nothing could be saved, the only decent thing I had left was what I was wearing, and the bloody shirt was too tight!

It was an unmitigated disaster.

The smaller bedroom next to Sandra's was bad as well. Everything was ruined either by the fire or water. I prayed Sandra was well insured. With a heavy heart I walked back down the stairs, to see what damage was caused, and thankfully it was not as bad as I had expected, although there would need to be extensive damage assessment to the ceilings and major refurbishment.

The neighbours that phoned for the fire service invited me in for a cup of tea and were gracious enough to offer me a room for the night, which I declined. I had to go and see Sandra and had some phone calls to make to their family to let them know the situation, and reassure them that she was alright although very badly shaken by the incident.

The 'boarding contractors' came out within twenty minutes and secured the three bedrooms, which meant I could now leave the house safe in the knowledge it was well secured.

I just prayed Sandra was alright and that she hadn't broken anything when she fell. That would be the last thing I needed, trying to help her about the house for six weeks or so, I reckoned that as long as she fell on her head she wouldn't be too bad. It might even knock some sense into her!

CHAPTER 12

UP THE CREEK

Sandra Potter was pronounced dead at 3.30 am, on Sunday, the 30th of January.

I still haven't got over the shock. I can't even begin to come to terms with the loss. When she left in the ambulance she was distressed, agitated, but she didn't look that serious, certainly not at death's door. She was lucid, responsive and I was more concerned with the fall down the stairs.

I miss her and her outrageous ways. She was a larger than life character with a heart of gold. I've only known her for a few short months, but I honestly feel like I've known her for years, she had a great attitude toward life, very ' laissez faire,' laid back, cared passionately for the ones she was close to and never let anyone down. She even cooked a mean chilli con carne and a decent Christmas cake.

For a while there was no consoling Irene and I think a part of her died as well, she didn't even get the chance to say goodbye, to embrace her, to tell her she loved her, not even a parting kiss .I honestly feel for the first time that Irene actually welcomes death. She was the one that was expected to die first, that's the way they had planned for the eventuality, so the suddenness of it all was a devastating blow to a woman who was already facing up to her own mortality.

Sandra will be buried tomorrow, Friday, at the Strathaven cemetery in a plot next to her younger sister Catherine.

Irene was supposed to take care of all the arrangements in a situation like this, but ill health made it impossible so Mary suggested that they should help with some of the funeral preparations. She was happy with this which I think showed considerable trust on her part. I think they were genuinely concerned about her deteriorating health and wanted to help, wanted to be supportive and treat her like one of their own family, they were very fond of her.

Friday is going to be a very difficult day for the family and I must admit I'm dreading it.

It was four days until I could move back into Laurel Place again and I was eternally grateful for the hospitality shown by Mary who kindly put me up for a few days. I found it difficult at first, probably because she not only looked like Sandra but she sounded like her as well.

So I'm back to square one again, my life is in a state of flux. Although I've returned to Greenhills, it's only a temporary measure, once the house is fully repaired and decorated it's going on the market and I'll be looking for a place to stay. I'm facing deracination once again. It was very kind of Mary to let me live rent-free for the time remaining and I hope they don't sell the house quickly.

I feel like I'm a dispossessed soul. I know I could move back in with my parents, but that's a last option believe me. Thankfully, Sandra was well insured, not only in her 'buildings and contents,' but also in her personal life, and after the funeral on Friday, her solicitor is due to read her last will and testament in front of the family.

The recent events, the upheaval of the last few days has taken its toll on me as well. It's hard being in the same house with those who have lost a loved one and the sisters and the rest of the family are inconsolable in their grief. I grieve for Sandra as well, think about her all the time and even feel guilty about the fact that I've not returned to work. I just don't have the heart for it at the moment. My financial situation, to put it mildly, is deleterious although I'm hoping to make a claim on Sandra's insurance which makes me feel guilty somehow.

The only item I salvaged was my metal money box which contained some personal papers, driving license, birth certificate, pictures and so forth and the princely sum of £450 which is the last of my earthly resources.

Penury looms in the distance.

What a depressing thought as I take a stock taking on my life. I've worked all my years, toiled, grafted, call it what you like and all I have got to show for it is £450 and the clothes I'm standing in.

Nothing else.

No possessions.

Zilch!

They say that life begins at forty, well, I'm a week off that and I can tell you this, it's not life that begins at forty, it's strife, with a capital 'S.' I've never had so many problems, anxieties in all my life, and for the first time ever I have absolutely no idea in what direction my life's moving, in fact I feel like I've been set adrift in a boat, no rudder, no oars, no compass, at the complete mercy of the elements and where I end up is anyone's guess.

Up shit creek without a paddle probably.

My lamentable musings were rudely interrupted by the phone.

"Hello."

"Hi, it's J and P builders, Stan speaking, can I speak to Alan please?"

"Sure, hold on a moment." I shouted up the stairs. "Alan, it's for you!" There was a four man team carrying out essential repair work upstairs and at times I felt like

I was the bloody secretary, have these guys never heard of mobile phones?"

After the gas, electric and plumbing contractors arrived earlier this week and 'made safe' the house, the builders arrived on Thursday to start the work after tea, sandwiches and a smoke, in fact they seemed to spend an inordinate amount of time in this particular pastime.

Less than five minutes later the phone rang again as I was in the kitchen making lunch for myself, with Sandra's stuff I'm ashamed to say, yet another guilt trip. I lifted the receiver and sighed audibly to register my annoyance.

"Yes."

"Hello Jack, how are you doing?" It was Irene. As usual my heart skipped a beat. She sounded very tired, lethargic, or was doped up on her medication.

"I'm doing alright, holding up," I lied.

She went onto relate in detail the funeral arrangements for tomorrow and asked if I would say a few words at the graveside which I was only too happy to do, I considered it a privilege. The service was to be conducted at the Rankin church by Robert Hastie, then the body was to be taken to the cemetery where she was to be laid to rest. They had hired the function hall in the Strathaven hotel so the guests could drink a toast to Sandra and have something to eat. Sandra would have liked that, she always said she loved a good funeral.

It always amazes me how people under great duress can organize and plan such a traumatic event like a funeral and still remain focused, all the painful phone calls to make, the liaising with the authorities, the funeral directors, the legal matters, they must be on automatic pilot or driven by sheer stress. It doesn't help that you're terminally ill and your own health is deteriorating, god knows where she gets the strength.

"Listen Jack, could we get a chance to talk tomorrow, I've a few things on my mind and I don't really want to talk on the phone, I'd rather speak with you face to face."

"Sounds intriguing, what's it all about?"

"Let's talk tomorrow after the funeral, it's just not a good time at the moment, I hope you understand."

"Of course, look take care and I'll see you tomorrow Irene." I was desperate for some insight, a single apercu, but I knew not to chance my luck.

"Okay, I'll see you tomorrow then, bye."

I hung up the receiver and my curiosity was aroused by the brief conversation, I had absolutely no idea what she wanted to discuss and I decided not to second guess myself, I know what I would like it to be, but I'm not going down that path again, rejection hurts.

I sat at the breakfast bar with my lunch thinking about what to say at the graveside. It was a big responsibility and the words had to be carefully measured and delivered with warmth and decorum. I flicked through some of the pages of one of Sandra's books which contained many beautiful poems that touched on the themes of 'sadness,' 'hopelessness,' ' the resurrection,' 'grieving,' and 'the human spirit,' great works from the masters like William Wordsworth, John Milton, W. B. Yeats, but I selected one that was penned by an anonymous writer which I found very puzzling, the poem was very profound, very emotive and one of the great word Smiths would have been proud to put his or her signature to.

That's the one, I was determined to learn it 'ad verbum' which would make the address more personal and hopefully moving, anyone can read from a piece of paper. The poem was quoted in a letter by a British soldier who was killed by the IRA in 1989. The words were fervid, impassioned and seemed to come from the soul of the writer.

It took me an hour to commit it to memory mainly because of the countless interruptions from the builders and the shock of seeing Sandra's Fanny walking into the kitchen looking bedraggled, bemused and ravenous. I knew the poor thing was desperate, it actually came up to me and rubbed itself against my leg, normally if a cat did that to me it would receive a swift kick up the arse, but I felt sorry for the poor beast.

I thought that it had died in the fire, not that I made an intensive search for it, or I was going to shout its name. Mrs Potter's Fanny survived, a bit singed but in reasonable health. God knows what will happen to it, maybe Irene would want it, if not it would have to be taken to a cat and dogs home, one thing was for certain, no matter doleful it looks, or pathetic it appears, or how friendly she was trying to become, I'm not responsible for it. No way.

In a magnanimous act of human kindness I opened a tin of tuna, emptied the contents on to a saucer, warmed some milk in the microwave and gave it to her as well. It consumed everything without looking up or even thanking me afterwards, when it was finished it trotted into the living room to park itself in it's favourite chair and sleep off the large feed and the harrowing experience of ingratiating itself to me for some sustenance.

You're welcome Fanny.

Ingrate!

CHAPTER 13

R.I.P.

Do not stand at my grave and weep:
I am not there. I do not sleep.
I am a thousand winds that blow.
I am the diamond glints on snow.
I am the sunlight on ripened grain.
I am the gentle autumn's rain.
When you awaken in the mornings hush,
I am the swift uplifting rush
Of quiet birds in circled flight.
I am the soft stars that shine at night.
Do not stand at my grave and cry;
I am not there, I did not die.

I recited the poem slowly, emphatically, letting every word pervade their thoughts, evoke feeling, and when I finished, it was difficult to hold back the tears. The moment just grabbed me by the throat.

Ambivalent feelings.

Fond memories.

The loss of a good friend.

I couldn't help think that I would be repeating this final act very soon for another person standing close to me, dressed in black, inconsolable, supported by her family and friends. Someone I loved, cared for, wanted to be with. I mentally chastised myself I was beginning to sound like a two dimensional character out of a Mills and Boon novel, get a grip, by manly! I was the last to speak. Mary said a few words after the minister, then Ann and Patrick. Irene started her eulogy but couldn't finish it, the emotion of the moment seemed to overwhelm her and for a moment I thought she was about to pass out, Patrick rushed over to support her and she was finally led away by her younger sister Jenny and her husband Scott.

It was the first time I had met her and was struck how similar they looked and even sounded. After the closing remarks of the minister, the family one by one threw a flower on her coffin and bowed in respect. The final goodbye.

The day had started off overcast and cold but as the last act of remembrance took place a small break in the clouds allowed the sun to shine through. I felt there was something symbolic, poignant at that moment as I remembered the words of Catullus, *'suns can set and come again; for us, when once our brief light has set, one everlasting night is to be slept.'*

Very powerful words.

We walked back to the cars in silence.

There was an open invitation for everyone attending the funeral to meet at the function suite in the Strathaven hotel, and when I arrived there was a considerable group of people already in attendance. Sandra was obviously a very popular person, the only one conspicuous by their absence was Mary's husband Bob, and to be honest I'm glad he didn't put an appearance in.

They had arranged a buffet and generously laid on a free bar. This was the bit I was dreading. At gatherings like these, under difficult circumstances I'm a bit inept at the social graces and I'm terrified that I say something inappropriate or incongruous, or even worse, laugh at something. It's just nerves that's all. I was grateful to get through the most onerous part at the graveside without making an arse of myself. I remember Neil telling me some of the things you should never do or say at a funeral and his flippant insights were starting to fill my head and I couldn't drive them out -

'you should never drive behind the hearse and continually sound your horn.'

'don't be tempted to put a hard boiled egg in the deceased's mouth.'

'don't listen to your personal stereo at the graveside.'

'don't go around the assembled group of mourners and inform them that they are not in the will, tough luck.'

'don't put a whoopee cushion on the widow's seat.'

'and never, hit the deceased body and then tell people that he started it.'

I tried to expunge those stupid thoughts from my mind as I queued for a drink. I made polite small talk to the gentleman in front of me who was a work colleague of Sandra's. I ordered a pint of lager and a single malt whiskey which I downed quickly to calm the nerves. I stood at the far side of the bar and watched as groups of people chatted and filled the tables. Out of the 120 or so I only knew a few them and was beginning to feel just a bit out of it until Patrick came over and invited me to their table.

"What are you doing standing there? Come and join us," he said.

"Thanks." I was relieved. I took a large gulp of the lager and reminded myself to slow down.

"It was a lovely service by the minister," Ann remarked.

Mary responded, "Very nice, he's a lovely man and his wife is also charming."

I could sense the tension at the table which was perfectly understandable. I thought the speech by the minister was purely formulaic and austere. Sandra was not, by any means, a religious person, the only time she attended was for the usual three important occasions, births, deaths and marriages, in fact she had a particular dislike for the man in the grey suit with the dog collar, the patronising voice and the limp handshake. The thing that really irked me was the way he spoke of Sandra as if he knew her personally and the condescending way he recounted stories that had been passed on to him by the family, it came across as disingenuous rather than sincere, maybe I'm just a bit cynical.

"Sorry Jack, but I don't think I've introduced you to my sister Jenny," Irene said apologising.

"No, I don't think you have, pleased to meet you Jenny." I stretched over and shook her hand. It was as cold as ice. Irene smiled and spoke again.

"And this is her eldest son Martin."

"Pleased to meet you."

"And Mark"

"Hello there," I said.

"And this is Scott, my husband, I think you met him earlier."

"Hi." Jenny's sons looked to be in their late teens and hardly said a word the entire time.

The last time I was in company with this group of people it was difficult to get a word in, the combination of Sandra's special punch and her 'happy cake' made for a boisterous time and some less than circumspect behaviour. Now the conversation was fragmented and clichéd. I needed another drink and asked the group if I could refill their glasses. I'm very generous with other people's money. I ordered doubles at the bar in an attempt to lighten the mood, I know it was a funeral but others around us were chatting and laughing as they recounted some of the stories about Sandra, I could tell a tale or two of her dubious exploits or strange habits. I brought the drinks over to the table.

"Help yourself to the buffet Jack. There's some lovely food. I'm going up, will you join me?" Irene asked.

"Yeah, I could eat something, excuse me folks." I was that nervous about reciting the poem and dealing with the occasion I couldn't eat. It doesn't happen very often. The table at the top of the room was beautifully laid out with some wonderful looking food and bottles of wine, they had obviously gone to a lot of expense to lay on something as attractive as this and for such a large gathering. Irene touched my arm.

"Your recital was very moving, I was touched by it."

"Thanks, your speech was nice and short." She smiled. I passed her a plate and asked.

"So how are you doing Irene?" It was a bloody stupid question, but I just blurted it out.

"Okay I suppose, the worse part is over. I still can't believe she's gone, I don't know how I'm going to cope without her, I loved her so much Jack."

"I know."

"I keep waiting for her to walk in through the door, or for her to phone for a chat.... it's difficult to put into words. I don't think I'll ever be able to fill that void she's left, it's"..... Her words trailed off and she wiped a solitary tear from her face.

"Irene if there's anything I can do, absolutely anything, please let me know, I want to help you, I know Jenny comes up often but I'm here for you as well."

"Actually that's what I wanted to talk to you about." She was distracted by a smart dressed woman in a blue pin stripe suit carrying a briefcase in one hand and a mobile phone in the other approaching the table. "It's Francis McQueen, Sandra's solicitor. She's early. Look, we'll talk a bit later, is that okay?"

"Of course, is this for the reading of the will?"

"Yes it is, I better get back to the table, I don't think that it will take too long, we've got a room next door for the reading."

"More stress, eh?"

"Yeah," she sighed, "I'll be glad when it's all over Jack."

Irene, Ann, Patrick and Mary politely dismissed themselves from the table and followed the rather brusque, business like solicitor into the adjoining room, she apologized for the intrusion and reassured us that it would not take long and this was what Sandra had proposed. I wondered if Francis Mc Queen was single as I nervously fiddled with my drumstick, the alcohol was only now beginning to relax me, but in my defence she was very attractive.

I was engrossed in conversation with Scott when they returned thirty minutes later to the table. I was dying to ask them about the will but decorum and decency prevented me from opening my big mouth, it was hard to tell how the meeting went by the look on their faces, they gave nothing away and the conversation returned to other matters. The following hour or so passed very quickly as we recounted some stories and anecdotes about Sandra, the mood lifted and it was warming to see them smile and laugh after such a heartbreaking morning.

The crowd began to thin out and I decided to phone for a taxi. I thanked everyone for their hospitality and hoped that the next time we met would be under more favourable circumstances. Irene caught up with me in the foyer.

"Jack," she said grasping my arm, " can we talk privately for a minute?"

"Sure."

"Do you have to be back in Greenhills this afternoon?"

"Not really. The builders have a spare set of keys, but I'm having two students for tuition on Saturday morning so I'll need to get the 8.30 bus tonight at the latest."

"I thought your instruments were ruined?"

"They were, but I got a loan of a guitar from Stevie, if you could actually call it a guitar, anyway the students always bring theirs."

"Can you come back to my place so we can talk in private?"

"Sure, no problem."

"Oh wait up, I need to say goodbye to Jenny and her family, I won't be long."

They embraced then Irene walked them to the door. There were tears in her eyes when she arrived back.

"Sorry about that," she sniffed. I handed her a linen napkin I had borrowed from the hotel.

"Thanks Jack, there's a taxi outside, let's go." The taxi took less than 5 minutes and we were back in Kirk Street. She made some hot Guatemala coffee as I admired the paintings in her living room and looked out on the busy street below, the buzz of traffic and the people outside brought a sense of normality back into our lives. She came back in with two mugs and some cakes. I got straight to the point as my curiosity was piqued by her earlier comments.

"So, what's it all about Irene, what did you want to discuss?"

"I've an offer to make you," she said sipping her coffee.

"I'm listening."

"Right, here we go, just bear with me. Sandra's house is being repaired just now, then it's to be decorated then put on the market, and the way property is selling at the moment we reckon it will go quick, we just want a reasonable price that's all, so your time there as you probably know is strictly limited I'm afraid to say."

"I know that Irene, it's not a problem, I'll just move back in with my parents until I get myself sorted out, I've got a few things planned at the moment," I said with an air of confidence.

"What I'm trying to say is, you're welcome to move in here for the time being, I've another spare bedroom but it's strictly a business arrangement."

"Go on" (outer exterior calm, inner voice shouting yes, yes! I'll take it).

"You do general work, like cleaning, shopping, decorating and so forth and you can stay rent free."

"Rent free, it seems a bit unfair on you surely?"

She sighed, "Money is no longer a problem Jack, you really would be doing me a huge favour, I've got to admit my health is failing, failing rapidly if truth be told, so I need all the help I can get and I want people around I can trust and rely on. Jenny has been brilliant but she's got her own problems and works full time so it would be good for her as well. I'm not doing this out of sympathy, it will work both ways."

I could see the way she was rationalizing matters and it was an offer I would have jumped at anyway even if she wanted rent. Here's the options, move back in with my aged parents or change residence to Kirk street with someone I have strong feelings for.

"I'll need to think about it Irene, ponder the variables" (did I actually say that?)

"Of course, take as much time as you need, it's a big decision."

Dirty Laundry

"Okay, it's a deal!" I said quickly. She laughed at the lame attempt at humour.

"Great, that's good news for me, I appreciate this Jack, you can move in whenever you like."

I tried not to sound too keen." Would tomorrow be okay? I've only a few things to organize, not much to move, let me see, one strong box, a few clothes, one naff guitar, and oh, I nearly forgot to mention, one other thing."

"What?"

"Fanny."

She looked bemused and slightly embarrassed. "Right! her cat, god I completely forgot about her, yeah you will have to bring her as well, she's lovely really."

She must have seen by the look on my face that I was less than impressed with the new addition, not only do I have a particular aversion of cats, they make my eyes water, oh well you can't have everything.

"Well that's it sorted then, I'll bring my belongings up on Saturday afternoon after I phone Mary and get things organized with her. There's still a lot of Sandra's stuff there downstairs that didn't succumb to the ravages of the fire, a lot of personal things you would want to go through yourself Irene.

"Of course I was planning to take a trip to East Kilbride tomorrow sometime to go through some of the legal papers and so forth. The only thing I really want are the photographs and Sandra's artwork, the rest of her belongings can go to the local charity shops.

"Art work?"

"Yeah, her two paintings in the living room, that's her work."

"I didn't know she painted them, they are absolutely fantastic, especially the one depicting the cottage in the snow."

"That's my favourite as well, she had a real gift. I'm surprised she never showed you the sketches, she kept them all in that big unit in the living room, have a look when you get back you'll be impressed with her work especially the portraits, they are so life like, so realistic you would think they were done by a professional, I think she's done one of you and a caricature if I remember rightly. Anyway, we can have a quick perusal when I come up tomorrow."

"Sounds fine, you can pick up some of the things you need and I'm sure Mary will organize the rest, although I think she'll want to throw a lot of it out, it's not damaged but it smells of smoke."

"Don't worry Jack we will get everything organized and it's just a matter of getting a taxi back up the road." She looked at me sympathetically and touched my arm. "All change again." I nodded in assent.

"I feel like I'm a wandering nomad but it would have been very difficult to stay at Laurel Place after what had happened."

"I understand, I'm dreading going back tomorrow, even just sifting through some of Sandra's things… it's just…well, very difficult." I could see her eyes welling up again and there was a terrible sadness about her, the inability to fight back against a terminal illness coupled with the loss of a close partner was like a cross that was just too heavy to bear and there was no one else that could be impressed into carrying it for her. She had accepted it with great reluctance and it seemed to be sapping her of her strength and will.

Irene refilled the coffee and passed me the mug.

"Isn't it amazing how quickly your life can turn around?"

I interrupted, "You're not joking."

"It's been a strange day Jack, I find it difficult to describe, I've lost someone who meant the world to me. I've been given so much love by my family and friends, so much support and consideration and from being in a situation where I've had to watch every penny, I'm now well off. But there's the irony of it all. I just don't have the time and health to enjoy it - isn't life paradoxical?"

"It is, but without sounding clichéd, you have to make the most of it because life is unpredictable, inconsistent. It was Nabakov that said, 'the cradle rocks above the abyss, and common sense tells us that our existence is but a brief crack of light between two eternities of darkness.' You could live to be a hundred and be miserable and unfulfilled or you can die early but have lived a full, complete life, it's your attitude towards it, that's my philosophy. *'Quem diable allait-il faire dan cette galere,'* as the French say."

"Say what?"

"It means,' whom the gods love dies young.'

"You know you are right Jack, life is precious, time is precious, it's only when you're facing death you appreciate that fact."

"Anyway money doesn't buy you happiness, but I suppose it will help you to be miserable in comfort." She laughed then replied in a serious tone.

"Sandra was well insured Jack, very well insured."

"Mary said something to that effect, she encouraged me to put in a claim for my losses which I did."

"Good for you. She had two insurance policies one for £100,000 and another for £85,000. She also had £ 71,000 in her bank account, then there's the proceeds of the house sale which we expect should reach £95,000."

"Good god, that's a lot of money." I couldn't help think with all that money in the bank she didn't even decorate my room.

"It was a bit of a shock to me Jack as you can expect. I inherit 50% of her estate. Mary and Ann were allocated 25% each. She must have been a shrewd investor."

"Well, I'm pleased for you. It's one less thing to worry about when you're so ill. It will ease the burden."

"So as you can see, money is not a problem, I would be delighted to have you here to help because I will damned if I'm going to spend my last days in a hospital associating with the living dead."

Dirty Laundry

I smiled at her choice of words, she was one determined lady and it made me feel a bit easier accepting her invitation, it would also help my financial situation in the long run.

We chatted for an hour or so before I departed for the No. 13 bus back to East Kilbride. After taking a cocktail of meds Irene needed to rest and would spend the rest of the day in bed recuperating for the stressful events of the day. Suddenly my life is back on track after yet another derailment. I had a new start in Strathaven, would be better off financially and was also waiting for the claim on Sandra's house insurance, which I'm not ashamed to say, was rather generous. Best of all, no more sleeping on the downstairs settee that was full of cat hairs. The only down side was the unwelcome return of Sandra's Fanny.

CHAPTER 14

HEADS I WIN, TAILS YOU LOSE

Ask a woman what's better than sex and they will probably say one of the following:

1. chocolate
2. alcohol
3. a vibrator
4. shopping

I'm taking a wild guess at this, but out of the four suggestions I reckon the greater percentage would opt for number 4, possibly combined with number 2. A certain sensual gratification that's on a par to an orgasm can be experienced while traipsing around the shops with money to spend and the thought of a liquid lunch with your best friend as you discuss in great detail what you have purchased and how you're going to hide the price from your husband. I think it was Adrienne

Gusoff that said, *'shopping is better than sex, if you're not satisfied after shopping, you can make an exchange for something you really like.'*

So when Irene and Jenny arrived back laden down with designer bags and boxes, they had that look on their face that suggested a 'good time' was had by all. It looked like they had combined all four on the ' what's better than sex list!' They had purchased so much stuff the taxi driver was assisting them as the meter was ticking away, no doubt he would receive a decent tip for his troubles.

I've never seen two women more excited in all my life, they were euphoric, not only did they buy masses of shopping they had also booked an expensive five star Caribbean cruise for themselves. Irene casually mentioned that with Jenny's assistance she had selected a small car, a Ford Fiesta, brand new from the dealer, which was due for delivery in three days time. I was gob smacked by their audacity and female scheming because I knew from our previous conversation very little of it would ever be repaid, which gave the shopping that extra dimension, no more looking for the bargains or worrying about money, just buy the best and damn the price, as they say, if you pay peanuts you get monkeys. Good on them!

Once they had offloaded the shopping in the living room it resembled an Aladdin's cave of retail treasures, the 'shop till you drop' marathon had been postponed many times because of ill health and I felt sorry Sandra had missed out on it. She's probably up there laughing at her partner's behaviour right now. I just wished they had asked me.

"Well, do I need to ask if you girls had a good time?" The expression on their faces said it all. Irene started laughing and hugged her sister.

"Now Jack," she said grinning, "We have not forgotten about you."

I replied, "You shouldn't have" ('yes you should have' I thought to myself).

"Now, now, this is for you." She handed me a catalogue from a musical instrument shop and said casually, "page 24 and page 98, I've marked the page and it's coming on Monday for you, it's my way of thanking you for all the help for the last month or so." I thumbed through the pages until I reached it - circled was a top of the range Fender acoustic priced at £2,229. I looked at her in disbelief.

"You've got to be kidding?"

"Nope," was the swift reply.

"Come on?"

"No, it's yours."

"You are unbelievable. This is fantastic. I don't know what to say."

Jenny smartly suggested, "Thanks would suffice. Oh, and a really big thanks to 'MasterCard.'"

"Alright, thanks very much, I'm overwhelmed."

"Now turn to page 98, I hope I picked the right one." After quickly finding the page I looked in delight at the wonderful keyboard that was equally as expensive as the Fender, it was something I could never afford on my paltry wages. It would be fantastic to play such beautiful instruments and I'm sure it would impress my students who made fun of my borrowed guitar and second hand Yamaha I bought in the local charity shop. I'm out to impress now! I just hugged her and kissed her on the cheek, I was really touched by her generosity, or should I say 'MasterCard's.'

"That's the wonder of plastic Jack," she said deviously, "it's all in my name so enjoy!"

"This calls for another drink!" Jenny cheerfully suggested, although by looking at them I think a few glasses of wine had passed their lips. I dutifully performed the task amidst piles of bags and boxes and left them to it.

I had spent the best part of the day decorating my bedroom and was just about finished. All that was left to do was to hang the new door which I would do after something to eat at the Waterside. Hanging a door is a bugger, I needed a drink first before I attempted the difficult DIY. Anyway, hard work should always be rewarded. Irene was going to Jenny's tonight so I would have a free house which would be a welcome break, looking after someone who is so ill was more than I had bargained for and I was thankful that her doctor was constantly in attendance to keep a wary eye on her although he was still adamant that she should be receiving palliative care because of the deterioration of her condition. Irene's mind was made up and there was nothing he could do to persuade her to attend a hospice although she did concede in hiring a part time nurse who provided an invaluable service.

For the first time in many months I feel very settled, have a purpose in life and working toward a goal, in the five weeks I've been here I've turned my life around, nothing drastic, just small changes that have made a difference , as one philosopher said, 'after all drops of rain make a hole in the stone not by violence but by oft falling.' I've sold half my window cleaning business (made £ 1,500) so I only have to work two days a week, while I've successfully managed to increase the number of students I teach through some shrewd advertising in the local papers. Living rent-free gave me the opportunity to save for a deposit for a sublet of my own in Strathaven when the time is appropriate.

I've hit a purple patch. Only this week I received a cheque for £2,152 from Sandra's insurance company which I accepted with good grace and a red face. Jill once described me as 'someone who sits on a hot stove then complains his arse is burning' - a bit unkind, well, not any more, I've taken a positive approach to life now I'm forty and I'm working towards loftier goals, namely, going back to college to get a degree in music, then eventually buying my own flat in Strathaven and finding someone good looking to share it with. I hope that's not being too optimistic.

It's so good to be back in my hometown again. I love everything about it, especially the people. They are warm and friendly, well, most of them anyway. The exception being old Jack who owns the newspaper shop on Kirk Street. He's still an old moan. He's Strathavens equivalent of Basil Fawlty. But then there's the lovely Rena, the lollypop lady, who still sees you across the road even though you're an adult, and it's great to see that the good looking bar staff at the Castle tavern hasn't changed either. Yes, there's no place like home. Where else can you wander about the ruins of a 15th century castle that's steeped in history and folklore? For example, there's the tradition that the wife of a past lord so greatly displeased her husband that she was walled up alive in part of the castle, and when a portion of the wall fell in the middle of the 19th century, human bones were discovered giving credence to the story. There are supposedly underground passageways leading from the castle to the mill brae and the 'tower,' an ancient watchtower about a mile or so out of Strathaven. You can also visit the cenotaph that crowns the hill and stands sentinel over the old graveyard that offers sweeping views of unspoilt countryside as far as the eye can see. Then there's the town mill that dates from 1650 which was built for the 2nd duke of Hamilton, as well as the old 'boo backit brig' with all its charm and history. There is also some splendid examples of 18th century buildings like the old house in western Overton, constructed in 1797 for general Lockhart, a hero of the charge of the light brigade at Balaclava. Some of the walls of the house are three feet thick. Another attraction are the imposing old churches which appear completely anachronistic in this modern day and age, with bells that peel early on a Sunday morning, reminding you that you're a sinner because you've never seen the inside of the place. Add to all this some beautiful walks, parks, and the best of all, my favourite attraction, Taylors bakery, the best in Scotland, although a bit on the expensive side. Did I mention the pubs?

In the last month or so I've also become quite the expert on the subject of cancer and particularly the 'care side'of it, I know all the medicines she's prescribed, the antiemitics, ones that relieve her nausea and vomiting, her morphine-based pain killers and the correct dosages and so forth. I found the history of morphine very interesting - the name comes from the Greek word for sleep 'morpheus' which is rather appropriate, it's derived from opium (morphine is ten times more potent than opium) and was used extensively by the ancient Sumerians who were aware of it's pain relieving effects as well as the mind altering states it produced. Hippocrates, the father of medicine wrote about the medicinal effect way back in 460 BCE, and by the 1800's the drug was used recreationally by many people including some of the great writers and poets like Keats, Byron, Dickens, Freud and Shelly. I think I might try a tablet or two myself if it's going to improve my writing. I understand the various treatments she was subjected to, the radiotherapy - treatment by radium or other radioactive matter that produces gamma rays that treat deep-seated tumours. Chemotherapy, which is basically treatment by chemical substances, has some terrible side effects. Irene suffers from pain in the lower back, bladder problems and nausea along with general dysphoria. The final indignity for her was losing her hair. I didn't know she was wearing a wig, but thankfully it's growing back in now.

I learned of the warning signs that the cancer is rapidly progressing ,the lethargy, cachexia, weight loss, a change in bowel habits that persist for more than two weeks, unusual bleeding and a loss of appetite. The doctor was considerate enough to give me information on the 'death signs' when it comes which didn't make for pleasant reading, nevertheless I was told to be acutely aware of the following and to phone him day or night. A patient who becomes confused, agitated and hallucinates, this is usually due to the combination of drugs and their suppressed immune system; vision failing is another indicator of the death sign. Fingertips and toes that develop a bluish hue, an indication that the circulation is failing and their skin feels cold to the touch and finally a change in the colour of the urine and breathing difficulties.

I was advised on the dosage of what's called the 'double effect.' If she was in intolerable pain and near death and no medical person could make it, the dose would induce an artificial coma. Her doctor assured me not to worry about the later stages of her illness, and that someone would be in attendance in her final weeks. That was a huge relief to me, I could not have coped with it, there would be so much to consider - the bathing, feeding, toilet care, medication and pain relief, most of which would be carried out by her newly appointed nurse.

All I could do at the moment is offer practical help and assistance around the house and I knew the time for greater palliative care was not too far away. The symptoms were already there. Within a month or so I've notice a discernable change in her physical appearance, she gets tired very easily, is losing more weight which I find quite alarming and is always complaining of the cold. My heart goes out to her.

After a quick shower, I put on my best trousers and a smart new shirt and headed in the direction of the Waterside for something to eat, it would give the girls a few hours to themselves and give me a much needed break. Although the Castle tavern was less the 100 feet away and convenient, the Waterside inn had a wider range of food and I fancied something a bit different, something that wasn't a 'toastie'. After all, I am now a 'thousand heir,' if there is such a word, a man of considerable means.

I pushed the door open and walked in pretending not to care that I was alone and was about to dine in splendid isolation, at least I wouldn't have to think about conversation, all I had to concentrate on was the food and drink and enjoy my book. I asked the waiter for his best ' table for one' and was directed to a seat beside the window. He removed the other place setting and cutlery and asked in a courteous manner what I would like to drink. I requested a bottle of the most average priced house red and he smiled and departed from the table with my order.

It's not very often I go out for something to eat by myself, there's a certain kind of 'stigma' attached to it and you can see others in their cosy groups looking at you as they chat away. It's viewed as lonely or sad, but I'm getting used to it now and even enjoy my own company and witty reposts with the people that serve me.

He arrived back with a single glass and a nice bottle of red wine which he uncorked with due ceremony, he poured a small amount in the glass and handed it to me to taste. I did the normal thing and replied, ' yeah, that fine, thanks.' The glass was then filled up by the waiter. Just once I would love to say, 'oh god this wine tastes like sour shit, bring me another bottle immediately,' then make some hacking, coughing noises that annoy onlookers.

I was thoroughly enjoying my prime rump steak and reading the paper when, out of the corner of my eye I saw Jill walking in unaccompanied. Too late she had seen me, hopefully she was just in for a quiet drink. No such luck! The waiter brought her into the dining area and the only table available was about six feet away from where I was sitting. It just about put me off my food. She took her leather jacket off and put it around the spare chair then ordered.

What a ridiculous situation to be in, one of us had to say something rather than grin inanely at each other, it wouldn't have been so awkward if she had company. I read the same paragraph three times before I plucked up the courage to say something, even if it was just to defuse a tense moment.

"Hi Jill, I've got a nice rump here," I said pointing to my plate.

She smiled and replied.

"Hello Jack, we meet again, are you awaiting company or are you just by yourself today?"

"Just myself, I'm in for a meal tonight, I can't be bothered cooking."

"Oh, I see."

"Are you waiting for Bryan?" (Bryan, her adulterous, lowlife, bald boss who's scared of me as I threatened to rip his head off).

"No, I'm like yourself, a quick meal then I'm off to see a friend in Stonehouse." Silence ensued as I returned to my rump. It was Jill's turn to try and ease the constrained situation by politely asking.

"So how are you these days, I see you're back on your feet again."

"Yes, it's been off for a while, but I'm good, still working away, usual stuff."

"Still cleaning windows?"

"Yes, but only part time, I teach now," I said trying to impress.

"Oh, what are you teaching?"

"Music, just from the house, a bit of tuition, but the money is very good and I've got quite a few students on my books now."

The waiter interrupted, or should I say rescued a very laboured, self-conscious conversation by bringing her order which looked better than mine. This was stupid, we're two adults, have known each other for years and we're sitting at two separate tables trying to conduct a conversation and remain civil, I could see people from the other table looking at us. I was thinking about inviting her to join me at my table so we wouldn't look so ill at ease and we could talk privately, but it was Jill that took the initiative first.

"This is a bit strained Jack, trying to talk from a distance, there's no privacy, do you want to join me?"

I shrugged my shoulders, "Why not." I transferred my food and wine over to her table and joined her. "I suppose this is more convivial."

"I've heard you have moved back into Strathaven, Kirk Street."

"Yes, I share a flat with Irene, do you remember her?"

"Of course, you introduced us when we last met in here along with Sandra Potter. I was sorry to hear about her Jack." Word gets around very quickly in a small town.

"It was tragic, a terrible way to go. She was a lovely person Jill, I miss her."

She took a sip of water then asked.

"So how long have you been going out with Irene? I'm really happy for you."

"I don't have a relationship with Irene, it's a business one, not romantic, although I wish it was to be perfectly honest. It's a long story."

"Oh, I see."

"She is my landlady, that's all, although she was already in a relationship when I first met her. I wasn't her type."

"She's very pretty."

"Irene is a lovely person, we get on very well. We have a good understanding. I'll be moving on in a few months time whenever I get enough for a deposit for a flat or even a sub let, and I need to get a few things together because I lost everything in the fire."

"That's terrible, I heard about it. Did you lose your guitar, the nice blue one I bought you?"

"As I said, I lost everything apart from the red strongbox - the keyboard, clothes, everything, even my manuscript I spent six weeks working on, which was the hardest to take."

"Manuscript?"

"Yeah, I toyed with the idea of writing a novel, just finished as well. Not much luck, eh?"

"No, afraid not. Could you not write it again?"

"I just don't have the heart for it, I devoted so much time and effort into it and it was just perfect. I don't think I could do it again. I don't even have any of the original notes left."

I nervously looked across at her and took a gulp of wine. The intrusion was making eating difficult. She was looking good and always dressed with real style. I pondered whether to compliment her or not. I didn't know how she would take it, would she read into it? Women are very good at that type of thing. She's probably studying my body language as we eat. My mind started racing ahead, slipping quickly through the gears. For some inexplicable reason I was getting very nervous, edgy. I did not know how to handle the situation. It had just crept up on me. I blurted out the most stupid thing next that made her laugh out loud. I think it cut the tension.

"Your meatballs look yummy." What a conversationalist I was, Mr smooth-talker, golden tongue. When she stopped laughing she offered me one, which I took.

Sharing food? Was that not a sign of close friendship, even intimacy? How will she read this? in fact how do I read this gesture and the fact we're sitting at the same table being nice to each other after our bitter break-up? 'Just eat the damn meatball,' I thought to myself, stop trying to psychoanalyze every little thing that's going on. I was so nervous the meatball went down the wrong way and I went into a paroxysm of coughing and choking and after thumping my own chest part of it shot out of my mouth and another small piece evacuated through my nostril which wasn't a pretty sight.

I wanted to curl up a die, my excessive choking quickly got the attention of the other diners and an old gent rushed over to assist, saying he was proficient in the Heineken movement, I surmised he meant the Heimlich manoeuvre. How to impress a girl eh?- all I needed to do was to fart loudly and my humiliation was complete!

Once I had calmed down and apologised to Jill, I said with beads of sweat on my forehead, "the meat balls are good!"

She was gracious enough to laugh it off.

"I see you're still as clumsy and accident prone," she said mockingly.

"Yeah, afraid so, and by the way, the ankle."

Jill interrupted, "you broke it in Auldhouse, not the alps. I know, it's easy to make a mistake between Switzerland and East Kilbride." Caught!

"How did you find out?"

"Word gets around, I phoned Lynn to find out how she was doing and she told me the whole story, all the details. I did warn you about the dangers of cannabis didn't I?" She grinned broadly and was enjoying my considerable unease.

"Don't remind me Jill, I've not touched it ever since, well not intentionally."

"Well?"

"Well what?"

"Can you push a cow over with one hand while it's sleeping in a field?"

"Shut up and eat your meatballs!" I took a sip of wine to settle myself down and grinned at her.

"I was worried about you, Jack." Was that comment out of genuine concern or just common sympathy?"

"I'm sure you were," I replied with a nuance of sarcasm in the voice.

"I mean it Jack. I've kept in touch with Karen and Lynn. They are still my friends as well." The conversation died, a raw nerve was exposed. It had taken such a long time to get over her, if, in fact I ever had, you can't suddenly become emotionally detached from someone you have come to love and cherish. It's difficult to make the dichotomy without experiencing pain and equivocal feelings and tonight, just sitting here with her, was bringing it all back. I was confused. Wrong footed.

"Well, Jill, I'm doing alright now. I've finally got my life in order but I have to say I was really hurt by what you did."

"I'm sorry."

"No, not hurt, devastated."

She looked down at her glass and took her time replying.

"We've been through this Jack, let's not argue, it was my fault and I'm trying to say sorry for all the hurt."

"Look Jill," I interrupted, "sorry, we are not here to apportion blame, we said it all, we've had the fights the arguments, I just want us to get on, be civil, be adult enough to greet one another without any bad feeling, that's all. I'm enjoying just talking to you again. I'm enjoying your company, so let's not start with the recriminations and faultfinding. After all, we have to live in the same small town."

"I agree, a truce, I was just trying to say sorry, I owe you that much."

"Accepted, but it takes two to fight and I feel at least part responsible now."

Jill sighed, "no you were not, it was my fault, I was ambitious and completely taken in by the false promises and the so called good life with Bryan. I was foolish." She went quiet. Thank goodness, she talks a lot when she's nervous. It gave me a chance to evaluate the usage of the past tense she was employing in her language - correct me if I'm wrong, but was their relationship over? Armed with that thought I boldly asked, trying desperately to be nonchalant.

"So how is Bryan?" (as if I give a damn).

"We split up a few months ago." She never said anything else and I had the good grace not to pursue the line of conversation, but it didn't stop me cheering mentally or performing an imaginary Irish jig in my head, it was like River dance on speed. I moved into writer mode in order to impress her.

"Well, Jill, 'semel insanivimus omnes,' as they say."

"What's that mean?"

"We have all been mad once." Look, no one is perfect, we all make mistakes. It could have been me, look how attractive I am. We've just got to get on with it." I tried to sound philosophical but I sounded more like an agony aunt from a cheap tabloid.

"As usual you are very magnanimous."

"That's part of my charm," I said almost smoothly. I noticed her glass was empty, "would you like a refill?"

"A glass of wine would be great thanks." I went to pour her a glass but only a few drips came out. I motioned to the waiter and ordered another bottle. He arrived within a minute with the uncorked bottle and placed it between us. I poured her a generous glass.

"There we go."

"Thanks."

"So are you still in the same job?"

"No, I left about four months ago, after we finished up. It turned out he was having an affair with another woman as well. It just became very ugly when I found out, I told his wife, a woman scorned eh? What a mess, a bit like my life really, anyway it's in the past and I've working in the Royal bank in Hamilton and I'm a lot happier now."

For some strange, almost compulsive reason, I wanted to ask her what sex was like with him and what size his penis was, but thought that line of questioning might prove to be uncomfortable for her as she ate her dinner, I put it down to jealously I suppose. I went for the safer option.

"So how is the old house?"

"Exactly the same, except for the spare bedroom, that's been decorated, I've done a lot more to the garden, put in some decking, that type of thing."

The conversation went into banal mode which was pleasant enough as we talked and reminisced about old times and some of the people we knew. We then ordered a sweet from the menu and were now beginning to relax just a bit. There was no more awkward questions or dead air between us. Or so I thought. The next sentence hit me like a wrecking ball.

"Can I ask you something, Jack?"

"Of course," I said. I sensed nervousness, maybe even anxiety and interrupted. Don't tell me you have no money and you want me to pay for the meal."

"Don't be ridiculous."

"Ask away."

She took a sip of wine and looked directly at me. "I want you to move back in, start again, I miss you."

I put my spotted dick down and just looked at her incredulously.

"What?"

"I want you to move back in, listen I understand fully if you say no, god I wouldn't blame you, what

I've put you through. All I ask is that you think about it, consider it at least."

I was genuinely stunned by her request. I did not see that one coming. I was blindsided. I looked at her and replied. "I don't know what to say Jill, I'm taken aback."

"Say yes."

"I can't make such a serious decision on a split second, I'll need time to think about it. It's so sudden, I had no idea."

"I understand, it was unfair to spring it upon you , will you at least consider it? It will be different, we'll be different. I've changed, grown up in the past year or so. Please tell me you'll consider the offer."

"Of course I will, but you can understand why I can't tell you right now. I'll let you know tomorrow. I'll sleep on it."

"Thanks, that's all I ask Jack." All I wanted was a quiet glass of wine, a good meal and a read at my novel. Now I'm faced with all sorts of possibilities, life altering situations and I cant even begin to make such a decision. I'm standing at the crossroads once again. I'm happy right now, focused, with my own plans and modest aspirations, but what Jill was offering was something I had always wanted, security, a close relationship, someone to share your innermost thoughts and feelings with.

But could I trust her again? What would our relationship be like after her affair. Someone once said that marriage was like a precious ornament, something of real value, beautiful, but once infidelity had been committed the ornament was broken, you could always glue it back together again and it would still look good, but on closer inspection you would always see the cracks and it's value had diminished. The ornament would never be the same. I had forgiven her because I know the person who forgives gains the victory and there's no point in harbouring animosity or resentment, they're negative emotions, destructive.

Then there was Irene to consider, and this presented a whole new set of problems and conflicts of interest. She had been open, honest enough to let me know her true feelings about me and it was patently obvious there was no romantic side to it, but I valued her friendship, her trust and her generosity and it would be difficult to walk away from that especially considering the fragile state of her health and her dependency on me.

What a situation to find yourself in! My mind started filling with opposing thoughts, 'don't change horses in midstream' - 'a change is as good as a rest,'- 'as the tree falls, so it should lie,' the deliberations were in a state of turmoil and I knew it was going to be very burdensome to make the decision.

We parted friends before she left for Stonehouse and I promised to meet with her tomorrow at her house at 11 o'clock. She asked me if I knew the way.

I've heard it said that those who expect salvation at the 11th hour usually die at 10.30. I hope there's no truth in that saying.

I doubt if I'll get much sleep tonight.

CHAPTER 15

EAST, WEST, HOME'S BEST

After enduring more than 15 months in purgatory and being shunted from pillar to post, I'm finally settled and have a semblance of normality once again. The difficult decision proved in actuality, to be an easy one although there was an element of guilt when I moved out of Kirk Street a month ago carrying two expensive 'gifts'.

Irene took it well, but I could sense she was upset and disappointed by the decision. I still make it a point to visit as often as I can and help out which eases the burden of guilt, although I often feel like I was a rat deserting a sinking ship. But I had to consider my future and I knew in my heart I wanted to try again with Jill regardless of what had happened in the past. If I stayed at Irene's my future would have been uncertain and it would only be a matter of time before I had to move on again. I now understand how those gypsies, or should

I say 'travelling people,' feel. At least they have got a caravan.

Jill has been very understanding and tolerant of my relationship with Irene and even helps out occasionally when she has the time and I'm glad to say they have become good friends, but not too friendly if you know what I mean. We have even had the odd night out at the local when Irene is having one of her better days, which I'm sad to say, is becoming a rarity, most of her time is spent confined to bed heavily sedated. Jenny has been very concerned about her recently. It's now three days since she has eaten anything although she still manages fluids. It's been over two weeks since I last visited her and I still find it hard to believe it's the same person I met just before Christmas. Irene seems to have aged dramatically, her face is pale and gaunt and she's painfully thin which, according to her doctor, is probably due to the cachexia which interferes with the normal absorption of food. When I look at her now I could weep.

I know death has a thousand doors to let out life and we all find one, but I hope to god when I go it's not through cancer, there's nothing more dehumanising or debilitating when it gets a grip on you and doesn't relinquish. When I go I hope its something quick, sudden, that's the door I would readily accept. Death is an inevitable part of life. I hope my eventual demise is as quick and painless as my grandfather's. William died in 1945 just as WW II was drawing to its conclusion.

Dirty Laundry

He was stationed somewhere in Poland, I think it was Warsaw and was assisting in the 'food and aid' programme that was set up to provide essential supplies for the people, it was a simple operation, the food was dropped from a plane, picked up, then distributed to the people. Unfortunately for William, during one drop, he was hit on the back of the head by a case of 'Spam' that killed him instantly. Death by Spam, what a way to go! My father had always told us he died a war hero but conveniently forgot to give us the salient details of his untimely demise. I had always imagined he died in the line of duty in some fierce hand-to-hand combat or perished trying to save a wounded companion, or trying to secure a strategic bridgehead.

Yeah, something quick, something unexpected would suit me fine, maybe dying suddenly during a vigorous sex session. I guess my grandfather William was a modern day example of those luckless ones that met their maker after a bizarre incident. For example Zeuxis, the great painter, who died of laughter at the sight of a hag which he had just depicted in one of his paintings, or the Greek writer Aeschylus who was killed by a tortoise which had fallen out of the sky and struck him on the head (it was dropped by an eagle) or Saufeius who chocked to death while supping the white of an under boiled egg according to the great historian Pliny the elder. Death truly has a thousand doors to let out life.

I suppose when I think of Irene, its with a sense of hopelessness, not being able to do anything that could make a difference or influence the future, and I also feel for some reason, a sense of guilt because I have managed to turn my life around and I've got the health to enjoy it to the full. Yes, I'm glad to say life is good once again, I've adopted a positive outlook and I aim to stay in that frame of mind, it's all about perspective, I think it was Fred Hoyle that said, *'space isn't remote at all, it's only an hours drive away if your car could go straight upwards'*, now there's optimism for you, someone with an unblinkered view on life and what's achievable through positive thought. No longer am I nursing the unconquerable hope, clutching the inviable shade.

I had just finished an hour of tuition with two of my students when the front door bell rang. I opened it and a cold blast of air assaulted me. It was Jenny and she looked agitated.

"Come in out of the cold," I said.

"Thanks Jack, I tried phoning you but it's constantly engaged."

"Sorry, I take the phone off the receiver when I have students in, there's nothing more annoying when it goes off during a session."

"Suppose."

"Would you like a quick coffee Jenny?"

"No thanks I have to rush back, Scott has been called out on an emergency so I'll need to get back to get some things organized, he's off to somewhere in France, can't remember where he said - listen Jack, the nurse is just away and she will be back in a few hours, could you maybe look in on Irene, she if she needs anything, you don't have to stay, just check occasionally that will be fine until I get myself sorted."

"Sure, that's not a problem Jenny, I'm free this afternoon. I'd love to help." She looked very relieved and I could see she was under considerable stress.

"She's just had her meds. They have been increased by her nurse because she is in a bit of pain and discomfort, so you don't have to worry about that. When I left she was sleeping, god that's all she seems to do these days. She looks terrible Jack. I'm worried about her." I had to interrupt just to calm her down.

"Listen don't worry, I'll take a walk over. I'm quite happy just to sit with her for a few hours, I've got a good book, so don't rush back and if the nurse is returning then she'll be fine, you can come back tomorrow, it will give you a break." She nodded her head and smiled.

"That's great, I really appreciate it. I have to go, but I'll phone you whenever I can just to check up." She left in a hurry. I found a good book, put on my jacket, left Jill a note and headed out to Kirk Street with a sense of foreboding. I feel like the grim reaper watching over someone that's bed ridden and so ill, the last time I visited she slept the whole time and I don't think she was aware of my presence. At one point I thought she had stopped breathing and went into a blind panic, I thought I would be able to cope with the situation but I was hopelessly out of my depth. I bent over her, put my ear to her mouth to listen for breathing sounds and when she grabbed my arm I nearly hit the ceiling and let out a yell. 'I'm not dead yet,' she said sarcastically.

I stopped in at the florists in the common green for some flowers to cheer her up, then Victoria wines for a bottle of white wine for later tonight , Jill had made her special chicken dish and a good Chardonnay was the order of the day. I opened the front entrance to her flat then walked up the stairs with an increasing sense of unease.

"Hi, it's just me," I shouted as I entered the flat. The place was very warm, uncomfortably so, it was warm enough to grow topical fruit. I shouted again. No answer. I then chapped her bedroom door.

Nothing, no response.

"Irene, its me, Jack." I pushed the door open. She was lying face down on the bed. My heart started racing as I approached her. I touched her shoulder to rouse her and she jumped which scared the hell out of me.

"Jesus. Irene… sorry, I knocked the door, there was no answer, sorry, are you alright?" It was an effort for her to turn around and acknowledge me, her voice was weak as she replied.

"Oh, hi Jack, drifted off again, can't get comfortable… help me sit up will you?"

"Sure." I gently lifted her into a sitting position and was shocked by how thin she looked, she was that diaphanous, that fragile looking, I was scared I would break one of her bones just moving her. The deterioration in her condition was appalling, there was no words to describe it. She spoke again, very softly as if even speech was an arduous task.

"Thanks you are a darling. Can you pass me my water over, I'm thirsty."

"Of course, there we go. Do you want me to put some ice in that, it looks like it's been sitting out for a while?"

"Please, thanks." I returned with a tray of ice cubes and the flowers which made her smile. She tried to fix her hair and apologised for the way she looked.

"Can you pass me the mirror and my bag? It's on the chair over there."

"No problem" The bedroom was so uncomfortably warm and the air was that heavy I suggested opening a window.

"No Jack," she replied "it's cold in here if you don't mind."

It was difficult to look at her without welling up. She cut such a pathetic figure yet she tried to make herself presentable for me as she fussed in the mirror.

"Can I get you anything else Irene? Could you maybe manage some soup or something? Jenny said you've not been eating much...."

"Can't face food at the moment. I feel too nauseous, but thanks anyway. Water is fine at the moment." A weak smile graced her face. "I'm afraid I'm not very good company right now… too tired. You know, the damn morphine…."

"I understand." She took a few sips of the iced water then put the glass down on the unit beside the bed, everything looked an effort. I didn't know what to say, the conversation was painful, normally it's very difficult to shut me up but under these circumstances words would just not come and it was obviously a real effort for her as well. I think she sensed my unease. I decided the best thing to do was to let her rest.

"If you need anything, anything at all, just shout, I'm going to sit in the living room for a while, I've got a good book, I'll leave you in peace Irene."

"Before you go Jack, could you be a darling and bring me my photo album, I think it's sitting on the coffee table, Jenny and I were reminiscing. It was nice, although I think I was beginning to bore her."

"Irene how could you possibly bore anyone, you're delightful." Another smile appeared. I think it was one of appreciation. There was three albums on the table and I brought them all in for her.

"Here we go, which one did you say you wanted?" I asked.

"The blue one, please." I left it on the bed and walked back into the living room. I opened the curtains to let some light in as it was shrouded in semi darkness, then settled down with a George Orwell book, 'Down and out in Paris and London,' a story that enlivens the spirit.

I completely lost myself in the novel. Two hours had passed and I decided to check on Irene and then get something to eat. Orwell's description of stale bread and margarine washed down with cheap French wine was even beginning to sound appealing.She was fast asleep.

The fridge, to my consternation, contained very little in the way of provisions, a small piece of cheese, not even enough to bait a mouse trap, some cold meat, a few eggs, milk and a Tupperware box which I investigated. It was empty.

I put my jacket on and headed for the common green to get a few things in for Irene and something for my own lunch, scotch pies, my favourite, heart attack cuisine, they say the quality of the pie is determined by how far the grease runs down your arm when you're eating them - delicious, it was better than what was on offer at Irene's place. The pink-faced butcher warmed them up in the microwave oven and I walked back up the road enjoying the greasy treat.

I checked in on Irene again then settled down on the chair to continue in the adventures of George Orwell. He captures the mood perfectly of Paris and London in the 1930's, the time of the great depression, especially the poorest classes in society. You can imagine what it was like to sleep on the cold stone floors of the doss houses, cheek to jowl with other down and outs and miscreants, worrying about infectious diseases, tuberculosis, or even the unwelcome advances of homosexuals. You begin to understand how hunger reduces an individual to a *'spineless brainless condition'* as he describes it as it saps the energy so it's physically difficult for them to work or even think rationally, their thoughts were constantly pre-occupied with food. You can practically smell the aroma of hot bread coming from the small back street bakeries, or the vast gruyere cheeses that looked like grindstones, huge piles of food that were unattainable for the very poor, and you can imagine the torment of the hungry as they view the contents of the window - Orwell described it as, *'a snivelling self pity that comes over you at the sight of so much food.'* You can empathise with the really desperate when they had to sell their clothing for the sake of a meal and you can appreciate how this inhuman condition produced complete inertia and a lack of will to live.

It's amazing how quickly a story can captivate you and invoke such strong feelings and emotions. I'll never moan about TV dinners again even if they are rubbery noodles.

The time had passed fairly quickly and the nurse was due in twenty minutes or so. I phoned Jill to tell her I would be back soon and was looking forward to a nice quiet romantic dinner and that I had remembered the wine that was chilling in Irene's fridge.

I marked the page in the book then decided to check on Irene again to see if she needed anything, like the last time I was here, she had slept most of the time. No doubt she would be grateful when the nurse arrives, she could get a bath, change into fresh clothes and receive her meds and therapy.

I knocked the door.

"Irene," I said quietly, "just me."

I pushed the door open and she was still sleeping. The photo album was open and there was a few individual photographs lying on the bed.

"Irene, Irene," I said a bit louder. I gently tapped her shoulder.

No response. A deep sleep. I tried again, but I couldn't stir her.

Panic now set in and I could feel myself shaking.

I lifted up her painfully thin arm to check for a pulse, then checked her breathing, but I knew it was an exercise in futility, she was dead.

I started to weep over her as I looked at what she had become, death was a relief for a person in her condition. She wasn't living, merely existing, just waiting to pass away. After I calmed down and composed myself (I couldn't stop my hands shaking). I phoned the doctor first, then Jenny, which was a very difficult thing to do. She was hysterical and felt guilty that she had not been there at the end with her to offer comfort, love and strength.

I told her Irene just slipped away. Peacefully, quietly.

I felt a sense of guilt somehow. I should have sat with her, been more attentive, tried to talk with her, but it was an awkward situation and she looked so lethargic and I thought it was best for her to rest.

I looked at the photographs that she had removed from the album, there were ones of her family, I presumed her mother and father, pictures of Jenny and her loved ones, snap shots that were obviously associated with happiness, fond memories, images to cling to. There were many of Sandra and Irene together, pictures of a holiday somewhere abroad, pictures of them laughing, celebrating, without a care in the world, great memories, snap shots of life.

The person lying in bed looked like a shadow of her former self, there was practically no resemblance to the one in the photographs. The cancer had stripped her of her former beauty and left a ghostly apparition in her place. On the bedside cabinet one of Sandra's sketch pads was open. It was open at a picture of herself. It was one that made me laugh. It was a very personal picture, very erotic, and I was quite taken aback when she let me see it. It was a wonderfully detailed picture of her as an angel, completely naked, with two wings and a halo. She was smiling and had a cigarette hanging out of her mouth and she was holding a bottle of Jack Daniels, to some it would have presented an offensive image, something iconoclastic, but I suspect it was done purely tongue in cheek, it seemed appropriate somehow. It was a striking image and it's the face I remembered when I first met her, bright, beautiful and full of life.

Death was a relief, because pain is a more terrible lord of mankind than even death itself. Now she is sleeping. Now she is at peace.

It was just then something dawned on me and it literally made my blood run cold, I recalled the conversation I had with Rose and the prediction she made during the reading of my palm. She stated with absolute clarity that someone with the initials I. B. would pass away peacefully and that I would be the only one in the room at the time. Her augury was accurate. I had always presumed that it would be my own aunt, Isobel Barns that would be the one to pass away, she had been ill for many months and there was concern among the family over her failing health, the fact that she was 95 was reason enough to be worried.

It was however, Irene Black that had passed away peacefully in my presence, that somehow gave me some comfort, assuaged the feelings of guilt especially as I left her alone as I went out, I was only away twenty minutes or so and I prayed she hadn't died when I was absent, not that it would have made any real difference.

I lifted the photographs up and put them back into the album. As for the sketch pad, I was determined to take it back home, I wanted something to remember her by as well as Sandra, I had a few photographs, but this was something more personal, more intimate, something intrinsically valuable to me.

The doctor arrived within fifteen minutes, followed shortly by the nurse. He politely asked me to leave the room and performed an examination, took a few notes, wrote the certificate and pronounced her dead. Quick and clinical. I went into the living room, closed the curtains and waited for Jenny. I was dreading the moment she walked in, I knew she would be inconsolable with grief as they were so close and so protective of each other ever since their parents died in a car accident. The sisterly bond was always in evidence. I suppose that's how they survived, made sense of things. I found myself in a very uncomfortable situation, I didn't know whether to stay when Jenny and her family arrived, or just go immediately. I was a good friend to Irene but I wasn't family. I quickly phoned Jill on her mobile and let her know the situation and she suggested to leave them alone to mourn the loss and to pay respects in private, too many people would not afford them the dignity. I headed her advice.

They arrived with some other members of their family. I stayed long enough to explain what had transpired and to offer my sincere condolences. I promised to phone and reassured her of any help for the funeral arrangements and she thanked me with tears streaming down her face. When I left the flat I was emotionally drained and deeply upset.

I needed some solitude, time to get my head together and calm down. The events of the last hour or so were quite traumatic, something I would never want to repeat again.

Irene was finally at peace, it was now the turn of the living to suffer the consequences of a loved one passing away, the guilt, the loss, the recriminations, regret, the terrible void that's left that can't ever be filled.

My heart goes out to her family.

I stood outside the flat and took a deep cleansing breath before I could do anything else. I phoned Jill once again.

"Hi."

"Hello Jack, what's happening, are you on your way back?"

"I'll be home in about half an hour, I promise," I said.

"That's fine, are you alright?"

"Yeah I'm fine now."

"Are you sure?"

"Yes Jill, I just need to take a walk to clear my head that's all, it was just the shock, the suddenness of it all, it was terrible. I didn't even get a chance to say goodbye, or her family for that matter."

"I understand," she said warmly, "do you want me to come with you?"

"No it's okay Jill, honestly, I'll see you in a bit"

"Okay, darling."

I took a walk up to the Kirk Hill graveyard as it suited my sombre mood and it was also a peaceful place, very restful. I thought I would visit Sandra's grave as I hadn't been for a while. I felt it was the right thing to do under the circumstances. Two good friends deceased, within a very short period of time, it's hard to take, doesn't make sense. As I walked past the graves with their ornate headstones and the floral tributes I thought about Sandra and where she would be, there's so many conflicting viewpoints of the question of death. In fact, it's the one question humans would like a positive, definitive answer to - what happens to us when we die?

If you're a Christian then your soul departs into heaven, the ancients called it the spark of the stellar essence, the 'scintilla stellarir essentioe'. Other religions talk about reincarnation. You will come back in another form depending on the type of life you led, God knows what Sandra and Irene would come back as if that was the case, it beggars belief. Then there are other conflicting views, some teach that when you die, that's it. The body goes back into the ground, dust to dust ashes to ashes. Jehovah's witnesses teach that when you perish you go to the grave and there's only a strictly limited number of people that go to heaven, 144,000, according to them - is heaven really that small? And where can I get a ticket? Other groups like the Balts of Latvia teach a man's spirit is split into three separate components.

It's all very confusing and there's a multitude of beliefs and religious doctrine. The world of the dead is a very complex concept that seems to blend and fuse biblical imagery and teaching, medieval doctrine and non-Christian elements. It's one cosmic melting pot. Take your pick.

I don't think Sandra's in heaven. Not that she was a bad person by any means. I just think it would be too boring for her. There are no pubs, it's probably a non-smoking zone, and I'm not too sure how they view the bi-curious. Some might find her language a bit offensive. On the flip side I don't think she's in hell, Hades, Gehenna, call it what you like, although she would certainly brighten up the place and give the devil a hard time.

Maybe she's in purgatory, awaiting a decision, I can imagine a heated debate between God and Satan, none of them wanting to take responsibility for her, too much trouble either way, a hot potato.

Wherever you are Sandra and Irene, I hope you have found peace and are with each other again, regardless of where it is.

It started to rain as I laid a single flower on Sandra's grave. I'm ashamed to say I 'borrowed' it off one of the graves as I passed, no one complained. I didn't have any money left and certainly didn't want to see her empty handed. Sandra would have liked that gesture. The gentle falling rain is probably the tears of the angels, weeping for my two good friends. I'm slipping into writers mode again. I told Sandra everything that had happened today and apologised for running out to lunch, I'm sure she would understand, she was a very tolerant, sympathetic type of person. I touched her headstone and wished her well (a bit difficult when you're dead, but she would have got the sentiment I'm sure).

I knew I would be back here again within a very short period of time once the funeral arrangements were finalised and would have to go through more emotional distress when Irene is finally laid to rest.

More despondency, grief, and pondering over the meaning of life and it's purpose. It sometimes seems so futile, so transitory, just like a breath. I think it was the Roman writer Antoninus that said, *'time is like a river made up of the events which happen, and it's current is strong; no sooner does anything appear than it is swept away, and another comes in it's place, and will be swept away too.'*

Jenny had asked me at Sandra's funeral if she could have a copy of the poem I read. She said it was very affecting, very moving and seemed to express the sentiments she was experiencing. I was only too glad to do so.

I still remember every line of the poem, every word, and it fills me with sadness when I recall them. When I die, and pass from this mortal coil to god knows where, I would love those poignant words read at my graveside. I would really like that.

Do not stand at my grave and weep
I am not there. I do not sleep.
I am a thousand winds that blow.
I am the diamond glints on snow.

Dirty Laundry

I am the sunlight on ripened grain.
I am the gentle autumns rain.
When you awaken in the mornings hush,
I am the swift uplifting rush
Of quiet birds in circled flight.
I am the soft stars that shine at night.
Do not stand at my grave and cry;
I am not there, I did not die.

THE END

Printed in the United Kingdom
by Lightning Source UK Ltd.
111103UKS00001B/10-36